Generations

TO ALYSSA AND AMY

GENERATIONS

Virginia Owens

A LION BOOK

Hannah's Family

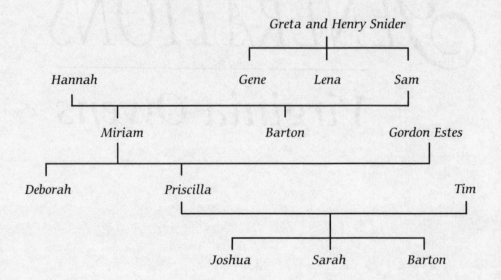

The author asserts the moral right
to be identified as the author of this work

Published by
Lion Publishing plc
Sandy Lane West, Oxford, England
ISBN 0 7459 3458 7
Albatross Books Pty Ltd
PO Box 320, Sutherland, NSW 2232, Australia
ISBN 0 7324 1430 X

First edition 1996
10 9 8 7 6 5 4 3 2 1 0

A catalogue record for this book is available
from the British Library

Printed and bound in Great Britain
by Biddles Ltd, Guildford and Kings Lynn

1

Miriam could feel the entire Palestinian coastline attached to the flesh on her shoulders by thin, steely wires. They stretched, taut and thin, as the plane banked to the left, starting its ascending spiral before heading northwest out across the Mediterranean. The sun was already turning the sea pink below them; the ships, glinting silver, pointed toward Haifa like filings toward a magnet. Herod's Caesarea. The eighty thousand armored Crusaders buried at Akko. The wall of submerged stones undergirding Alexander's causeway to Tyre. Ashdod to the south. The bones at Ashkelon. That world was falling away beneath her, darkening as the plane headed toward the sun they'd never catch up with.

At a certain altitude—she knew because it always happened—the wires would grow thinner and thinner till they not so much snapped as dissolved. Her ears would pop, the sounds inside the plane's cocoon would change, and what was real to her would pop too. Suddenly the life she'd been living on the dry surface of Israel's stratified history would then seem a distant mirage. She'd be headed home.

Now, she thought, it's about to change forever. When I come back—if I come back—everything will be different. The plane lifted and settled into its cruising altitude.

Miriam let out a long breath and pushed against the seat back. Actually, everything had already changed before she even got on the plane. The neatly folded sheet of graph paper with Yigal's note she'd found yesterday afternoon propped against her computer screen had marked the dividing line.

propped against her computer screen had marked the dividing line.

After their last encounter she knew it had cost him something to write such a portentous message instead of delivering it in person. He never would have entrusted it to any of the others at the dig site, reserving that intimacy for himself. Whatever had passed between them these last few days, leaving a note about a family emergency would have violated his sense of the seemly. Only the Cairo conference would have induced him to leave without telling her in person.

Otherwise, she would have heard about Hannah hours later when the team returned to the kibbutz guesthouse in town. By then it might have been too late. It might already be too late. It had probably been too late a long time ago.

Miriam had tried to talk Hannah into coming with her to Israel this year. "You've always wanted to visit the Holy Land, Mother." She'd even made herself say "Holy Land."

But the Gulf War had still been too fresh in her mother's mind. And Miriam's son-in-law Tim hadn't helped any, with his horror stories of 130-degree temperatures and his forecast of Armageddon still hanging fire over Baghdad. "That's the same city as Babylon in the Bible, you know, Gram," he said, inching forward on Hannah's sofa. "And Hussein claims he's the next Nebuchadnezzar. That old buzzard's still just sitting there, waiting for a comeback."

"Really, Mother," Miriam had countered. "We'll be hundreds of miles from Baghdad on the Mediterranean coast. Look on the map, for crying out loud. Your chances of getting mugged in Houston are a lot greater than being killed by an Iraqi missile in Israel. I've been there, remember? Take my word for it."

But Hannah's imagination grasped eschatology more easily than statistics. Her mother and Tim used the same vocabulary of arcane cosmology—the Rapture, the Millennium, the Battle of Armageddon. "Tim's been there too," Hannah persisted.

"Not to Israel, he hasn't. He was in Saudi Arabia."

"And Kuwait."

"Whatever. It doesn't matter."

But Miriam had been surprised, actually, by how much it did matter. To her, anyway. Taking Hannah on this trip had seemed urgent, crucial in a way Miriam hadn't expected. Not that she'd been prescient or sensed any impending threat to her mother's health. The past was Miriam's specialty, not the future. She left portents to her daughter Priscilla and Hannah. They were the ones who had premonitions about everything from the cat disappearing to the gas well explosion in Brenham. Miriam had merely wanted to give her mother something memorable, extraordinary, a gift on Hannah's own terms.

She'd even been prepared this once to violate her own sensibilities for her mother's sake. On the whole, Miriam despised the way Israel was turned into a theme park for religious fanatics. For several summers now she'd come alone to work on archaeological digs, immersing herself in the tedium of unearthing domestic detritus, labelling broken pottery, cataloguing sherds on computer disks. Which would themselves then be labelled and catalogued in an infinite regression of indexes. That's what she loved about archaeology: its dehydrated and infinite regress. It dealt with acts, consequences, failures which had already happened, the ripples of their animation having died out long ago. You didn't have to worry about changing anything, fixing mistakes. It comforted her to think that one day her own failures would fade out and be forgotten as well, just like the blunders of the people who had shaped and broken, filled and emptied, the pieces of clay pots she labelled now. She relied on this long slow study of the already-dead to steady her every summer so she could face the classrooms full of youthful, needy faces each fall.

At first she'd only come for two or three weeks to the bigger sites in the Upper Galilee, what the Israeli tourist bureaux liked to call their Switzerland. Then two years ago she'd come across the advertisement for the Ashkelon expedition in a professional journal. The dig at that port city needed trained volunteers who could stay all summer. North African goddesses were Miriam's academic specialty, and she was currently working on the permutations of goddess figures ringing the Mediterranean. It had seemed a natural fit. "It's the desiccation I like," she assured Yigal when he apologized for the short supply of fresh water at the site. Ashkelon, after all, was where she had come to dry out.

During her first weeks at the dig, the team director had not paid her much notice and, despite the resolution which had brought her to Ashkelon, Miriam found herself irritated by his disinterest. Once he discovered, however, that— unlike the usual volunteer on these digs—she would be staying all summer, perhaps might even want to return the following year, his attention had swung in her direction like a gun turret—inevitable and dangerous. She could feel his eyes on her during the day like a weight, his presence rolling into her consciousness like a juggernaut.

There was absolutely nothing complicated about Yigal. He was made up of equal parts of hard flesh and sheer will, and his will regarding her had been clear. His face, smoked by the glaring biblical sun, and the iron-grey hair, stiff as springs, would once have made her capitulate. Or bristle. She took pains not to bristle—a response, she had learned, that only signalled engagement in a skirmish destined to end with acquiescence. She hadn't come all the way to Ashkelon to capitulate.

For his part, Yigal had stared at her over the rim of his wineglass, paid for her lunches in the Kikar Medumim when they went up to Tel Aviv, and suggested nothing. From other members of the team she discovered he was divorced and intent on moving soon from the Israel Antiquities Authority to a full professorship at Harvard. Though he was neither a devout nor a practicing Jew, his character had nonetheless been forged in the white-hot flame of that ancient tradition, then hardened in the dark waters of his country's modern history.

By that first August, she found herself baiting him, using Tanit, the moon-goddess whose particular ties to Ashkelon she was documenting. "It was that boy-emperor in Rome who imported her from Carthage," she told him one evening as they lingered over a late dinner on the terrace overlooking the sea. She could hear the clatter of the kitchen and a few voices she recognized from the team, still arguing indoors.

"Third century, wasn't he? She would have found Astarte and Aphrodite powerful rivals then," Yigal said, trying to show a polite interest.

"Well, when you're the emperor, you get to say who's god. And since he'd been named for some obscure Syrian god, guess who he chose."

"But your Tanit... how does that explain her appearance?"

She waited till Yigal's polite smile grew less pronounced. "It seems that this Syrian god had at some point married her. The timing on that's not too clear. You know how all those divine escapades happen outside of time. Anyway. He brought her cult-image to Rome too. I guess having a wife makes even a deity more respectable. Richer too, since he ransacked Carthage to pay for Tanit's dowry."

She had waited till the next week when she'd gone back to Tel Aviv before she brought up Tanit again. Yigal helped her find a small apartment in a co-op in Old Jaffa she could sublet for the summer, a place where she could both write up the team's field notes and get some of her own work done in peace and quiet. He came on Fridays, as a matter of course now, to take her to lunch. Usually they went to the Yamit and ate on the terrace overlooking Andromeda's Rock just offshore. Miriam had kept her tone mildly academic, in the manner of a colleague reporting on the next stage of research. "Tanit's stock went up all over the empire, of course," she said, leaning her elbows on the table. "That's why you find evidence of her in Ashkelon."

Yigal kept his eyes turned toward the sea, saying nothing.

"The emperor was only fifteen. And bisexual, you know. He must have looked like a combination of Cleopatra and Michael Jackson." She held up a slice of orange and considered it idly before biting it. "He wore makeup. Outlined his eyes with black kohl, painted his cheeks. Then he'd cruise the public baths, shopping for male lovers to have delivered to the palace. If he liked them well enough, he'd give them government jobs. But actually his mother handled the more mundane arrangements." She sat back and sighed. "Just keeping her boy happy, I guess."

Yigal's shoulder flinched. She dropped the limp orange peel onto her plate. "Of course, that was all by the by," she continued, still pretending to speak as one scholar to another. "Naturally he married—four times, in fact. A new wife for every year he was emperor. Once to a Vestal Virgin he claimed was Tanit in human form. And he was an avatar of his namesake, of course. So when he and the Vestal Virgin did their thing, well, it was divinely inspired fornication— no, it was more than that. They were actually manifesting on the physical plane the spiritual copulation of the gods. Sacramental sex, I guess you could call it."

Yigal's heavy fingers drummed on the glass table top, his eyes turned toward the outcropping where Perseus was supposed to have rescued Andromeda from the sea-monster.

"Strange, isn't it, that after all that late Greek in-tellectualizing of the gods, turning them into some kind of abstract life-force or Idea of the Good, the Romans finally reverted to the most primal sort of paganism."

She picked up her glass and held it out to be refilled. "Please," she said, smiling and lifting her face toward him as she caught at a strand of hair that had blown between her lips.

Yigal glanced at her, then fixed his attention on the dark green bottle. "I think next time we try the Golan Chardonnay," he said, frowning.

She went on speaking eagerly while he poured, lifting her shoulders, pretending not to notice his attempt at diverting her. "Unfortunately for Tanit, though, the emperor and his mother got killed off by a jealous aunt." She paused to nod her thanks, then sank back against the chair's cushion with a sigh. "I still like the Gamlah Riesling myself. Anyway. Poor Tanit sank into obscurity, as they say, after that. In fact, it wasn't long till Constantine killed off all the old gods—and goddesses." She hazarded a sidelong glance at Yigal who had topped off his own glass.

"It won't do, you know," he said with abrupt disgust. "Your Tanit and Ishtar and all those other earth-mothers. I defy you to name one goddess who was a totally benign figure."

Miriam smiled in the direction of Andromeda's Rock and lifted the collar of her thin blouse away from her neck to let the dry air circulate inside. She sometimes found his eclectic speech patterns, a mixture of Israeli rhetoric and dated British public-school phrases, as charming as his leathered face. "Actually the part I'm interested in is divine marriage. Whether it inevitably proved fatal to goddesses. They have this tendency to disappear after they link up with a male god." She tilted her head and rolled the stem of the glass between her fingers. "Another correlation between the divine and the human."

The pent-up breath erupted from his chest in a blast. "There is God and there is man. And they are separate."

"And there is woman also?" she asked mildly.

"Woman also. Yes." He swivelled his gun-turret head toward her, his eyes hooding themselves again as he sat back, appraising her intentions. A smile lifted one side of his wide mouth. "Ah, and you would like to think maybe that woman is the connection, the conduit along which man must pass from earth to heaven?"

"The notion's not limited to prehistoric cultures, you know," she answered, a little too quickly. "The nineteenth century was full of it. The 'better half.' The ennobling influence of women. What else was that?"

He shook his head, the skin around his eyes corrugating in a smile. "Sentimentality."

She lifted her shoulders. "The modern world's name for religion."

He had laughed outright at that and immediately steered the conversation into safer waters. She had laughed too. But that was last year, before they'd uncovered the bones.

Miriam opened her eyes and pulled the airline magazine halfway out of the seat pocket in front of her. The paper's bright surface, slightly sticky, clung to her fingertips as if it were coated with some kind of albuminous protein. She pushed the magazine back into the pocket and rubbed her hands along her thighs. She shivered and closed her eyes again.

"Rabbit run over your grave?" the man beside her asked, closing the paperback he was reading over his thumb.

She opened her eyes and stared at him blankly.

He shrugged and opened his book again.

She studied the watch on his wrist. She'd seen the style before, one with two crescent moons on the face. What did the moons do anyway? Did they track the lunar cycle some way? What would a man like him—a salesman? a dentist?—either know or care about the waxing and waning of the moon? He probably hadn't looked at anything but his Rolodex and the thick bottom of a shot glass in months. She turned her head away.

All of a sudden everything inside this plane seemed suffocatingly irrelevant—the glossy magazines, the man's watch, even the contrived wispy hairdo of the flight attendant coming down the aisle toward them. What was she doing here herself, anyway?

Miriam had just come back to the small camper trailer they used as an office at the site, to finish charting an elevation on the new graphics program, when she'd found the note propped against the terminal screen. She'd been thinking about how thick the walls of these ancient Near Eastern buildings were, and how small the rooms, at least in private homes. Of course, people were smaller then too, and they did their cooking outdoors in the courtyard. But still. A ten-foot-square room would make her claustrophobic, especially without any windows.

She'd picked up the sheet of graph paper, almost afraid it might be an apology from Yigal, not sure she had the strength for another refusal. *Miriam*, she read instead, *call your daughter Priscilla immediately. Your mother has been taken ill. Take the Land Rover up to Tel Aviv. I will pick it up at your flat on my way back from the Cairo conference.* The phone number he'd included didn't look familiar. She assumed it was for a hospital. That was all, except, under his initials at the bottom, *Where have you been?* He'd planned to leave before lunch. She must have just missed him.

Four hours later she was going through the Tel Aviv apartment like a sleepwalker, trying to focus, checking to see if she'd forgotten to pack anything essential. She glanced at the computer drawing that for some reason she'd brought with her from the site. It could wait. Everything would have to wait.

In the kitchen she dribbled water around the geranium and basil she kept in pots on the windowsill over the sink. By the time she got back they'd be dead for sure. She lowered the blinds, hoping the plants wouldn't dry out as fast if the sun was blocked, but the thought of those ancient small dark rooms made her pull them again. Half a world away, she would want to picture this place full of light.

Light was one of the things she and Gordon had always argued over. He was the one who wanted the heavy drapes they eventually ended up with. They cut out too much light, she told him. She'd compromised with curtains at first. With curtains, some light always came through.

In the bathroom Miriam went over her mental checklist. Hairdryer. Antihistamine. Estrogen. She spotted the blue-and-white vial holding her contact lenses and stuck it in her skirt pocket. The air in the plane was always too dry for contacts.

In the bedroom, she opened the closet door one more time, then closed it without looking in. Clothes wouldn't be a problem. The girls could always lend her something to wear. She riffled once through the papers in her briefcase, spotting the letter to Yigal from the expert on bones at Hebrew University. He'd insisted she read it. She slipped it out of the file folder now and put it in her handbag.

Checking to make sure she'd unplugged the computer—yes—and turned off the thermostat—no—she paused with her finger on the control. Miriam gazed around at her white-walled refuge, so full of light and dry air. The first place she'd ever been obliged to explain to no one. She didn't even have curtains now. Then she rummaged again in her handbag to make sure she had her passport—her ticket would be waiting at the airport—looked one last time at the place she'd been most satisfied in her whole life, pushed her suitcase through the door, and locked it behind her.

Max, the concierge, had already called her a taxi. He was standing on the sidewalk, leaning into the passenger-side window. The driver was an old friend of his. Max took messages for her and collected her mail when she was down at the dig site. He didn't water plants, though. Now he straightened and took the suitcase from her.

"Sattled up and ready to rite?" Max had never gotten over the fact that she was from Texas, a place as mythical to him as Israel had been to her three years ago.

"You'll let the *ozzeret* know she won't need to come next Thursday? Not till I get back."

Max gave an exaggerated nod, humoring her anxiety. The cab driver got out and put her bags in the trunk. "Ben-Gurion," she said to him, as if Max hadn't already told him.

Max opened the rear door for her. "Well, so long, pardner. Your modder. Not to worry. She be all right." He kissed Miriam on both cheeks before she ducked into the cab. "Adios!" He was still waving as the cab made the corner at the end of the street.

The flight attendant was working her way down the aisle, taking drink orders. Miriam closed her eyes, pretending to be asleep. Judging from the girl's hairdo and the way she was made up, she probably harbored fantasies of being a rock star. All the modern world offered girls like her—pretty, but not enough to be a top model, with a certain ripe willingness, but no particular talent—were jobs like this. Attendants. For airlines, for tanning beds, for game show hosts. Background, like flowers or music. Peripheral, only marginally relevant.

Miriam could have told the girl she wouldn't have been irrelevant three thousand years ago. In Ashkelon, for instance, she might have been a sacred prostitute at Tanit's temple. That economy had needed girls like her, painted and costumed to represent Tanit, functioning as a kind of metaphysical modem that connected earth and heaven. Through them, farmers fertilized the goddess herself, who in return gave them good crops and healthy flocks. Her job would have been important then, indispensable even.

Miriam used a harsher word than "fertilized" to describe what the farmers did to the temple girls when she gave this lecture to her Intro to Anthropology class every fall. If the girls were drunk or drugged most of the time, she explained, it wasn't so much to keep them from running away as to keep their own mental activity from disrupting the psychic current that flowed between the physical and spiritual realms. Her students would frown, not quite sure if this was meant ironically, especially when she added that "raping the earth" had been, quite literally, the main point of most ancient Middle Eastern religions. Afterwards she showed slides of bulbous-bellied stone fetishes, pregnant goddesses, their blank faces smoothed and featureless. Some of the world's oldest religious artifacts, she told them.

"Goddesses," Yigal had scoffed, "don't tell me you swallow that ridiculous theory—a golden age of matriarchs when all the world was young and green."

Miriam had smiled wryly at the stark, dry angles of Ashkelon and his alkaline-roughened fingers tapping her arm as he questioned her. "Whatever this place looked like three thousand years ago, it's certainly not young and green now," she said, turning to face him. "And neither am I."

A baby cried from one of the bulkhead seats up front, the sound cutting through her drowsy thoughts like a razor. Miriam unbuckled her seat belt, crawled over the man with the lunar watch, and made her way down the aisle to the lavatory. Sliding the latch closed inside, she leaned over the sink and splashed water on her face.

"Mother," she said, staring at her image, "wait for me."

2

Miriam made her way back to her seat, crawling over Lunar Watch Man who drew his knees up, making a point of his irritation. She settled into her seat again, hoping to sleep, but her mind refused to shut down. Ben-Gurion, as always, had been a madhouse. Six separate security checks to go through. As soon as she answered "Ashkelon" when the guard asked her where she spent last night, she'd known she was in for it. Anyone who'd been that close to Gaza got the full treatment. Luckily she'd packed light or she might still be there, some zealous customs agent dismantling her luggage.

By the time she'd reached Priscilla at the hospital it had been after midnight in Houston. The wail in Pris' voice kept replaying in her head. *Oh, Mother, I'm so glad they found you, out there in the countryside*. The way she said "countryside", Miriam knew her daughter was envisioning Israel as some green and flower-studded slope dotted with people in striped bathrobes, people she would have identified as "the multitudes".

"I've got an emergency stand-by seat in three hours," Miriam told her, trying to read the notes from the travel agent she'd scribbled down. "That's if I can make it through security in time. Can someone pick me up—let's see—it looks like sixish your time. I guess that's tomorrow evening."

"Deb can come," Pris said. "I'm not leaving Gram till you get here."

Miriam ignored the implied reproach. "What hospital?" She didn't recognize the name Pris told her. There were so

19

many in Houston now, all in different sections instead of downtown. "What's the address, Pris?"

"Address?" Pris repeated as if it had never occurred to her that a hospital might have one. "Don't worry. Deb'll know how to find it, Mom. She's the organized daughter, remember?" Again, that edge of reproof. Leaning her head against the plane window now, Miriam gave a muted groan. The filaments attaching her to the darkened coast were gone, but she could feel the steel bands of home already tightening.

It was Houston she pictured now. The setting sun would be turning its geometric skyline pink and pewter. Except it wouldn't be sunset there now but—what? Time zone differences always defeated her. But whenever darkness fell, a timer would switch on the porch light at her mother's small white frame house on the north side, the same house her mother had lived in for almost forty years now. The house Hannah had come to as a still-young widow with two children. Even at twelve, Miriam had known that they were there for good, that her mother never intended to leave Texas again.

Her father she barely remembered now. He'd been a navigator flying supply missions out of Okinawa during what people called the Korean Conflict then, the same job he'd had ten years earlier in the South Pacific. Miriam seldom pictured him as he appeared in the World War II photograph on her mother's dresser—a cocky grin lifting his cheeks, his garrison cap tilted just off the level. Instead, in her memory he was always dressed in civilian clothes—a flowered shirt loose outside his khaki trousers—the kind of clothes he wore when they went on family outings to the Okinawan village outside Kadena Air Force Base. His dark hair winged back from his broad forehead, and a little moustache outlined his upper lip. She'd known even then that the native women called out to him from their stalls in the open-air market because of those easy good looks. His mouth would twitch in a half-pleased, half-embarrassed grin, and he'd whisper something secret to Hannah. Her mother's own mouth would stiffen.

They only left the base when her father was at home, so these trips to the village Miriam recalled as special holidays. She couldn't even remember the name of the place now, only the smells. Aromas so rank they shoved aside other sensations. Bananas, plantains, dead-ripe tomatoes, dried fish, plucked chickens, rice cooking. Thin, whining music from overhead speakers threaded through the redolence.

Her little brother Barton, not yet six, stared into the gloom of the open bars, round-eyed. Miriam, though, already knew enough to mask her fascination with the foreignness. A woman sitting at the bar, black hair halfway down her back and her turquoise dress split to the hip, propped one high heel on the rung of the bar stool and smiled at Barton. Miriam pulled at his arm, hissing, "Come on. Don't stare."

Her mother turned and frowned at them both. "You all go wait in the car. We're almost ready to go." But her father had just spotted one of his buddies from the base and was calling to him. Hannah looked at him and then back to her children. "Go on," she said. "We'll be there in a minute."

Miriam grabbed Barton's hand. He jerked away and ran ahead of her up the dusty street to where the car was pulled into a rutted alley. He jumped in the back seat and tried to lock all the doors before she could get there, but she jerked the front door open before he could reach it and slid into the driver's seat, calling him a Japanese name she'd heard at school. She leaned her head against the doorpost and practiced the way she would look when she was old enough to drive.

A couple of young airmen turned into the alley, jostling against the car door as a jitney honked its way past them.

Had they been drinking? No one drank in her family. She turned her head away, just enough so she could still see them in the side mirror. One of the airmen, his face flushed and his eyes feral, grabbed his friend's arm and pointed at her. His friend turned, raised one eyebrow, and whistled. The first one winked, as if he knew she was watching them in the mirror.

Miriam looked away quickly, her face reddening. The airmen laughed and moved on down the alley. She glanced into the back seat, but Barton, playing with a little tin airplane, hadn't heard. She turned her eyes to the mirror again and studied her face, her streaky blond hair, pulled to one side in a barrette. She made a pouting, sulky face at herself. Was she pretty?

The next Saturday her mother had called her into the bedroom. Miriam remembered her parents' bedroom as the one room in the house, no matter where they lived, that never looked settled. There were no pictures, no doilies, no little figurines, none of the decorative touches her mother bestowed on the rest of the house. Her parents always seemed to be perpetually camping out, their belongings only half-unpacked.

Hannah was sitting on the bed, covered only by white sheets, holding a stack of large, grey-bound books on her lap. "Sit down," she said, then paused and cleared her throat. "You're old enough now." She lifted the books from her lap and set them on the bed between them.

"I want you to look at these," she went on, opening the top one. "Especially the pictures. This tells you all about how it happens. I checked them out of the library for you. It's not good for girls to be ignorant about these things."

Miriam stared at the engraved picture on the page where her mother had opened the book. Arrows led to numbers and the numbers were repeated below the picture, followed by strange, foreign-looking words. It took a moment to figure out just what she was looking at. Except for the hair, the illustrations looked more like plants cut in half with their seeds and core exposed. Apples or bananas. Even more like the soft, tropical fruit that ripened, dropped, and spoiled almost overnight here. Hannah got up from the bed after a few minutes and started rearranging the clutter on the top of the dresser—bills, keys, coins.

Male Reproductive System, Miriam read silently. Of course she knew in a general way what boys looked like. After all, she had a little brother. It was the style of the drawings that affected her, not what they represented. The black engravings on the slick, ivory paper looked as if they'd been drawn by someone who found the human body repulsive, grotesque.

Hannah pulled open the top dresser drawer and took out a small flat box with a cellophane window. The bed sagged as she sat down again and handed the box to Miriam. "You'll need this." Only a strip of elastic and a metal triangle showed through the cellophane window. She turned the box over and showed Miriam the diagrams on the back. "These are a lot better than we used to have. Everything will be on the top shelf of the bathroom closet for you so it'll be there when you need it." She shook the little box. "It's nothing to be worried about. It happens to all girls eventually."

Miriam felt a vague sense of dread. Surely there must be some way of stopping this.

"It probably won't be much at first. Just a little spotting. Blood stains are hard to get out, though. Always use cold water. Hot water sets them."

But nothing happened until that summer, the polio summer, when no one on base under the age of sixteen was allowed in public places. No swimming pool. No movies. Nothing. Miriam had been sitting on the front steps, staring dully at the flame tree in the front yard, wondering what had become of the leeches that clung to the bark during monsoon season. She felt heavy and sluggish, as if it would take an enormous amount of energy just to get up and walk around the house. Barton and the little girl next door were playing horses in the back yard. Their neighing noises made her vaguely spiteful. She was the one who had invented the game. Horses had been her idea, not theirs. Last week she'd been a coal-black stallion named Blaze for the white streak on its nose. Blaze appeared suddenly on distant horizons and battered down fences to free other penned-up horses.

But she didn't feel like Blaze today. In fact she felt like she'd never run again. Her body seemed swollen and heavy, her real self trapped inside it, like a princess turned into a toad. There was a vague pain in her stomach. Maybe, she thought with a sudden thrill, it was polio.

Later, when she went inside to the bathroom, she found the fold of toilet paper smeared with a pink stain. She frowned and wiped herself again. There was more. Miriam leaned back on the toilet seat, her heart beating rapidly.

Miriam slipped her shorts and panties off, got the boxes down from the top shelf in the closet and opened them. Standing on the cool bathroom tiles, she tried pulling the elastic thong up around her waist. It felt alien, like a kind of harness. She took out one of the gauze-covered bundles and turned it over, examining it closely. She flinched as the gauze rubbed inside her thighs. Then with a jerk she stripped off the elastic harness. Other people maybe, but not her.

She was sweating. She sat down on the toilet again, naked, and propped her bare feet on the edge of the bathtub. She'd just sit here until it stopped. It was cool and dark in the bathroom, the sun only a muted square filtered by the vines at the window. Maybe she should have been a boy after all. She picked at a scab on her knee with her fingernail, considering the possibility. She wouldn't like all that stuff hanging out instead of being tucked neatly inside like girls. The scab flaked off in crusted bits, revealing pink, slick skin beneath. There was a trick to picking at scabs; if you went too far, past the healed part, the raw flesh would ooze tiny drops of blood. Then it would have to dry and scab over again.

Boys, of course, had to do lots of hard things that girls didn't. Work outside in the hot sun, for instance. They had a yardboy now, but once they went back to the States, Barton would have to mow the grass. Ironing was just as bad, and she'd have to do that too when they no longer had an amah. But at least ironing you did inside, out of the sun.

The worst, though, was war. And sport. Sport was bad enough, but war was worse. People throwing balls at you was one thing, but bullets and bombs killed you. This war was over an invisible line somewhere in Korea. It made no sense. So maybe after a while they moved the line. So what? Birds could fly across it.

Then too, you might have to kill somebody else. She had tried to imagine what it would be like, pulling the trigger on a gun and watching a person's face or chest erupt in a geyser of blood and meat. She didn't think she could do it. Her muscles would freeze. But boys were expected to. On the other hand, a lot of them seemed to like it. Some of them fought all the time, even at school.

Not that being a girl didn't have its drawbacks—and more than just this. She drew her feet up onto the toilet seat, trying to find a more comfortable position. Having babies was about as bad as war. She had already figured that one out though. She just wouldn't get married.

Eventually, she'd had to give up and put on the elastic harness, and get dressed again. She'd tried folding toilet paper inside her underpants, but that hadn't worked. She could see she was trapped. This harness thing was going to happen over and over. For the rest of her life.

When school started again, she began to catch on to cryptic remarks made by her friends and to understand the sighs and lifted eyebrows as signals between them. She learned the code words you said to the school nurse when you wanted to retreat to the cot in her office. She had joined, whether she liked it or not, the universal, secret society of women.

Miriam sometimes heard her parents arguing in their stark bedroom, Hannah's voice dropping to a lower register as if to offset her husband's increasing volume. The fights always seemed to happen right before he left on a mission. They were always about money or Barton.

The last one had been the worst. Miriam had waked up, confused, thinking it was morning when actually she'd only been asleep a couple of hours. The light was on in the hall, and she could hear their voices in the next room, more muted than usual, but talking fast. Finally their bedroom door opened and she heard her father hiss something back over his shoulder as he passed through it. Then the light in the kitchen came on, and later the front door slammed.

Her father's plane had gone down just short of Kyoto. The bodies of the crew were never retrieved. There was a memorial service at the base chapel, but no funeral.

In school, Miriam had read about New England sea captains in the nineteenth century who sometimes didn't come home from their voyages for years while their wives and children waited and watched the sea. She had already decided that, if her father's plane ever went down, she would think of him like that—away on a long trip. And the lack of a body had made it easier to pretend he was still on a mission. She told herself that, like the New England sea captains, he would be home someday. He was, in fact, safe and alive somewhere. His ship just hadn't made it back yet.

But he was coming. The loss was easier to bear that way. You could stand someone being gone if you just didn't think it was final.

She never told anyone else about the New England sea captain trick. And it had worked, more or less. Later, after she and her mother and Barton had returned to the States and the little white house, she modified the story slightly in her mind. She pretended to herself that her father had survived, had been picked up by a fishing boat and taken to the interior of China. There he lived on in an imaginary prison camp, her memory of him growing ever dimmer, until at last he was only a dusty shadow. When she thought of him at all now, it was like coming across the memory accidentally while rummaging through old boxes in the attic, a possession she'd forgotten she ever had.

Her other losses, however, had not been so easy. The sea captain trick hadn't worked when Barton's body had come home from Vietnam. It hadn't worked with Gordon either. He was still out there somewhere, a derelict vessel adrift like the Ancient Mariner's phantom ship, one that still sailed through the miasma of her dreams. Or maybe Gordon was the sea captain and her self-deception had come true.

After Hannah had bought the little white house in north Houston, the backwash from the city's growth began accumulating around them. Instead of moving to a better neighborhood though, her mother had merely put extra effort into keeping the house painted and the grass cut. Miriam, meanwhile, grew up, went off to college, and married Gordon. Eventually, after two years of graduate student apartments, they bought their own house. Not in Houston, but closer to the coast, in Freeport, where Gordon had gone to work for Dow Chem.

Come to think of it, that was where they'd had their first disagreement about the curtains. As soon as he'd deposited his first paycheck, Miriam had gone to the fabric shop, lightheaded with the unaccustomed affluence, feeling for the first time in her life like a person of position, a chatelaine. She'd bought twenty yards of waffle-weave pique, gold and orange paisley on a white starchy background. Ordinarily Miriam didn't like orange, but she imagined how the curtains would give a sunny glow to their dim living room shaded by a huge live oak in the front yard.

Her fingers still remembered the pique, the deep texture running through them as she guided the folds under the needle of the sewing machine. The way it had piled up in luxuriant heaps on the floor. The material had cost her forty-five dollars, an enormous amount in 1964, especially after they'd been used to living on Gordon's fellowship stipend. Deborah had crawled around on the hardwood floors Miriam polished to a high sheen with Johnson's paste wax, plucking at the gold and orange mounds with her sticky baby fingers. The floors had been the main attraction of the house for her. Gordon had wanted wall-to-wall carpet.

"Why can't we just have regular drapes and carpet like everybody else?" he protested. "Then you wouldn't have to go to all this trouble."

She had stared at him. "Because."

"Because why?"

That was the day—they'd been married two years then—when she'd figured out how pointless it was trying to explain these things to Gordon. He'd already supplied the answer himself: then they would be like everyone else. But being like everyone else suited Gordon just fine. Not because he was a conformist or cared what other people thought. It just saved time and energy. To Gordon, thinking about floors and walls and windows and what to put on them was a waste of time. He expected those to be a given, part of the supply-package of life. Gordon only liked thinking about two things. Other things he liked to do, as long as they didn't take up space in his brain, but the only things he actually enjoyed thinking about were carbon chains and politics.

Was it drapes or politics that had been the root of their problems? she sometimes wondered. Eventually, when they moved into the new house, Gordon had gotten his way. Then, ironically, she'd lost her husband to the same part of the world that had taken her father.

The sea captain trick only worked if you stayed at home, not if you were the one who went away. And the sea captain trick would never work with Hannah either.

Miriam's eyes felt dry and scratchy. Her mouth too. She unzipped her handbag, looking for eyedrops, mints, gum. The edge of the envelope she'd folded inside earlier scratched her palm. She pulled it out and stared at it a moment. Then she replaced the envelope in her handbag and leaned her plane seat back the two inches the modern world allowed for human fatigue. She didn't need to read it again. She had it practically memorized anyway. What she needed was sleep. She had to change planes at Heathrow. By the time her flight arrived in Houston she'd be a zombie. Thank heavens it would be Deborah picking her up. Cool, serene, efficient Deborah, who sailed through life self-contained, entire.

Around her elder daughter, Miriam always felt slightly askew. Messy and scattered, as if she were continually shedding bits and pieces of herself, leaving a trail of metaphysical dandruff in her wake. Deborah's brisk composure, her sense of mastering fate by a sheer exertion of will—she knew well enough what that felt like. It had been a long time though. These days she hoarded her energy, felt a keen sense of her limits.

She settled her head against the cold plane window and closed her eyes. Ah well. She'd be grateful enough for Deb's uncompromising efficiency when she reached Houston, jet-lagged, disoriented, and braced for grief. She fell asleep somewhere over Turkey, lulled by the drone of the plane's engines, easing her dread by imagining their reunion.

3

"Eighty-nine percent," Priscilla said. "That's what the success rate is, Deb. Would you jump out of an airplane if they told you one out of every ten parachutes wouldn't open?"

"I wouldn't jump out of an airplane under any condition." Deborah picked up the glass and paper plate she'd balanced on a stack of her sister's books—*The Strong-Willed Child*, a Bible atlas, and a government publication on how to start a small business—and carried them into the kitchen. She dumped the plate into the gaping jumbo plastic bag already overflowing with household garbage. Maybe she should get Pris a dishwasher for her birthday.

She could feel her sister in the doorway behind her. "Besides," she added as she rinsed out the glass, "we don't use condoms."

"Don't fool with that," Priscilla said.

Deborah turned off the faucet. "I was only trying—"

"I know what you're doing. You're trying to brush me off. You don't want to talk about it."

Deborah set the glass upside down on the cluttered drainboard with exaggerated care and raised her palms in a gesture of abdication. "Fine. Fine. Whatever you say." She wiped her hands on a dishtowel caked with dried cookie dough. "Barton's asleep," she went on. "Joshua and Sarah went next door to play with Arnold. Good heavens. Who names a kid Arnold these days?" But when she turned, Pris was still waiting in the doorway, her fists on her hips.

"Okay." Deborah leaned back against the counter and propped one bare foot against the inside of the opposite knee, a stance she'd developed in her gawky junior high stage. Up to this point she'd kept her tone intentionally light; now she lowered the pitch and put an edge to it. "You've apparently concocted this speech and intend to deliver it, come hell or high water."

"What do you mean by that?" Priscilla's stare wavered for an instant before it locked onto her face again.

"Come on, Pris. It's pretty obvious. Eighty-nine percent? Parachutes? It's not like you can do math in your head. Go ahead and get it over with. But cut to the chase, okay?" She glanced deliberately at her watch.

Pris' fists dropped from her hips and uncurled. Her bottom lip twitched slightly. "You can joke about it if you want to, Deb, but do you realize how small an AIDS virus is?"

Deborah crossed her arms and kept her own gaze steady. "Something tells me I'm about to find out."

"If condoms fail—what, eleven percent of the time? A virus, you know, is—" she spread her arms, "hundreds and hundreds of times smaller than a sperm."

"Oh for heaven's sake, Pris." A sperm? Wasn't that a collective noun? Deborah pushed away from the counter and went back into the living room where she stepped into her sandals and began gathering up her papers off the coffee table. "Scott isn't gay and he doesn't shoot up. He's hardly likely to have AIDS."

"You don't get AIDS just from men, Deb. I don't imagine you're the first woman he's slept with. And transfusions. Don't forget transfusions." Pris had followed her back into the living room. "He could have had an operation before you met him." Her head was cocked to one side and thrust forward. She always took that stance whenever she was losing an argument—half pleading and half cornered. With her dark hair frizzing around her forehead in the high humidity, she looked like an overpowered Pomeranian. This was the point where Mother had always intervened in their childhood arguments. *Now, Deborah. Don't tease your sister like that. It's not fair. Remember, she's younger than you.*

Abruptly Deborah sat down on the sofa. She could feel her niece's *Waldo* book poking from beneath the cushion. "All right. I'll tell Scott he has to get tested for HIV. Then I'll have them send the lab results directly to you. Will that satisfy you?"

Her sister turned her head away and stared out the picture window still streaked with the remnants of snowflakes the children had stenciled on with shaving cream last Christmas. The sprinkler rotated hypnotically in the front yard.

"I'm sorry," Pris finally said in a voice tight from pinched-back tears. "It's not right to ask you to babysit and then use the opportunity to—" She broke off and made a gesture meant to fill in the blank.

"Especially considering I might have AIDS. I wouldn't think you'd want to take a chance I might infect the children." Deborah could stand her sister's apologies even less than her lectures.

Priscilla's head whipped toward her. "Don't be a turd."

"Don't you be, Pris," Deborah said. She got to her feet again. "Look. I'm two years older than you. I think you can safely assume I know how to take care of myself. Besides, it's not AIDS you're worried about. You just don't like the thought of my living in sin with Scott. Why don't you just admit it?"

Priscilla looked down, flexing her toes in her sandals. "I just thought when you got baptized—" she said stiffly.

"Confirmed," Deborah muttered under her breath. She started stuffing the papers into her briefcase. When she glanced up again, something about her sister's dark eyes, overbright with tears, made her savage. "What did you expect, Pris? That I'd suddenly dump Scott for Jesus? That my glands would miraculously stop functioning?" She straightened up. "Everyone's not as lucky as you, okay? Even if I married Scott—not that he's asked me—I still wouldn't be as lucky. So don't go around shoving your good fortune in everyone else's face, all right?"

Deborah had picked up her briefcase, stepped around the clutter on the floor, and given her sister's shoulder a quick squeeze as she left, a mute signal for a truce.

And that very night—could you believe it? (she still asked herself the question every time the scene started rolling in her mind)—Scott had told her he was leaving. Moving to Mexico, he said, to help set up a maquiladora for his father's firm.

"What I get for taking Spanish in college," he'd said with the sardonic twist to the left end of his mouth, an expression he practiced to perfection, one his tawny skin and long, thin lips seemed created for. The look conveyed at once resignation to fate and his own lack of culpability, while also warning you not to press him too hard. It said, Hey, what's a rich, handsome, well-connected, not to mention clever guy to do? It was the look that had challenged her when she first saw him come into the district courtroom, buttoning his double-breasted suit, and disarming the judge, a woman old enough to be his mother, with a contrite nod.

Deborah had pulled the sheet to her chin and stared at the ceiling.

"So?" He rolled over onto his back and put his hands behind his head. "Hablas espanol?"

She glanced over at him without turning her head. "When?"

"That's the really bad part. Short notice. A couple of days. We've got to move fast on this so we can get things in place and grandfather in before some new federal regulation goes into effect."

"When?"

He didn't even hesitate. "Day after tomorrow I leave for the first stage. Of course I'll be back again in two weeks to get whatever I'll need for my office there. After that—you can come down and see me. Lots of cheap flights to Mexico. Weekends anyway." He turned toward her and propped his head on one arm.

"How long is this going to last?"

He twitched a shoulder. "Hard to say. At least a year. Maybe longer."

She could feel her face tightening. The mixer with the dough hook was his, she was already thinking, as well as the coffeemaker. The undershorts and t-shirts mixed up with her things in the clothes hamper—should she wash them before she gave them back?

She turned on her side, away from him, frowning. This was God. She was certain of it.

Ever since she'd started taking instruction with Father Botts in the spring, she hadn't been able to make up her mind what to do about Scott. Or rather, she knew in a general way what to do but not how to bring it off, how to make it work. She had felt at an impasse, equally powerless to make Scott propose marriage or to risk hurting him by asking him to move out. He'd never understand, not after the three months they'd already spent together. Even an egotistical, self-indulgent person can still feel rejected. It would give him a bad impression of God. He already felt threatened on the mornings she got up early and went to Mass.

Now, however, it appeared that God was taking care of the situation, getting rid of Scott for her. Okay, she thought, taking a deep breath. I can do this. I can handle it.

"Come on, Deb," he murmured, his lips brushing her ear. "There's not much time left. Let's make the most of it."

She felt his hand slide along her thigh. The bastard.

Deborah rubbed her forehead as the scene faded and resolved into the screen-saver exploding fireworks on her computer screen. "I'm not getting anywhere with this, am I?" she said to the woman at the other desk.

"If it was me, I'd just go ahead and leave," Arlene said. "It's almost four already and your mama's plane gets in at five-twenty. Traffic'll be getting bad soon."

Deborah checked her watch. Ten till four. Hank Crawford wouldn't be back from the courthouse for another hour. "He's not going to like it if I'm not here," she said to Arlene. "He'll want to deliver his usual blow-by-blow account. Replay the entire courtroom scene." Deborah knew that for Hank Crawford, pushing seventy and trying to ignore an enlarged prostate, she made the ideal audience for his reenactments of courtroom triumphs as she sat across from his desk, her long legs slanted demurely to the left, showing just a rim of white, even teeth between her slightly parted lips.

"How can you sit there and look so wide-eyed and innocent while that old coot lies to you like that?" Arlene had asked her after he'd spent an afternoon recounting how he'd defended Sam Rayburn against a libel charge cooked up by the John Birch Society in the late fifties. "I wouldn't be surprised but what he was a Bircher then hisself. Him and Hoot both."

"For the same reason you call them 'Mister Hank' and 'Mister Hoot'. It's what we both get paid for, Arlene."

Arlene had raised both her eyebrows and expelled a long whistling breath. "I see. Well, just so's we understand one another."

That had indeed been the beginning of their understanding. Three months after Deborah was admitted to the
firm as a junior partner, Arlene had acted out for her the
scene of Hank Crawford and Hoot Jasper deciding to hire
her.

"Why can't we get a man?" Hoot had objected. (Raising
her voice to a thin, nasal whine, Arlene used a magic marker
to demonstrate how he'd chewed his cigar.)

"We gotta keep up with the times, Hoot. I'm a-telling you,
ever' firm in Houston's got them a woman now."

"We got Arlene."

"Hell. You know she ain't a real lawyer. Besides, she's
black."

"So? Even better. Black and female. A two-fer." Arlene
slapped her spread thighs.

"So how's that look? We show up in court with a black
woman paralegal, first thing you know, they're saying
we're exploiting her, that we're racist."

"You told me when we hired her it was so they wouldn't
say we're racist."

Arlene pulled her chin in close to her neck to show how
Hank's jowls gathered volume when he was intent on
making a point. "That was seven years ago, Hoot. It's more
complicated now. Besides, we need these offices redecorated.
The carpet's worn clean through out there in the waiting
room. And I ain't paying no limp-wristed decorator to come
waltzing in here, charging us an arm and a leg, neither."

Arlene coughed and pretended to spit into the waste basket
like Hoot. "All right," he'd finally agreed. "But if we gotta
have one, get us a nice, well-brought up young lady. You
know what I mean." And she cocked her head and gave an
exaggerated wink.

The firm of Crawford & Jasper hadn't been Deborah's first
choice out of law school. She had wanted to work for a firm

that specialized in environmental law. But so, it turned out, did every other new L.L.D in Texas. Consequently, she decided to settle for something in state government. But men with fifteen years' experience in Austin were losing their jobs. So she spent three months in Dallas, living with friends, looking for anything at all, growing ever more desperate. The only nibble she got there was from a guy in a one-room office in Oak Cliff who advertised $59 divorces in the sports section of the newspaper.

Finally, she'd given up and gone back to Houston—the place she'd sworn she'd never return to, a city in perpetual decay. Ever since she could remember, Houston had been rotting. The fetid odor of decaying vegetation from the drainage ditches around her grandmother's little house had permeated their summer visits there.

Gram's house sat up on concrete block pilings, and the exterior walls had to be swabbed with Clorox every spring to wash away the green mold. The lush Saint Augustine grass was full of chiggers, and the pink azalea hedges swarmed with mosquitoes. Deborah and Priscilla had played outdoors with the neighborhood gang of muscular children, muddy-colored from spending long hours outdoors. The sweat never dried from their bodies all day.

When she was about ten, Deborah had asked her mother why Gram lived in such an annoying place. She'd just learned the word from reading *Alice in Wonderland*.

"Annoying?" her mother had echoed.

"You know. Sticky. Icky."

Her mother had stared at her a long time, so long that Deborah thought she'd forgotten the question. They were staying at Gram's the entire summer while her parents got their divorce.

"Being annoyed isn't the worst thing that can happen to you," her mother finally said. "If annoyances were all I had to worry about—" And she went back to picking out matching buttons from the jar Gram kept in her sewing box. Mother never sewed except when they visited Gram in the summer.

Deborah scratched at her mosquito bites, waiting. "Then what?"

"What what?" her mother said absentmindedly.

"If annoyances were all you had to worry about, then what?"

Her mother frowned at her. "I'd be a happy woman. Now quit bugging me and go find your sister."

Deborah had slouched outside, almost but not quite letting the screen door bang behind her. Pris and her dumb little friends were playing "Overs" with a tennis ball on opposite sides of the carport. It wasn't a good place to play the game because you could see through the open sides of the building and tell which way the other kid was going to run, but Mother wouldn't let them throw the ball over the house roof. She said the noise would bother Gram, though Deborah knew it was their mother who had the headache. She always had a headache now.

Inside the carport Deborah slumped onto the cool, damp concrete beside her grandmother's ten-year-old turquoise Ford Fairlane and began scratching her initials into the whitewalls with a nail that had come loose in the siding. Deborah Elizabeth Estes. When she got to the second E, she hesitated. Would her last name still be Estes after the divorce? Would her mother still be Miriam Susannah Estes, or would she go back to being a Snider, like before she was married? And if she did, then what would her and Priscilla's last name be? Who would they belong to? Dad wouldn't change his name. He'd still be Gordon L. Estes. Would she and Pris still belong to him if they changed theirs? Would his feelings be hurt if she and Pris became Sniders?

Deborah frowned at the first two letters she had already scratched in the white side of the tire. D.E. She couldn't leave it like that. For initials to look good you needed three. She was considering the possibilities when she heard the lady next door calling her kids to come home for lunch. A moment later, Pris wandered into the carport and plopped down beside her on the cement floor.

"What you doing?"

"What's it look like, dummy?"

Pris cocked her head to one side, thoughtfully. "Writing your initials?"

Deborah hesitated, not wanting her sister to see her misgivings. "No. Wrong."

"You are too. D. E. Deborah Elizabeth."

"I am not either. Don't be annoying."

"You are too done it. You put little periods after the letters. That means they're initials. Go ahead. Put another E."

"An E?"

"Sure. I asked Gram. She said we're still going to be Estes. You and me anyway. She's not sure about Mother." Priscilla was shading her eyes with one grimy hand, squinting into the sun that had crept into the shade of the carport.

Deborah took a big breath and let it out slowly in a slow sigh. "I already told you," she said. "It's not my initials."

"So what is it then?"

"A word," she said. And she picked up the nail and scratched a lopsided A and then a D onto the tire. DEAD. It was the first word she could think of that started with DE.

Avoiding Arlene's eyes, Deborah pushed her desk drawer shut carefully to keep from slamming it.

"It's a long drive from the airport out the Southwest Freeway. You could tell her then," Arlene said.

"I don't intend to tell her my problems the first thing off

the bat. She'll be too worried about my grandmother."

Arlene spread her elbows along the rim of her desk and leaned forward. "Got to tell her some time. Now that she's here."

"Not necessarily." Deborah picked up her briefcase and headed for the door. She stopped with her hand on the knob. "You're worse than Pris, Arlene. You know that?"

"You sure better not tell your baby sister. Shoot. She'll have her whole church praying for you."

Deborah pulled the door shut behind her without answering. She'd already told Pris.

"My parachute didn't open," she'd said three days ago, still sitting on the toilet holding the cordless phone in one hand and in the other the little stick on which the dot had just turned, incredibly, pink.

There had been a minor pause. "Oh, sweetheart." Pris had breathed the words into the phone in a muted moan.

Deborah could feel her throat constrict. "I can't talk now," she managed to say before she pushed the disconnect button. She was still sitting there, dazed, when the phone in her hand trilled again. She stared at it a moment, then answered.

"Where's Scott now?" Pris said.

"What?"

"Scott. Where is he?"

"I don't know. Monterrey, I think. Pris, no."

"But he needs to know, Deb. He needs to—"

"Just stay out of it, Pris, okay?" Her voice had cracked but she wanted to get this over with. "I've got to make up my own mind. I don't want you telling anyone, you hear? Not Scott, not anyone. Promise." And her shrill, fractured voice and torn breathing had elicited not quite a promise but at least a frightened silence from her sister.

She'd called Pris back that night after she knew the kids would be in bed. "I'm going to be okay," she told her. "Don't worry."

She could hear her sister swallow on the other end. "You hear me?"

"Deb. You need time to think about this."

"I'm thinking."

"Maybe you should go see—your priest." Not, for once, your minister, not "that" priest.

"Maybe." But she knew she wouldn't. Not till she made up her own mind. Maybe, depending, not then.

The possibility had been enough, however, to hold her sister at bay for the time being. And in the meantime, other things—God?—had intervened. The very next day, the very next morning, it was Pris who'd called her, frantic, from Gram's house, just before she followed the ambulance to the hospital.

What Pris didn't know, what Deborah never intended to tell anyone, was that she had in fact called Scott when she'd got back from the hospital that night. The sight of her grandmother, grey and inaccessible in the tangle of tubes had made her reckless. Some woman had called him to the phone, still laughing from the party Deborah could hear going on in the background.

"Yeah?"

"Scott?" Her voice sounded breathy, scared. She cleared her throat.

"Deb? That you? How's it going?" She recognized his ascent from vague dismay to hearty nonchalance. It helped her to steady her.

"Great." But suddenly she realized she could never tell him on the phone. "I was going to fly down for the weekend, but then Gram, she's in the hospital. Pris found her this morning. I don't know. It doesn't look good."

"That's too bad. I'm really sorry to hear that."

"I don't suppose you'll be coming back this weekend yourself?"

He made an interim humming sound to indicate a mental run-through of his calendar. She waited, feeling her body stiffen. "Let's see. Gosh. It's going to be another month before I have a weekend back there." A chuckle, finally, sounding forced. "They're running me ragged."

There was a pause she didn't try to fill. Somewhere behind him a man was speaking, the rhythm of his voice indicating the wind-up for a joke, then a scatter of laughter.

"So," Scott said, a slight edge to his voice now. "You want to say, what, four weeks from this coming weekend?"

"I don't know," she said, her own voice harder now, but threatening fracture. "I'll let you know."

"Gee, Deb, you know I would like to see you, but—"

"I'll let you know," she repeated, and saw the tiny red light go dead as she pushed the button.

4

"**P**riscilla?"

Gram always called her Priscilla, maybe because Deborah had teased her about her name when they were little. "Prissy Priscilla, eating armadillo," she'd mock. Then she'd make a face. "It sounds like ruffles." But when Gram pronounced her name, she made it sound as if she'd just whisked it off the ironing board, all the wrinkles in the word pressed smooth.

As a child she had tried to reproduce the way her grandmother said her name, whispering it to herself in bed at night. She never could get it exactly right, though. In her mouth it sounded strained rather than smooth. The way her grandmother pronounced her name embodied an ideal she yearned to equal—graceful, composed.

Gram was struggling to sit up in the hospital bed now, trying to push the pillow back against the metal headboard. Pris caught the water glass just as the edge of the pillow bumped it.

"Wait, Gram. Let me crank it up for you." She moved the glass to the far side of the nightstand, then pushed and pulled the knobs along the bedframe until the upper part of the mattress began to rise. When the incline seemed right, she grasped Hannah under the arms and tugged her from the middle of the bed where she'd slid into a huddled heap. Priscilla was strong from wrestling her children into bathtubs and high chairs, but their compact, elastic bodies had more give, more flesh. Hannah's long frame felt brittle and fragile. If something broke inside her, Pris didn't want to be the one who did it.

"Sorry to be such a bother," Hannah panted. "Seems like I can breathe better propped up."

"Come on, Gram," Pris said, "Joshua could handle you, light as you are. You must be feeling better if you're wanting to sit up." She wedged a pillow behind Hannah's back. "Feel like eating anything?" However she tried to temper the hopefulness in her voice it came out sounding like a plea.

"Joshua's really shooting up, isn't he?" Hannah said, ignoring the question. She had to stop for breath before she added, "How old is he now?"

"Seven, Gram. Seven in May."

"Yes, well. With three now it's harder to remember."

"I can hardly remember myself."

There had been times during the past few days when Priscilla wasn't sure just what her grandmother remembered. Maybe because they'd doped her up so much right after they rushed her to the hospital, Gram had kept calling for her son. Priscilla had just started first grade when her uncle had been killed. Pris had sat between her mother and grandmother at the funeral. Gram had wanted to open the big box with brass handles down at the front, but they wouldn't let her.

"It's better this way," her mother had said. "You want to remember him the way he was."

"I want to see," Gram insisted. And Pris, wondering what was inside, had silently concurred. If Uncle Barton had been shot, would there be a hole in him that you could see all the way through like in cartoons? Or if he'd been blown up, were there only pieces of him inside, stacked up like firewood? Would his eyes be closed? Could you dream when you were dead? Or think? Did he know they were going to cover him up with dirt?

But not being able to see him, her mind refused to fill up the box with Uncle Barton. Instead she pictured it holding the things he'd left behind. His books, a basketball trophy, the jumble of oversized shoes at the bottom of his closet, his Beach Boys records. If she tried hard, she could make out the uniform he'd worn when she saw him last—the khaki shirt and trousers, oddly crisp after his frayed jeans and t-shirt. But in her mind, the uniform was empty, folded neatly at one end of the box.

She had wanted to marry Uncle Barton when she grew up. She'd never even told Tim that. She had been fascinated by the way her uncle moved slowly and kept up a constant humming through his delicate nose. She liked to sit in his lap and listen to the vibration coming through his chest wall. When they were married, they would have a dog, a cat, a kitten, and goldfish. She would cook him hot dogs and tater tots for supper.

When she was even younger and they went to visit Gram in the summer, he always took her along on his trips to the Seven-Eleven, the junkyard to buy parts for his old car, his girlfriend's house. She felt sorry for the girlfriend. Pris could tell from the way he laughed and took a step backward and said "Hey!" as they were leaving that the girlfriend didn't have a chance.

The girl, blond and unbuttoned so that the freckles showed between her breasts, followed him down the sidewalk to where Pris had already climbed in the car. "Your niece is so cute!" The girlfriend leaned in the window. You could see down her shirt.

Uncle Barton turned the key in the ignition and jerked his chin up, smiling. "See ya." After they pulled away, he reached over and shook her knee. "How 'bout some ice cream, kid?" Then he'd start singing. "I could eat a goose-moose burger, fifteen pickles and a purple plum!" A song she'd taught him.

He was drafted the next year.

"What's drafted?" she asked Deb.

"When you go to Vietnam." Which to Pris was only a place on television. "Where Dad goes," Deb added.

Deb had already told her she couldn't marry Uncle Barton. "He's your uncle, nu-nu."

"So?"

"So it's a rule. They'd send you to jail or something."

How were little kids supposed to learn these things? she wondered then. How had Deb known?

It was that way with all the most important things in life—you had to discover them on your own. No one actually taught you. You had to pick up information from an offhand comment, an exclamation, a joke. Something would come together in your mind and you'd suddenly know what "ground wire" meant, for instance, or God.

She'd had to discover about Dad on her own too. Even Deb wouldn't talk about that, not until much later, after they were grown. That dark gap in her understanding had almost kept her from marrying Tim.

She was still having misgivings, right up to a few days before the wedding. One night she told Tim he better be awful sure about marrying her, because she would never divorce him, no matter what. Not even if he got drunk and beat her or ran around with other women.

Tim had looked stunned. "Beat you? What other women?"

"I just want you to know. I don't believe in divorce. That's just the way I am. I'd die first. Well, I mean I'd call the police, of course. And Deb's going to be a lawyer. She'd get a restraining order or whatever. And I guess if I got mad enough I might even shoot you. But I'll never divorce you. I just thought you should know that."

"But Pris—you don't think—I mean, what way is that to—"

Closing her eyes, she'd shaken her tangle of dark hair and held up a palm to stop his protestations. "People can do all sorts of crazy things you wouldn't believe they'd be capable of. 'The heart is deceitful above all things, and desperately wicked: who can know it?' That's my life verse, Tim. I mean it." They'd met at a Youth for Christ summer camp.

"Well, that makes me feel really great. I mean we're not even married yet and you're already talking about me beating you and running around with other women." He threw up his arms, then turned and walked away a few steps. They were in the darkened back yard. With the wedding so close they didn't trust themselves to sit in his car, having desperate, half-naked conversations any more.

She started to take a step toward him and then stopped. "I was only trying to be honest with you. It could be me just as easy."

"Be you what? Beating me up? Sure." His voice sounded husky and offended.

"No. But sleeping around. I mean I have it in me, you know. Not now, of course. But say you went to, oh, Saudi Arabia for months and months. I might take a lover." Tim had been working on his uncle's drilling rigs that summer.

"Pris. Really. You always try to turn everything into some kind of story." But the timbre of his voice had changed and he'd turned back toward her, shaking his head. "Just because your dad—"

She went to him then, her head down, looking up from beneath her spray of bangs. "All I meant was I'll never leave you. Never. No matter what."

And of course she hadn't. Not even when she found out she was pregnant for the third time. Bart had still been in diapers. And then they'd called up the National Guard and sent them to the Persian Gulf.

Gram stirred, then gave a low moan and opened her eyes,

struggling to pick up the thread of the conversation. "And Deborah. What about her and her young man? Are they still on the outs?" Her eyelids, puffier than the day before, slid shut.

Pris didn't answer, thinking her grandmother had drifted into sleep.

But Hannah's eyes opened again. "She needs to hurry up if she plans on having any babies. How old is she now?" Then as if to avoid another reminder, she added, "A woman shouldn't try to have a first baby after she's thirty."

"I don't know, Gram," Priscilla said carefully. "Modern medicine..."

Gram had always been her ally, the one who would listen to her complaints about her older sister. When Deb had gone over to the Catholics, Gram had taken it as a personal rejection. "Baptists must not be good enough for her anymore," she'd said, though Deb hadn't gone to a Baptist church since that last Vacation Bible School the summer of their parents' divorce.

"Oh, she's just putting on," Pris had said, using one of Gram's expressions. Their shared criticism of Deborah always felt to Pris like balm running in oily rivulets over her crusted wounds of rivalry.

The first Christmas Deb came home from college, Pris had told Gram about the birth control pills she'd seen in her sister's handbag. Gram was replacing a button on Pris' skirt with her in it, and she'd snapped the thread off with an incisor before she spoke. "Some day," she said, her voice taking a curving plunge on the last word.

They both had understood the words not so much as a prediction of disaster for Deborah as a pledge that their world—hers and Gram's—where moral consequences had the same inevitability as gravity, would in the long run outlast the self-indulgence of her sister's. When Gram's "some day" came, Deb would open her eyes and look around blinking, surprised that things had turned out more or less like Baptists had always said they would.

Hannah had paused, the thread she was wrapping around the spool momentarily taut between her fingers. "Still," she'd hesitated before she began winding again, "we shouldn't judge."

At the time Pris had taken the admonition as either one of those talismanic statements with which believers hedge their bets or as a boundary marker, a reminder that Hannah had kinship obligations to Deborah also.

Pris scraped her chair closer to the hospital bed now. "I'm not sure Deb even wants any children, Gram. Maybe she's just not cut out for it." She made a sound almost like laughing. "Who is? I mean who in their right mind would give up—"

"You give up nothing!" Hannah's head had turned on the pillow and her eyes were staring at her with a ferocity she hadn't the energy to sustain. She turned her head back to blink at the ceiling. "That's a good way to make bad mistakes."

Pris swallowed. Hannah's anger was rare. "What way, Gram?"

"Always thinking about what you want. What you might want isn't always what's good for you." She struggled for another breath and then went on in a calmer voice. "My children were all I ever had, the only thing I lived for."

Pris looked down at her lap and made a humming noise in reply.

"It's going to be harder for her, Priscilla." Gram's eyes had closed again.

"Having babies, you mean? After thirty?"

"Life."

"Ahh." She relaxed a little at the generality.

"It never does turn out the way you expect. Even when you don't expect much."

"Maybe that's best, Gram," she said, forcing the cheer. "Then you can be surprised."

Hannah gave a weak snort. "Not all surprises are good ones, Priscilla. Things happen some time." Her grandmother's eyes were open again, staring across the room. "Things you hadn't intended."

Pris frowned but said nothing.

"I was already a widow when I wasn't much older than Deborah is now."

Pris trapped a deep inhalation and let the air out of her cheeks slowly. In her mind's eye she tried adding a dozen years to the photograph she had of a young Hannah shading her eyes in front of a stone pavilion. The war again. The real war. One where people actually died.

"You're lucky, Priscilla," Gram murmured. "You know that, don't you? You and Tim."

Pris pressed her lips together, and her cheeks slowly inflated again. Why were people always telling her that? And why did it invariably sound like an accusation?

When Tim had been suddenly snatched and sent to Kuwait, she thought she'd heard those words for the last time. Seven months pregnant, she had defied anyone to call her lucky then. She'd sat glued to CNN for weeks, straining to see his face among the tan-splotched soldiers the camera panned. Night and day she'd been haunted by the fear that the baby she was carrying would never see its father.

She and the boys had taken to eating all their meals on the sofa in front of the television set. "Is that Daddy?" Josh would ask. And she'd get down on her knees in front of the set, straining to see the figures in the background. Of course it never was. She couldn't offer her sons even that consolation.

Mom called every few days to reassure her. "I don't think you have anything to worry about, sweetheart. The fighting will be over soon." She didn't have to add, "It's not like Vietnam." Pris could feel the comparison hanging in the air. Or like Korea. Or World War II.

And Tim wasn't Dad.

The morning after she'd been to the doctor and got the news, Pris lay in bed gazing numbly at a troll doll, its green hair sticking to the gummy spoon beside the cough-syrup bottle on her bedside table, and thought of all the things she might have been besides a mother. An undercover police agent. A medical missionary giving TB tests in Bangladesh. A helicopter pilot. Then it would be her going to Saudi Arabia, leaving Tim behind.

She had one arm tucked up under her head, and she could smell her own rancid sweat, the reek making its way up the flannel tunnel of her nightgown sleeve. It mixed with the faint whiffs of burnt toast wafting from the kitchen where Tim was making the children's breakfast. He was feeling particularly guilty about this pregnancy. No bacon, she'd told him. The smell of frying fat made her stomach lurch.

"Why did you do this to me?" she said in a small choked voice. It took her a moment to realize that the words were not directed, not even in her imagination, to Tim.

"Two was enough. What are you trying to do to me anyway? Bury me?" She pictured herself under washerloads of sheets, diapers wadded with wipey-dipes, crumpled paper towels oozing pureed baby food.

"I'm uneducated. I don't know anything. The only thing I'm an expert in is childhood excrement. I feel like a—like a—slug. No, no, a sow. And that's what I'll look like in five months. A big fat sow with its belly all flopped out in front for the little pigs to come suck on."

She sat up suddenly, slammed the pillow against the wall behind her, and leaned back against it. "Just a holding tank," she whispered fiercely between her teeth. "That's all I am to you."

She threw back the sheets and stomped to the dresser in her socks and flannel nightgown, then stood staring at herself in the mirror. Her skin looked sallow, yellow almost. Even the freckles seemed smeared and indefinite. She pulled her nightgown up to her neck and looked at her creamy body. Stretch marks ran diagonally upward from her pelvis. Her nipples stuck out like the brown centers of yellow susans.

"And that won't be the last of it either. Then I'll be the milk tank. Just turn the spigot and I supply. That's all I've been for the last five years anyway. A container. A vat. Is that all you made me to be?" She started to cry. "Human tupperware?"

She let the nightgown fall. Deb's body had never looked like this, and she was two years older. Her sister didn't wear flannel nightgowns and socks to bed either. Pris could hear Joshua and Bart laughing in the kitchen, the kind of giggling that meant they were probably poking holes in their toast and using it for masks. Why wasn't Tim paying attention? What good was it for him to fix breakfast if he let them make a mess she'd have to clean up after he was gone?

After he was gone.

She turned away from the mirror and backed into the narrow space between the bed and the window, sinking to the floor and leaning her head against the mattress. For a long time she stared vacantly at the dust motes floating in the shaft of sun that fell on her legs, not thinking, only feeling space open up around her, as if the world itself had defected, cut all its ties to her.

"Why did you even bother to give me a brain?" she muttered after a while, wiping her nose on her sleeve. "Everyone thinks Deb's so smart. And what does she use all her brains and education for? Figuring out how to sleep around without getting pregnant." Her lips puckered and then straightened. "Well, I've got a brain too—for all the good it does me. You gave it to me. Me! I'm the one who tries to do right and live by the rules, remember? Your rules."

She wiped her nose again on the tail of her nightgown and tried to follow a single floating dust fragment through the air. Maybe people were just so many frogs' eggs after all. So many of them, and most of them living and dying like flies. How was she any different? Millions, maybe billions of people were alive right now. A long, slimy string of endless frogs' eggs, most of which never even made it to the tadpole stage. All the ones who didn't matter. Only a few ever survived and most of them didn't matter.

She frowned, feeling calmer, and scratched the instep of one foot. What about all the Ammonites and Jebusites and whatever other ites he'd wiped out to make room for the Israelites in the Promised Land? What about those African babies with their distended stomachs? Maybe God could afford the waste. Maybe it was all just percentages with him. Either you were at the right place at the right time or else you ended up part of the squandered excess. Maybe that was the way it worked after all. So he knows every sparrow that falls to the ground. Big deal. It still falls.

She sighed and leaned her head back, only feeling dull now, the way she usually did after a long cry. She could have sat and stared at the drifting motes all day, her mind as empty as the shaft of sunlight hitting her leg.

"All right," she said out loud after a while. "If that's what you want, fine. That's what I'll be. Just this idiot membrane holding nutrients for all the really important people." She got to her feet, went into the bathroom, and turned on the shower, feeling a certain grim pleasure at having surrendered to her fate. "Okay," she said. "Go ahead. Screw me. See if I care."

She jerked the shower curtain back and watched the water swirling down the drain. God's concubine, she thought recklessly, that's all I am. He keeps me around to use for his own purposes. If she was going to be blasphemous, she might as well go all the way.

She dropped her nightgown on the floor and stepped into the tub, kicking a plastic dinosaur to the back as the water began to wet her crinkly hair. Before she shaved her legs, she lifted her breasts, pushing in a little, to see if they were growing tender yet.

Now that she thought about it, that was a pretty good way to put it—a concubine, submitting to God's will. Like the Song of Solomon. *Let my beloved come to his garden, and eat its choicest fruits.* But then. To be the apple of his eye.

She ran her fingers over her abdomen, imagining the clump of cells already growing inside her, translucent. Like frog eggs. But more. Marked already with herself, her self. She might have added, marked with Tim as well, except that just then she thought of the clump as having been implanted there, inside her, intentionally. Tim hadn't known what he was doing. But *he* had known the very instant the cells united.

The thought, whirring enormous in her head, made her dizzy. She had to put out one hand to steady herself. Then slowly she slid down the slippery shower wall till she was crouching in the tub, laughing at the pellets of steaming water pounding her the way they had when she and Deb used to spray one another with the hose in summer as children.

Fifteen minutes later when Tim came into the bedroom to ask where the new bottle of Flintstone vitamins was, he found her shaking out her damp tangle of curls. She was smiling faintly as she turned from the mirror and let the pink towel she'd wrapped around her slide to the floor. "Behold the handmaid of the Lord," she said.

5

The arrivals screen in the international terminal showed the flight from Heathrow would be an hour late. The delay suddenly seemed more than Deborah could deal with.

"What's the problem?" she demanded of the man at the British Airways desk.

He mumbled something about the weather, keeping his eyes on his computer screen as he punched up a ticket for a college student checking a backpack and duffel bag.

"Really? I thought the weather was fine. I checked the weather channel this morning."

The man looked up at the student. "Checking through to the Orkneys?" he asked.

Deborah turned away abruptly and stalked down the corridor toward the nearest restroom. A gaunt woman in jeans and a skimpy tank top was changing a baby on a pull-down table. The baby was crying thinly. Deborah scanned the row of sinks, pretending to be looking for something she'd left behind, then turned and hurried out again.

The next restroom along the corridor was deserted. "Calm down," she muttered to her image in the mirror as she bent over the sink. "This could take hours. And do something with yourself. You look a wreck."

She pulled the makeup bag from her handbag and unzipped it, setting it on the edge of the sink while she splashed water on her flushed face. Reaching to turn off the faucet, her hand brushed the bag, and its contents clattered onto the floor. A cylinder of mascara rolled under the door of one of the stalls.

She swore under her breath as she bent down to retrieve the tube. When she stood up again her head was swimming. She tried to steady herself against the stall door, but it swung inward, almost spilling her onto the floor. She dropped onto the toilet seat and drew a deep, shuddering breath. "Get a grip, Deborah," she whispered shakily.

Pris would pray now, she thought. Aloud. She was always so damn cozy with God. But then Pris had never found out she was pregnant right after her lover had left her.

Deborah got up wearily and went back to the sink, dumping the spilled makeup back into the bag. Rummaging toward the bottom of her handbag, she found a small brush and ran it through her hair. Just last week she'd spent a hundred dollars—a price she knew to be exorbitant—to have a gay hairdresser duplicate the streaks of blond she'd had in junior high. He'd massaged her neck every time he came to check the long foil-wrapped bundles of hair, his long thin fingers trailing sensuously along her throat, stroking upward. It was that she'd been paying for.

She stared at herself in the mirror. The skin under her eyes looked dark and bruised. There were lines like incised parentheses on either side of her mouth, and a double furrow on her forehead. Where was this glow you were supposed to get when you were pregnant?

She flipped her long hair to one side and snapped her handbag shut. She needed a drink. Maybe several.

Out in the corridor again, she glanced both directions at the overhead pictographs, looking for the glass that indicated a bar. "Chapel located on second level," the one to her left said. For a moment she pictured herself sitting, demurely reverent, on a molded plastic seat in a darkened room the size of a largish closet with a backlit generic altar.

Maybe there'd be some peace and quiet where she could pull herself together. Sure. More likely there'd be some woman dressed like a Mennonite, her eyes magnified by thick glasses, who'd want to be helpful. Or worse, a grinning volunteer pastor with his shirt buttons gaping. The sort she'd joined the Catholic Church to escape.

The cocktail-glass logo was on the next sign along the concourse. She saw with relief that the bar had windows at the back where she could watch the planes, away from the neon lighting. She stopped at the bar and picked up a scotch and water, then sank into a chair at one of the platter-sized tables by the glass wall, setting her handbag on the floor by the chair.

Taste hadn't been her only reason for converting, of course. She'd needed something to stabilize the world, to save her from the vertigo of her isolated subjectivity. At least you always knew where you stood with the Catholic Church, she'd told Father Botts. How many degrees wrong you'd gone and just what you had to do to get back on course.

She didn't like scotch and had only ordered it thinking she'd drink it more slowly. After a while the muscles in her shoulders and arms begin to loosen. Maybe she should eat something too. She asked for peanuts and a gin and tonic, figuring she'd earned it after the scotch. That's probably all she'd have time for. Surely two drinks wouldn't be enough to cause fetal alcohol syndrome. She'd had nothing to drink since Scott left.

The frosted glass was still half full when she began to imagine Scott walking into the bar, just off his flight from Mexico, newly tanned. Her head would be turned away, looking out the window, but he'd recognize her by the long loop of hair across her shoulder. He'd want to sit down, but she'd look up at him, almost smiling, and say she was just leaving, meeting someone else's flight.

Or no. He'd walk in—they'd never have met—and he'd see her sitting there alone and—what would he say? What line would he use? Haven't I seen you somewhere before? Appeals court, wasn't it? I knew it! You're an attorney, aren't you? What firm? Mind if I sit down? And she'd lean back, motioning to the other chair with a gesture somewhere between languid and indifferent, taking in the rolled cuffs, the Italian loafers, the blond hair just below the little dip in the sternum, though the shirt wouldn't be unbuttoned the extra obvious notch. But most of all taking in what money couldn't buy—the long perpendicular bones in his face, the oblique bar from his ear to his eye, the deft indentation at his temples before they rose to the sleek forehead, sloped only enough to give the impression of forward movement. Bones, her mother had always told her, are the most important part of beauty. You're either born with them or you're not. And they last the longest.

Deborah had good bones too. Both she and Scott had good bones. She shuddered involuntarily. She wasn't a brood mare. Still, she would have been willing. Glad, even. Carefully, she set the glass down and began composing a letter to him in her mind. Dear Scott, The baby has beautiful bones.

Down below on the tarmac, a man with headphones around his neck was talking to a long-haired guy in jeans who had one foot propped on a wheeled conveyer belt. How did they bear the heat? The acres of concrete must be like the bottom of a stove. The window between her and the men was faintly tinted, giving the false impression that the empty sky was always about to rain, making it appear cooler outside than it was.

She'd forced herself to tell Father Botts about Scott. It had been the first real test of her new religion. At first her Protestant-bred soul had dug in its heels. But she'd been prepared for that reaction. Sister Edwina who had catechized her when she was a law student at Saint Mary's had warned her, "Sin is never a private matter, Deborah. Everything we do, for good or ill, affects the fate of the whole world. Confession is like a mirror. It gives us a truer picture of ourselves than the one in our heads."

And she'd been right. When Deborah told Father Botts about Scott, it was no brazen rebel that had looked back at her from the mirror of his eyes but a pathetic, desperate woman. She'd felt more shame than guilt.

But she hadn't given up Scott. And gradually she'd found herself actually wanting to go to confession, seeing it as an emotional trade-off—the humiliation before the priest somehow making up for the pleasure of Scott. Or maybe it was just the humiliation itself she enjoyed. She wanted him to plead with her: *Deborah, sweetheart. Don't do this. He's not worthy of you.* That had frightened her. So she'd simply stopped going to the altar after Easter, hoping Father Botts wouldn't notice. She didn't want the poor man to feel like a failure. She wouldn't be officially obligated to go to confession again till Advent, next November. She had expected things to be settled with Scott, one way or another, by then.

As it turned out, it had been a good decision. Now she wouldn't have Scott on her conscience anymore. And the pregnancy would be a vindication for the priest. *Deborah, darling. I tried to warn you...*

Assuming, of course, she actually had it. She'd confessed to unchastity, but she knew she'd never be able to tell Father Botts about an abortion. She wasn't even sure just how many degrees wrong that was or what you could do to get back on course after that.

Three men with briefcases peeled off from the river of forms flowing steadily along the concourse and eddied into the bar. They picked up their drinks and moved to a table where they could see the local sports news on the TV set suspended from the ceiling. One of them—a short, wiry fellow in a suit with western points—was protesting that Dorene would be waiting for him down at the baggage claim area.

"She'll keep," said one of the others. "No telling when we'll all be on the same flight like this again."

The third man snorted. "Yeah. Time we did a little male bonding here."

She could tell he was looking at her. In her peripheral vision, she could see him turn in her direction, one arm leaning on the table. His forehead was narrow and his jawline, what there was of it, had long since been swallowed up by his double chin. The glass he was rotating between his thick fingers seemed fragile and inconsequential.

Staring steadily out the window, she picked up her glass and propped her elbow on the arm folded across her waist, her daydream draining away as she gathered her defenses. The man's attention had driven away the pleasantly detached, fuzzy sensation. Lecherous bastard, she thought.

She swallowed the last inch in the glass, glanced purposefully at her watch, and left. Out in the concourse, she'd reached the sign for the chapel before she remembered her handbag. She marched back into the bar and past the table of men. Half crouching to retrieve the handbag from behind the table, she felt a snag in her pantyhose pop open over her left knee. She straightened quickly; a strand of hair caught in her mouth. She took a wobbly step back and pulled it loose, a flush starting along her throat. The chinless fellow stood up, took a step toward her and caught her elbow.

"You all right, ma'am?"

"Fine. I'm just fine."

"Sure?" His thick fingers squeezed her elbow.

She straightened and gave him a courtroom stare. "Thank you, I can manage." She slipped the handbag strap over her shoulder and started toward the concourse again, walking carefully, forcing herself not to hurry, pulling her shoulder blades together, raising her chin. Putting as much expression of disgust into her back as she could.

"Ice queen," she heard the man say as he dropped down at the table again.

"What's the matter? Couldn't melt her down, George?" one of his buddies asked.

Deborah squeezed her eyes shut, her hands gripping the stock of an AK-47. As she reached the concourse, she swung on them from hip level, scattering them backward from the table in flying pieces.

The crowd closed around her. She bumped against a lady using a tripod cane. "Sorry," she muttered and moved to the right, against the carpeted wall.

The AK-47 had become her weapon of choice after Dad had brought one home from one of his trips when she was in kindergarten. She'd watched him break it down, laying the pieces out on the kitchen counter while he explained its superiority to their own M14s. Dad was always happy when he was explaining things. An eagerness, innocent and glad, possessed him then. She'd understood nothing of his explanation and remembered only her surprise that guns came apart into pieces. That and her mother's voice sounding so hard as she said, passing through the kitchen, "Is that what G.I.s are using to shoot villagers now?"

"Of course not," Dad had answered with a certain guileless irritation, "this is Russian. One of the Lurps brought it out of a spiderhole."

Deborah had frowned, trying to picture this.

"Told me I could have it, but I'd have to check with intelligence first." He'd laughed at some obscure grownup joke.

She must have been almost seven when he brought the casing from an early TOW missile home, old enough to sense even more keenly his excitement and to connect it to the glass that was never far from his hand any more.

"See, Deb, there's wires that roll right up in here, attached to this joystick, and when you launch it—"

She remembered pondering the word "joystick"—could he bring her home one of those?—while he went on with his explanation, gesturing, mimicking the missile's trajectory.

Her mother slammed the dryer door shut. "An ersatz penis."

Deborah stared at the dark olive cylinder, frowning. What were they talking about?

Then her father gave one of his short, barking laughs. He looked sideways at her mother, "We'll shove it right down those gooks' throats. Wham." He struck his fist into his hand.

Miriam's face had gone rigid. "You're disgusting, Gordon. That's your own child you're talking to like that, for God's sake."

His head nodded unsteadily on his long neck, like a bloom too heavy for its stalk. He slid off the stool he'd been perched on at the counter and started toward the door of the laundry room.

"Get out of my way, Gordon," her mother said. "Deborah, go make your bed."

Deborah had waited for her father to protest on her behalf, but his back was to her. He was hanging with one hand onto the doorframe. As she slipped down from the other stool, she heard her mother say, "Forget it, Gordon. Don't even think about it."

He took a clumsy step backward as her mother pushed past him.

"Come on, Deb," he finally mumbled, his gaze still on his wife, "I'll show you what I brought back for you. A nice little star sapphire I picked up in Hong Kong. Maybe your mother can get it set for you."

Deborah still had the stone, unset. Even years later, after she'd figured out that she and Pris had been the battleground for another war he must have seen from the beginning he would lose, she couldn't bring herself to get rid of anything he'd ever given her. The lacquered jewelry box inlaid with ivory and jade. A silk kimono the shade of green he knew she loved best. It had been made for an adult, but she put it on once when she was thirteen and it had fit perfectly. That was three years after the divorce, when they'd moved to Denver. Her mother had been studying for comps.

"Look, Mom," she cried, twirling from the mirror. "Madame Butterfly."

Miriam twisted her neck first to one side and then the other. She had a headache. "He probably got it from some Japanese whore all right." It was the one remark Deborah had never forgiven her mother for.

All his gifts had been glorious and completely inappropriate for children. Before the divorce, before the war—she could remember this better than Pris—he had bought them racing bikes. One Christmas, an elaborate science kit that generated electricity and ran a little fan. She sat patiently at the dining room table, watching him assemble it and explain in words she had no meanings for, knowing that her attention, submerged as it was in a lake of ignorance, was nevertheless essential to him.

Later, the gifts had stopped altogether. For a couple of years Mother had made excuses. He was probably travelling. He'd been sick. Once he was in the veterans' hospital. Pris had wanted to go to him then.

"Jesus commanded us to visit the sick, Mom," she'd declared. "And he's our father after all."

Miriam had stared out the window a full minute before she answered. Deborah could sense her mother groping for words to reply. "Look, sweetheart," she finally said. "It's not an ordinary kind of disease your father has. It's—"

"Alcoholism," Deborah rushed in. "They won't let anybody see him right now. He's being dried out." She had to get it over with. She couldn't stand the way her mother dragged out explanations. "So just shut up about it, Pris."

Her mother and sister had both stared at her, stunned. Deborah got up and stalked from the room, impatient with their shock, sick of the whole messy subject. Dad was gone. He'd been gone a long time. He wasn't coming back. They'd all gotten used to it. So why couldn't everybody just shut up about it? Life was simpler without men anyway. They only complicated things.

Why hadn't she stuck with that attitude?

She had almost passed up the British Airways counter before she recognized the large red letters. The man she'd spoken to before wasn't there. Too bad. She could have used her AK-47 on him too. Instead, a girl with smoky eyeshadow and bright lips told her the plane was on its approach now and should be arriving in fifteen minutes. Deborah found the right gate and settled into a seat facing the runway.

To be fair, she had to admit Scott hadn't known she was pregnant when he dumped her. And she'd make damned sure he'd never know now. An oblique revenge, but the only one left to her.

"What is it with women?" he'd said to her once when she'd made up some excuse for not having dinner with his parents. "If you don't want to go, why not just say so? Why can't women just say what they want up front?" She'd replied with a heavy sigh and sidelong look. Much as she hated to admit it though, he was right. She had always come at what she wanted indirectly. When had she ever had another option? When had she ever been strong enough simply to enforce her will the way a man could? She was always justifying, marshalling reasons—actual or invented—automatically, instinctively.

She leaned back, stretching out her legs almost to the window, and closed her eyes. Maybe this was for the best after all. Scott had left—smug, but ignorant. In the Bible, it was always a man who "knew" a woman. Well, this time, buddy, the tables were turned. She was the one who knew. He was unaware of his own child. Maybe ten years from now she'd come across him unexpectedly, possibly at the natural history museum where she'd take their son to see the dinosaur skeletons. Scott would be with his wife, a blowzy socialite with champagne-pink hair. Hello, Deborah, he'd say. I didn't know you were married. This is your son?

I'm not, she'd say. And this is Scott, Jr. Doesn't he have lovely bones?

It really is better this way, she told herself again, sliding further down into the seat so she could drop her neck across the back. This way she could raise the baby the way she wanted to, without any interference from him or his family. She'd have it baptized at St. Christopher's. She'd be wearing a suit, sedate but not staid, navy probably. The baby's christening robe would hang clear to her knees. For some reason, in her mind's eye she was also wearing a hat with a veil. Mother and Pris would be there too, just behind her in the shadows of the cavernous nave. Father Botts would look at her with a mixture of sorrow and sweetness on his beagle face while she held up her head like Hester Prynne with little Pearl in *The Scarlet Letter*. Undaunted.

She'd feed the baby imported meusli for breakfast. Read him Christopher Robin stories. Get rid of the television set. Could she afford a nanny? An older woman who wore cotton housedresses.

She could raise a child by herself. After all, she and Mom and Pris had made out all right on their own. Without Dad. In fact, they'd all been relieved when he finally left for good. Except maybe Pris. But then she'd only been eight when the divorce happened—an event Mom, for some reason, had always linked to Nixon signing the peace accords in Paris.

Over the years, her sister had devised her own history of their parents' marriage, one that attributed its failure to their political differences over the war. Dad, Pris maintained, being a man, naturally supported the war. He'd even worked for Army Intelligence. Mom, on the other hand, had a woman's innate distaste for war. It was a version that allowed Pris to absolve them both.

But Pris didn't remember as clearly as Deborah did the unhappy times in that house in Freeport. Tiptoeing around Dad, unconscious on the living room floor, the drapes drawn against the morning sun. The screaming and shouting and anger so heavy it made the air hard to breathe. Mother taking guns and a rifle out of the closet and from under the bed and locking them in the trunk of her car. What had become of the guns after that? Their disappearance had presaged his own.

But that was later. Deborah had only been about three herself when they moved into the new house. Five years old when Dad began to go away, at first for a few days, then later for longer stretches, until finally he was gone for weeks at a time. Feet Numb, she thought her parents were telling her, until she learned to read and could identify the name of the place in the newspaper headlines.

She must have been in second grade the day she discovered Vietnam was a dangerous place to be. Her mother had been studying for a test at school when the news came on. She looked up, listened a moment, then stiffened. Suddenly she picked up her textbook and, with a cry, hurled it at the television set as she sprang up to turn it off.

Priscilla's large dark eyes followed her across the room. "Was it Daddy," she asked in a whisper. "Did they kill Daddy?"

Deborah was sitting on the floor dressing a Heidi doll— Mother didn't allow them to have Barbies. "No, dummy," she muttered to her sister. "Didn't you see? It was gooks."

Suddenly she felt herself jerked upright and shaken till she couldn't get her breath.

"Don't you ever, ever let me hear you use that word again! Do you hear?"

She stared at her mother's face, hardly recognizing her. Her long, straight hair, parted in the middle, hung around her face in a lank curtain. The breath was whistling through her nose and her jaw was locked.

Deborah's eyes fastened on her mother's, refusing to blink. A surge of adrenalin shot through her. "Dad says it." She braced herself, holding her neck rigid, expecting to be slapped. Even wanting it. A vindication. She could already feel the tingle on her cheek.

But her mother's hands fell away and she took a step back. Her lips twitched several times, as if she were about to speak. But nothing came out. Then she turned and went into her bedroom and shut the door.

Pris stared after her, then turned to Deborah. "What's a gook?" she whispered.

Deborah shrugged with one shoulder. Suddenly she felt slack and sick. "Somebody you kill," she said indifferently.

She had been ashamed later when she heard a teacher explaining that "gook" was a word like "nigger," a word she would never have used, even at seven. But she didn't let her mother see that she was ashamed, even when Miriam apologized for shaking her. And she never talked about Dad when he was away anymore after that.

She was eight when he finally came home for good. Or what they had hoped would be good. But by then he was already a stranger to her, not simply because of his prolonged absences but because he had changed from the person he had been, the one she couldn't even remember clearly any more, only sensing his mutation.

All she retained from that earlier time were pictures in her mind. Her father putting together the metal poles of the backyard swing set, his heavy eyebrows meeting in the middle as he frowned at the white square of paper spread out on the grass beside him. His thick, dark hair, clipped too short to curl, its pent energy fascinating her. Him swinging Pris up into the air, tossing her beyond his hands so that Deborah was breathless with fear that her little sister would fall. She had wanted to be flung upwards like that too, but her mother had said she was too big now. Had he played with her like that when she was a baby?

Mother must have still been happy then, or at least Deborah had been too young to know if she wasn't. But restless. Waking her and Pris up at dawn to see the sun rise, the three of them sitting on the back deck, watching it burn off the early fog through the trees. Painting their faces with flowers and butterflies. Keeping them up past midnight to watch the meteor showers in August, and telling them the stories of the constellations.

Once they'd made a camping trip to the beach—had there been more than one?—where they all crouched around the fire Dad built in the sand after dark. Suddenly Mom had jumped to her feet and, with one arm stretched toward the bay, had given a cry that made Deborah's heart stop. They all looked toward the dark Gulf waters where she was pointing. A narrow band of pale greenish light began to glow, rise, then descend and break apart. Another rose behind it, then another. In a moment, the glowing bands had reached the shore and spread themselves like a skirt on the sand.

"A phosphorus tide," Mother breathed almost reverently.

"ATP," Dad said, standing up. "A phosphorus compound. It ignites when it's exposed to air."

"Come on, girls," Mother said, catching Deborah's hand and scooping Pris up onto her hip. As they ran along the edge of the water, Deborah saw the sand glow with her mother's footprints. Then she looked down and saw her own footprints, gleaming pale green behind her. Dad had followed more slowly.

"Is it okay?" she asked him, still uncertain.

He shrugged, his hands jammed in his pockets. "It won't hurt you. It's just lots of little organisms, sweetheart, like fireflies, only underwater."

Mother had set Pris down on the sand, and the baby was staggering in circles backward, staring at her own tracks. "They're not organisms, Gordon. They're magic!" Mom had laughed.

Maybe that had always been the difference between them, Deborah thought. Dad always wanted to explain things, like a scientist. The model electric generator. Assault weapons. The phosphorus sea. Mother, on the other hand, moved through a world of signs and wonders where every visible object was a metaphor for something else, something just beyond the range of sight. She tried to make more out of everything. Dad wanted to know how things worked. Mom wanted to know what they meant.

"You are what you eat," she'd told them a thousand times the year they were vegetarians in Denver.

"So I want to be a cow," Deborah had replied.

"Oh, you're just like—" Her mother stopped abruptly. But Deborah knew she had been going to say "your father." Just like your father. But what was her father like?

After the war ended, he wasn't even a scientist any more. He didn't try to explain things to her when he came home. He didn't go to work either. Mostly he sat at the kitchen table and drank until he moved into the living room and finally passed out on the carpet.

Some days he'd stay at the kitchen table, watching her mother move from the refrigerator to the sink, her back steadfastly to him. He'd say things calculated to make her angry—"When are we going to eat? Why can't you have dinner ready on time?"

"At least I'm doing something. Which is more than I can say for you."

"Really? Who's paying the bills here then, I'd like to know?"

"Not you, Gordon. The Defense Department's only sending you checks till they figure out what to do with you. We're just living off the government."

"Oh, you mean the same government that burns babies? The one you despise so much? What's happened to your scruples?"

"Better it go to feed people than kill them. After all, I pay taxes."

He snorted. "No, sweetheart. *I* pay taxes. You've never earned enough to pay one month's light bill. The government doesn't owe you anything. But it owes me. Big time." He watched her closely as she froze, resting her wrists on the edge of the sink. Then he added, "And it's not the only one."

She turned, a handful of wet lettuce dripping onto the floor. Deborah watched the drops make a little puddle on the tiles. "And just what do you think I owe you, Gordon?"

There had been a long pause. "Respect," he finally said. It had sounded like he was spitting.

"Respect? My God, Gordon, look at you."

After that they'd begin to yell. Sometimes Mother would run to the bedroom and slam the door, leaving their dinner half finished. Sometimes she'd hustle her and Pris out the door to a neighborhood park where they'd swing or seesaw morosely for an hour till they could count on his being asleep on the floor.

Whenever he left the house, her mother would make furtive calls to a friend on the bedroom phone. Deborah could hear her through the closed door, crying. The phrases were repeated so often she learned them by heart. "I'm losing my mind. I don't know what to do. What should I do?"

During one of his long absences, her mother had started back to school. After he came home to stay, she still spread out her books on the dining room table, the way she had when he'd been gone, and tried to work there. But Dad would turn the TV up loud and then fall asleep in front of it, only waking up, startled, when someone turned it off. When Mom left for evening classes, she always looked worried. "Be good girls," she'd whisper so he couldn't hear. "Take care of Daddy."

Deborah raised her head from the chair back, puffed out her cheeks and blew, as if expelling her frustration. Then she sat up and rummaged in her handbag for breath mints. Mother still clipped articles out of magazines linking alcoholism to heredity and sent them to her. Her way of completing the phrase she'd never actually spoken. Just like your father.

She yawned and checked her watch again. Funny that Pris, who actually looked so much like Dad, was as much of a romantic as their mother. People said Deborah favored her grandmother, though it was hard for her to see the resemblance herself. For one thing, Gram would never be sprawled half tipsy, her stocking sprung, in some airport lounge.

The last they'd heard of Dad, he was someplace in

New Mexico. If Gram died, Deborah hoped her mother wouldn't insist on trying to contact him about the funeral. It was impossible to retrieve the original Gordon Estes. She'd never know now if she were like him or not.

She sat up and brushed at the wrinkles in her skirt. She could never do that to a child—bring him up with only a blank, a void where his father should be, his own identity leaking away through that hole.

From somewhere overhead and behind her, a voice was finally announcing the incoming flight from London. Deborah took a breath, her head suddenly clearing. She stood up, catching at her hair and pulling it to one side, over her shoulder.

She moved toward the ramp doorway, straining to see over the heads of people crowding forward to greet travellers. In a few more seconds Mom would be coming up the passageway, her head bobbing and disappearing again behind the other passengers, one shoulder sagging under the weight of a carry-on bag, her eyes vague as she searched the waiting faces, her expression ricocheting between anxiety and expectation.

The stream of passengers was thinning to a trickle. Mother had enough to deal with already. Deborah shut her eyes. She'll be next if I don't look. Don't look yet, don't look.

There was no way. She couldn't do it, not right now. It was time to stop fooling herself. Stop all the fantasizing. She was in no position to take care of a baby. Not the way it ought to be. So what was the point in even telling Mother?

6

Miriam could feel the inside of her chest cavity sweating cold moisture like the brick walls of an old well. It was both better and worse than she'd expected. Better because her mother hadn't died and, at intervals, was conscious and able to speak. Worse because Miriam had never seen her look so helpless.

Hannah lay stretched out on the hospital bed, the escarpment of her clavicle jutting above the hollow where the cartilaginous shaft of her neck began. The knob of her wrist bone overhung her hand. She looked eroded. Miriam had expected her to look gaunt. What upset her most was simply seeing her mother horizontal. Hannah had never taken naps during the day, had always been the first one up in the morning, didn't lounge. This shift of axis contradicted everything Miriam knew about her mother. She who was the definition of upright, of perpendicular. She was the steady needle on a gauge. A flood marker sticking above the turbulent water, twigs and bits of debris forming a parabola around her as she leaned into the current.

After Miriam had finally made it to the hospital last night, dizzy and jet-lagged, Hannah had opened her eyes and smiled weakly. "How's my girl?" she'd whispered, just as if she were still the one on her feet. Miriam knew she was really saying don't make a fuss, don't add any weight to whatever's about to burst through the dam. So she had merely lifted her mother's long hand—Hannah hadn't even the energy for that—and dropped into the chair Pris had pushed up beside the bed. The air whistled shallowly in her mother's chest which lifted with a jerk at each breath.

"Don't talk, Mother," she'd said. "In the morning, when you're feeling stronger." Hannah had closed and opened her eyes, a substitute for a nod. Then she'd seemed to relax a little; the hand had gradually gone limp in Miriam's hand. After that, Hannah hadn't waked, had hardly even moved. Numb from travel and feeling as if her soul had been left behind in some foreign baggage claim area, Miriam had finally gone back to Deborah's apartment and slept the clock around.

Now she sat by the hospital bed again, absorbing the contours of her mother's leveled body as if she were studying an aerial photograph of a dig site and telling herself it was stupid to be angry. At the girls for not letting her know sooner. At herself for having left the country. At Tim for spoiling the plans she'd made to take Hannah with her. At Hannah for looking like this.

She wasn't ready to let Hannah go. She wasn't even ready for her to be seriously ill. She figured her cosmic accounts were all paid up for some time to come. She'd lost her father, then her brother. Not to mention a husband. She could remember not only losing them, but when they'd first come into her life. She couldn't remember the world without Hannah, however. Like air and water, she had always simply been. Though they differed on many points, Miriam had given up arguing with her mother long ago. About Gordon, the girls, about God. You didn't argue with air and water.

She sat now, listening for the dry hiss of sand, blowing in and settling grain by grain, filling the clammy cavity inside her chest. This was the way the earth covered loss. Graves, houses, cities—everything disappeared eventually under the literal sands of time, Yigal had said to her. He had been pointing to a large depression at Ashkelon, supposedly the Well of Abraham.

"They didn't have the technology to dig wells straight down, of course. Instead they made a sort of terraced crater," he explained. "Later the Romans turned this one into a tiered theater. Lately, it's been used for dog shows." He put his hands on his hips in a military stance and squinted off to the horizon. "Everything happens on top of something else in this world. Every child is conceived over someone else's grave." He gave a laconic snort at his own aphorism.

Life was full of holes, she remembered thinking then. With luck, the hole filled up.

On the other hand, what she liked about archaeology was that it reversed that process. It dug things up, made holes instead of covering them. Excavation, she figured, wasn't exactly resurrection, but it was as close as you were likely to get in this world. Maybe what you dug up wasn't life, wasn't living, but at least those pieces of broken oil lamps, crusted jewelry, hinges from a door long since rotted were evidence that couldn't be ignored, reminders that the past was real, that someone had been there.

Miriam stood up and went to the sink near the door and ran a trickle of water into a paper cup. She carried it to the window beyond the bed and stood drinking slowly, a sip at a time, the way she'd learned to do in the desert. She wanted Hannah to wake up now. Pris would be back soon, her own fear and need like a compressed spring.

And Deb would be here later in the afternoon. Even through the fog in her brain last night, Miriam could tell that something was bothering her elder daughter. Deb had come to the door as Miriam was crawling into bed, and stood, one hand holding an alarm clock, the other resting on the doorknob, hesitating just as she always had when she wanted to talk.

"Mom?"

That single plaintive syllable had sent fibrillations clear to Miriam's elbows.

But Deb's lips had only twisted in a tight smile. "Sleep as late as you like. I'll probably be gone when you wake up." She ran a hand through her hair in what Miriam recognized as a sign of anxiety. "Let's see. Tim's dropping off his car for you. It'll be in my parking spot out back. So. Sleep well." And she'd closed the bedroom door.

Worrying over a grown daughter was as bad in its own way as dealing with one as a teenager. The wanting and not wanting to know, the knowing and pretending not to. Miriam glanced back at the white sheet making a sierra of Hannah's bony shoulder and upthrust hip. How much, she wondered, had Hannah figured out about that summer before she'd married Gordon?

At the time, Miriam had been relieved that her mother was too distracted with Barton to catch on. She hadn't even felt guilty at the time, hadn't been fully aware that her deception was breaking forever the alliance between them.

She had, however, been aware that she was only passing organic chemistry because she was sleeping with Gordon, her lab instructor. She had, in fact, signed up for the course—one not in her degree plan and for which she had no preparation—only after discovering that he was the graduate assistant for the single lab section still open. Her roommate Lanell had pointed him out in the student union during spring registration. He was smoking and talking intently to a guy in an ROTC uniform at a table close to the snack bar.

"Too intense," Lanell cautioned her. She was a biology major hoping to be a nurse.

Miriam was a sophomore and hadn't settled on either a major or a career. She felt restless and unfocused. She'd read *Lady Chatterley's Lover*, *Thus Spake Zarathustra*, and *Coming of Age in Samoa*, all in the last two weeks.

"I love intense men," she said, staring at the triangle of heavy black hair Gordon kept pushing back from his forehead.

And he was intense. He had talked passionately about the Bay of Pigs on their second date as he fumbled with the hook on her bra. She hadn't known it was in Cuba.

Still, another month passed before she could tell Lanell they'd gone all the way (they still said that in the early sixties), and even then, only after she agreed to help him raise money on campus to ransom captured rebels from Castro. From Gordon's point of view, combining sex and politics was a real timesaver.

Miriam liked it when they talked about politics. All she had to say was "Che Guevara" and he'd start unbuttoning her blouse. It was definitely better than studying organic chemistry.

She'd been scared to death, of course, about getting pregnant in those pre-pill days. Strangely, for all his scientific expertise, Gordon hardly seemed aware of the possibility. When she brought it up, he merely shrugged and said if it happened they'd get married.

But Miriam wasn't at all sure she wanted to marry Gordon. She wasn't sure she wanted to marry anyone. Life was just getting to be exciting, after that long terrible stretch of high school and her first awkward year of college. She had this sense of herself standing on some high overlook with all the world spread out shining before her. As soon as she took a step forward though, she would plummet earthward. That sparkling panoramic view would be lost.

But once she'd started sleeping with Gordon every weekend, she found she couldn't stop. What she craved was not so much her own satisfaction as seeing Gordon turn into another kind of creature altogether as soon as he touched her. The emotional distance between them would suddenly collapse. His aloof preoccupation vanished and he would plead as shamelessly as a starving man. Miriam felt as if she'd discovered some kind of mystical power, one she hadn't known she possessed until then and still only dimly understood.

She had Lanell figure her fertility cycle precisely; on the risky weekends she went home to Houston. With Lanell's chart and glops of the spermicidal cream she made Gordon buy, she had managed. Even now, the scent of Delfen had an erotic effect on her.

"I got accepted at Purdue," Gordon said one evening as he rolled over and reached for a cigarette. They'd been watching William Buckley on his little black and white TV. It was almost time for her to get back to the dorm before Sunday night curfew. She had started to dress, and her red plaid skirt was halfway over her head. The zipper caught in her hair.

She yanked it loose and sat down on the bed, the mattress sagging under her, and picked up her stockings from the floor. She'd intended to stuff them in her handbag along with the garter belt. It was too much trouble to put them on again. "Purdue?"

"I told you, remember? I applied to their doctoral program." He paused, then added wearily, "Purdue's in Indiana."

"Indiana," she repeated, trying to picture what piece that was in her old wooden Map of the USA puzzle. One of those midwestern states, but not a square one. All she knew for sure as that it was a long way from Texas. And Hannah.

"Are you going?" Her voice sounded small.

"Not till August."

"August? Gordon, it's already May! Finals are next week."

He shrugged and stubbed out the cigarette in the old mayonnaise lid on the window sill beside the bed. "That's three months away. Don't worry."

"What do you mean, three months? I'm going home after finals, remember?"

He got up and started putting on what she called his Kingston trio pants, the ones with the little buckle across the kidneys. "Yeah. I forgot."

"So is this going to be it? After next week I may never see you again?"

He sat down and started to put on his shoes. "I suppose you could go with me," he said.

"You mean—" she hesitated, "get married?"

He stood up and put his hands on his hips. "I guess that would be the easiest, wouldn't it? Hurry up. We're going to be late." He checked his watch.

It was the only proposal she ever got.

They rode back to the dorm in silence. She was too stunned to speak. He was thinking about either polymers or precincts or whatever went on in his head. Certainly not her. When they pulled up in front of the fake Georgian columns, the dorm mother was already blinking the lights to signal the couples outside.

"Let me know soon," he said, not even switching off the ignition. "I'll have to contact the graduate housing office to reserve an apartment."

She nodded numbly and got out.

She hadn't said yes. She hadn't said anything. She told Lanell, of course, who squealed with delight, then asked if she were pregnant.

"Of course not," Miriam answered, sounding wounded. Already in 1962, virtue consisted in successfully avoiding consequences.

"Ah-h-h," Lanell sighed in naked envy. "I can't believe you, Miriam. You saw what you wanted, and you just went and got it. Sex and everything."

Miriam hadn't liked that. Even then, "sex" sounded too truncated, too blunt.

"I wished it worked like that for me." Lanell was still writing to her high school sweetheart back in San Angelo and going bowling with the college class at her church.

Miriam, to her knowledge, had never been envied before. She found it produced a certain pleasure, in itself almost erotic.

"My folks don't want me to get married till I've finished college," Lanell went on. "They say they want me to have something to fall back on."

Miriam hadn't even mentioned Gordon to her mother yet, for fear of giving herself away. Hannah was practically psychic about sin. Still, she couldn't just announce out of the blue that she was getting married. And was she? Was that what she really wanted?

One day she did and the next she didn't. She daydreamed during class about living in a graduate student apartment with Gordon, going to parties with other couples, having her own dishes and towel sets. She could picture herself picking Gordon up at the lab in the car, keeping supper hot for him in the oven, making flagrant love on the sofa to "Face the Nation" on Sunday mornings instead of putting on high heels and stockings for Sunday School. Then she'd see a poster on the French department bulletin board for study abroad and decide she was crazy. There was still too much to do, too much to find out.

She couldn't make up her mind.

Then, in the middle of the following week, the buzzer sounded in the dorm room about nine-thirty in the evening. Gordon rarely called her at the dorm, especially on weekdays. She picked up the phone at the end of the hall with her heart in her throat.

Her mother's voice sounded thin, strained through static and distance. "I just wanted you to know so you could be praying, sweetheart. Your little brother's in the hospital. They're not sure what it is yet. You know those bad headaches he's been having for several months now? Well, he passed out at school yesterday."

As Hannah talked, Miriam could feel her head growing clear and cold, as if she were waking from a dream.

"I'm in his room now. I'd let you say hello to him except they've already knocked him out. They'll probably operate first thing in the morning." Her mother's voice had taken on the austere edge it always did when she was determined to keep it under control.

"Should I come home, Mother? Do you want me to?" Now, from the vantage point of thirty years of motherhood, Miriam knew she should never have put the offer in the form of a question.

There was only a moment's hesitation, however. Then Hannah said, "No, sweetheart, no. You've got your finals coming up, I know. You stay there and do well on them. I'll keep in touch, and if there's any danger, I'll let you know. I promise."

"Are you sure, Mother?"

"Yes. Certainly. I've already arranged to take next week off from work and Lucille's coming in the morning to stay with me."

"Well, if you're sure."

"Yes, baby. You just stay there and do well on your tests. You're going to need that scholarship next year. If Barton has to have an operation, it's going to take all our savings, even with insurance."

"Don't worry about that, Mother. You just take care of Barton. And yourself. I love you, Mother."

The next morning the doctors removed a tumor the size of a stuffed olive from behind Barton's left eye, and Miriam walked out of her history final knowing she'd flunked it. She had been unable to concentrate. She had never actually failed anything before.

That afternoon she took the French final. The words swam before her eyes, not words at all, but little individual animalia with legs and a life of their own. After half an hour, she turned the paper in almost blank and left.

So much for the scholarship. The world was coming apart. Whatever had glued it together till then was suddenly dissolving or drying and cracking. She had never felt so shaken, clear down to her roots, not even when they'd gotten the news about her father. She could scarcely walk.

In a daze she made her way across campus to the Student Union and found Gordon in his usual spot close to the snack bar. She hadn't seen or talked to him since he'd brought her home Sunday night. Without a word, she reached into his shirt pocket and extracted a cigarette from his pack of L&Ms and waited till he lit it for her.

He shook the match out, frowning. "When did you take up smoking?"

"You'll have to come home and meet my mother," she said.

He shrugged. "Okay."

"And my brother."

He looked at her with mild surprise. "You have a brother?"

"If he's still alive." And she began to cry.

They drove down to Houston that weekend in Gordon's '52 Chevy. Barton was out of danger by then, but the doctor said it was too early for a prognosis. Gordon stayed with a friend in the Heights, and when he came over for Sunday dinner, he asked Hannah very politely if he might marry her daughter.

Miriam, of course, had already told Hannah about his proposal the night before while they were folding the week's laundry. She watched her mother's face closely. Would she be surprised, disappointed, suspicious?

Hannah only looked dazed after a week of sleepless nights. Uncertain and tired. "This is awfully sudden, baby."

"It won't be till the fall," Miriam said. "I've known him almost five months now. That'll be almost a year."

"Is he a Christian, Miriam?"

She heard the steel slip back into her mother's voice. "Of course, Mother." Actually, the only religion they'd discussed was Kennedy's and its impact on the last election. It had made for a memorable Saturday afternoon.

"What does he do? How can he support a wife if he's still a student?"

"I already told you. He's got this graduate fellowship to work on his doctorate in chemistry at Purdue next year. We have to sign up for married student housing by next week."

"And he gets paid for being a student? Enough to support a wife?"

Miriam had no idea how much the fellowship paid nor how much it cost to support a wife. "Of course."

"What about his family?"

"His parents were killed in a car crash. He's an orphan." She'd been saving this. The very word had an immediate softening effect on Hannah. "He's been brought up by two old maid aunts in Dallas."

"Really?" Hannah's hands smoothed the pillowcase in her lap slowly. "How old was he when he lost his parents?"

"Around eleven, I think."

Hannah tilted her head sideways as she stacked the folded clothes in separate piles for different rooms and drawers. She made a sympathetic clicking sound with her tongue. "Almost the same age you were when we lost your dad." Then she looked up at Miriam, worry wrinkling the fine skin between her brows. "What about school?"

Miriam shrugged. "I'm sure I can transfer most of my credits to Purdue." She didn't mention the disastrous finals.

Gordon appeared at the door at twelve-thirty the next morning, just as Hannah was tying on her apron after church. Her mother's face had that timid-cordial look Miriam had hoped for. With the financial difficulties brought on by Barton's surgery, Hannah could hardly insist that Miriam stay in school. Indiana, they had both agreed last night, was a long way away. But by that point, Miriam could tell, as with every other hardship that had befallen them, her mother had made up her mind to make the best of it.

Gordon had even bought a ring. It was the one thing he had ever done that surprised her. After that, she forgot about the rest of her finals and the fertility cycle. Not that she had any desire to get pregnant. Babies bored her. But now that she'd made up her mind to marry Gordon, the fear of pregnancy, which had been linked in her mind to not being married, foolishly disappeared.

Miriam stayed at the university for the final weeks of May while Gordon finished up his projects at the lab. She told her mother she was helping to close up the dorm.

None of the girls Miriam knew then lived openly with their boyfriends. Staying at Gordon's apartment made her feel like George Sand. She had supper waiting for him every night when he got back from the lab, even if it was midnight. And she brazened out his landlady's sour looks when she went down to the front porch to get his mail out of the box. This, she decided, is stepping off the precipice. She felt the confines of her experience cracking. It was glorious.

Gordon hardly seemed to notice she was there, though he seemed glad enough for the hot meals. She sometimes fell asleep if he had to go back to the lab at night, and he didn't wake her when he came to bed. In the mornings though, he made love to her, pulling her legs apart hungrily and muttering into her neck about the Pathet Lao uprisings or Billy Sol Estes and the Department of Agriculture. She tangled her hands in his hair, knowing she was clinging to a heaving volcano that would finally erupt and leave her spent and sticky, but with the confident knowledge that her body was somehow essential to contain his profound interior fury.

When he was gone, she would lie in bed, running her hand over the thin skin of her thighs he'd reddened with his beard stubble. She was beginning to believe in her body. That it was more than beautiful—it was consequential. Gordon desperately needed her, needed those blind descents into a world he never gave any other sign of acknowledging. She would smile to herself, thinking how he depended on her, how his brain—the only part of himself he valued— would explode without the release her body offered. Then she would roll over, tangled naked in the sheets, and sleep till noon.

She turned on the radio as she made supper, memorizing the news that Kennedy had seen his first H-bomb on a B-52 at Eglin Air Force Base that day or that he was proposing turning Laos into a buffer zone. The day the Seventh Fleet reached Bangkok with 125 warships and five thousand troops moved west of the Mekong delta, Gordon came home for lunch and, for the first time, was late getting back to the lab. In later years, she thought of those last weeks of May as their actual honeymoon.

They were married in early August at the Baptist church where she'd spent years learning Bible verses on pink flashcards and cutting up on the back pews with her friends during revivals. Hannah had made her wedding dress, working on it late into the night after she came home from work. Barton, fully recovered, walked her down the aisle.

As they glided past the pews of friends and relatives, Miriam felt as if she were floating on some cosmic ocean, washed on a warm tide toward some green shore that promised parrots and mangos. When she turned to take Gordon's arm, she caught sight of her mother's stricken face in the second pew and felt as if she had suddenly bumped against something sinister submerged in the sea water.

After the ceremony on the way back up the aisle though, this time with both hands looped confidently over Gordon's arm, she saw that Hannah was smiling. Miriam's fear loosened and drifted away as the wave caught and lifted her.

"Miriam?"

She jumped at the sound of Hannah's voice behind her, and, for a split second, it seemed as if all the rest had been a mistake, a bad dream. "Mother? You awake?"

Hannah swallowed drily and motioned to a glass on the nightstand. Miriam filled it from the styrofoam-covered pitcher and held it for her, lifting Hannah's head with her other hand. After a couple of sips Hannah blinked and turned her head away to take a quick breath. Miriam lowered her head back to the pillow. "You've had a good sleep?"

Hannah waited till she'd taken another couple of breaths to speak. "I was dreaming." She closed her eyes and smiled slightly. "You remember Mrs. McMichaels, don't you?"

Miriam frowned. "No, Mother."

"Sure you do. She was my landlady, the whole time your father was overseas. We lived with her, you and me. In fact, she was the one who took me to the hospital when you were born." Hannah finished the last phrase in a breathy whisper, then struggled to replenish her spent breath.

Miriam drew the chair up to the bed again and sat down.

"She helped me pick your name. Don't you remember living in her house? Upstairs?"

Hannah could still see that upstairs bedroom, the low west window she worried about Miriam falling out of, the high bed with the metal bedstead and the chenille cover. Mrs. McMichaels had been her supervisor at the laundry, and when Sam had shipped out, the older woman had offered to rent Hannah her spare bedroom for next to nothing.

Mrs. McMichaels had sat beside Hannah's bed in the maternity ward, wetting her thumb and turning the pages of a worn Bible that slowly rained newspaper clippings, dried flower petals, and little poems typed on onionskin onto the wooden floor, as they searched for a name for the baby.

She'd first told Hannah the Bible story of the barren woman whose name Hannah bore. "Listen to what her husband told her," Mrs. McMichaels said, sliding her finger down the page. " 'Am I not better to thee than ten sons?' Wasn't that sweet?"

It sounded like the kind of thing Sam would have said himself, but Hannah already knew by then that her husband's love alone could never make up her internal deficit. Having a baby satisfied her in a way being married hadn't.

Mrs. McMichael's voice went on in the up-and-down inflection of scripture-reading. " 'And when she had weaned him, she took him up with her, with three bullocks, and one ephah of flour, and a bottle of wine, and brought him into the house of the Lord in Shiloh: and the child was young.' "

"How young?" Hannah interrupted suddenly.

The older woman considered, bunching up her lower lip between her fingers. "I'd guess about three. Women used to nurse their babies a long time, you know. Breast-feeding's supposed to keep you from getting pregnant again."

"She gave him away when he was only three! He was still just a baby."

The thin pages of Mrs. McMichaels' Bible fluttered as a breeze drifted through the ward's open window. "That was the deal she made. I guess it was better than nothing."

Hannah looked down at the infant sleeping on her chest. Their combined heat sent up a warm redolence of milk and sweat more sensual than anything she'd experienced with Sam. The baby's mouth had slipped from her engorged nipple and trembled now, dreaming. The flow of creamy colostrum filled the crevice between the pink lips and pooled in the dimpled corners. Three years—even three months—would be better than nothing at all. She gently shook the baby's fingers clinging to her thumb, rousing it to pull at her breast again before the nurse came to take her away.

"When you're dealing with God, you know," Mrs. McMichaels added, "it's not like ordering out of the Sears Roebuck catalogue. You take what he sends you."

Hannah nodded noncommittally. She didn't feel as if she had enough experience dealing with God to say one way or the other. To her landlady, God was like gravity or the government—a fact of life. Hannah wasn't sure she'd ever feel that confident of him.

"Now here's a nice one," Mrs. McMichaels went on. "I've always liked the name Sarah. That was Abraham's wife."

Hannah shook her head. It sounded too old-fashioned, like somebody in a sunbonnet without all her teeth.

Mrs. McMichaels ran her finger down the page, tilting her head back to see through her bifocals. "All right. Here. What about Miriam? That's pretty."

"Miriam," Hannah repeated, then said it again, more slowly, liking the way it felt, all focused forward on her lips. She rubbed the little whorls of fine gold hair up into a kewpie doll curl on top of the tender skull. "I like that one." She looked down at the baby's sleeping face. "Miriam."

7

"Okay. So I'm late. I couldn't help it, all right?" Deborah hoisted her briefcase onto her desk with a thud.

Arlene's stilt-like nails paused in their march through a drawerful of file folders. "And good morning to you too."

"How long does this part last?"

"Which part?"

"I threw up twice on the way here."

"Didn't your mama ever teach you nothing?"

"Sure. She got me birth control pills."

Arlene raised an eyebrow, extracted a folder, and pushed the drawer shut. "Ever' one's different. With Jake I threw up ever' single day for three months. Jamal—I never was sick." She went back to her computer terminal and swivelled her chair to face Deborah. "The first few weeks are the worst. The trick is to keep a little something in your stomach all the time. Crackers. Keep some beside the bed and eat one before you get up."

"That worked with Jake?"

"No. But then nothing works with Jake." Arlene had spent her income tax refund for Jake's bail when he was caught shoplifting cigarettes at Safeway. She turned back to her screen. "So what your mama say?"

"I couldn't do it. She went straight to the hospital to see Gram. I just couldn't do it."

Arlene made an indeterminate noise and tapped a series of keys, the screen flickering images in rapid succession. "Hoot wants you to interview a client—one that goes a way back."

Deborah groaned. "A good ole boy?"

"Otis Ruffner."

"Isn't he Alamo Assets? I thought Hoot was handling that himself."

Arlene was scrolling through a contract on the screen. She didn't look up. "He is. He just wants you to get some information out of him."

"But why me?"

"He said you should smile a lot." She hit a button and the printer sighed to life behind them. "Honey, you want to be taken seriously as a lawyer, you better cut your hair and put on thirty pounds." She paused and glanced up from the screen. "Forget I said that."

Like being invaded by some alien creature, Pris had described it once. Deborah closed her eyes, trying to sense the alien's exact location inside her. All she could feel was her diaphragm quiver. She lifted her head and rubbed her temples. "We have any aspirin?"

"On a queasy stomach? What you need is some breakfast." Arlene took her hands off the keyboard and pulled open the bottom drawer of her desk. A cellophane packet containing two soda crackers skidded beside Deborah's elbow. "Start eating those. Real slow. Just nibble a little at a time. I'll go down to the vending machine and get you a Coke."

Deborah watched dully as Arlene's tight red skirt moved past her. Arlene was always fighting her weight. The skirt was polyester. She got most of her clothes from the Avon sale catalogue. Every dime she made went for oversized sneakers and basketball camps. Four semesters of paralegal training had taken her four years. And that was after her G.E.D., going nights to a community college, leaving the boys at home, watching TV alone.

Arlene's high heels came tapping up the hall, then were muted by the waiting room carpet.

"Here." The long ruby nails snapped the tab open deftly and inserted a straw. "Just sip it slow."

Deborah pulled the dark liquid half way up the column, then said, "After Jamal, did you ever..."

Arlene, examining the pages the printer had ejected, took a deep breath. "Did I ever what? Get knocked up again? Want to get married? Have an abortion?"

"Yes," Deborah said, keeping the straw between her lips.

Arlene dropped the pages into a folder. "I had me two babies. What did I need a man for? To pick up after? Yell at me? Maybe knock me and my kids around?" She looked up, shaking her head. "You ever see a tom cat kill its babies?"

Deborah watched her go back to her desk and study the computer screen again. "So you just—" she finished the question with a little shrug.

"I mean," Arlene said measuring her words deliberately, "I never got pregnant again." She gave a little laugh. "But then I wasn't no Catholic either." The keyboard began clicking. "Old Otis should be here by ten."

For a while there was silence except for the irregular rhythm of the keyboard. Then Deborah added in a lower key. "I'm sorry. I'm just trying to figure something out, what to do."

Arlene shrugged and rested the ruby nails on the function keys.

"And I know—I'm thirty. Not sixteen."

"And you've got more to lose?"

"I didn't say that."

"Good. Because you'd be wrong." Arlene swivelled her chair half way around and her black eyes looked flat. "Two things won't ever change for me, Deborah. I'll always be black and I'll always be a mother." She turned back to the keyboard. "Ain't much in this world lasts for always."

After a while Deborah got up and went into the restroom across the hall. She breathed deeply to steady her stomach and stared at herself in the mirror. She hated that my-life's-harder-than-yours game everybody played with her. In fact, the more she thought about it, the angrier it made her. Like she hadn't worked hard to get where she was. Like everything had been handed to her on a silver platter.

Feeling the exhilaration flushing the nausea from her system, she allowed the anger to grow. Arlene, Pris, even Mom, implying comparisons with how hard it had been to get through graduate school with two kids and no husband. And Gram, the famous war bride, with her framed photographs of the Sacrificed Warrior. At least all of them had husbands. Well, not Arlene. But she'd sounded like some kind of black widow spider—*I had me two babies. What did I need a man for?*

She turned on the water, dipping a paper towel into the stream, then cooling the back of her neck with it. She had wanted more time to think this thing through, but she was tired of ricocheting back and forth. First yes, then no. It was time to get this over with. After she'd dropped her mother at the hospital yesterday, she'd looked up a clinic in the phone book and made an appointment. As soon as she finished with this Otis character, she'd go home, change clothes, and keep the appointment. Get it over with. They'd told her she might need to stay in bed the rest of the day. But by tomorrow she should be normal again. She could make it up to Pris and Mom then, do her part with Gram. It made sense.

Last night, after Mom had gone to bed, she'd toyed briefly with the idea of going to see Father Botts again. But there was no point in dragging him into it. She knew what he'd have to tell her. She loved Father Botts. He'd kept her sane during those first few months of dealing with Hoot and

Hank. He'd listened to her impatience with her mother, her frustration with Pris, and her bitter dismay about her father. She'd even, finally, told him about Scott.

"You understand, Deborah," he told her dejectedly, "you've now obliged me to tell you that you're not in a proper condition to take communion."

"I shouldn't have told you?"

"I didn't say that."

"You'd turn me away from the altar rail?"

"I didn't say that either." He paused, rubbing his thumbnail along the ridge of his long nose. "That would violate the internal forum."

"The what?"

He waved the question away. "Let me put it this way." He sighed and looked at the ceiling as though contemplating just how he could in fact put it. "Though we all," he dipped a hand in her direction as if to include her, "inevitably take advantage of one another, you're not a person who systematically sets out to do that. Despite the fact that you're a lawyer." He smiled briefly, attempting to lighten his unwonted austerity. "But by taking communion, that's what you'd be doing. Taking advantage." He lifted his eyes directly to hers. "And not just of me."

It had been a gentle remonstrance. She'd even asked herself later what she expected, after all. A special indulgence? Nevertheless, she hadn't been able to break with Scott. When Scott had gone to Mexico, however, she'd hurried to tell Father Botts about her conviction that it was God who'd arranged his departure.

The priest had smiled as if he found the notion naive but endearing. "Perhaps, my dear," he'd said, patting her hand with his own soft palm, "but think what pleasure it would have given the Lord if you'd thrown the bum out yourself. The Father condescends to our weakness, true. But he'd much rather you outgrew this particular weakness of yours."

They'd both laughed then. But if she told him she was pregnant now, well, she knew what he'd say. And she couldn't bear to disappoint him. Not after he'd invested so much time and effort in her.

Her eyes began to burn as she straightened and studied her reflection in the mirror. "I'm not going to cry," she said aloud, clenching her teeth. "I will not." She closed her eyes briefly and imagined herself resting her head on that black clerical convexity. "Good God! Why couldn't you make any regular men like him?" She gave a little shudder. Next she'd be fantasizing about Father Botts leaving the priesthood for her. This was probably some special category of sin— wishing you could marry a priest. "But why can't there be someone like him, someone I could trust?" she silently wailed at the mirror. And someone, she attached a mental rider, who'd be grateful, gratified to have her.

"Well, it's not going to happen," she whispered to her reflection, "so just shut up about it." She flexed her shoulders to loosen the tension in her back. "And leave the poor man out of it, all right?" You thought you were getting away with it when Scott told you he was leaving. Admit it. And now you find out you're not off the hook after all. You still have to pay. So just suck it up and get it over with.

Hoot Jasper had told Deborah before he left for court to use his office to interview the client. The man in the chair with his back to the door sprang up immediately when Deborah came in and closed the door behind her.

"Mr. Ruffner?" Deborah could still hear the leftover anger in her voice.

"Otis," he said, sticking out his hand. "You must be Miss Estes. Hoot told me you'd be a sight for sore eyes."

Deborah, pegging the creased cowboy boots and the straw Stetson he held, murmured something indefinite as she took his outstretched hand, shook it once firmly, then moved around Hoot's desk and sank into the creaking oak swivel chair. She positioned the list of questions Arlene had given her squarely before her and looked across at Otis Ruffner's upper forehead, two inches of startling white skin the hat usually covered. He leaned towards her, one forearm athwart a thigh, his grin showing tobacco-tanned teeth. "Ready when you are. You just go ahead, ma'am. Shoot."

Uncapping her pen and taking a deep breath to suppress her stomach's heave, she looked down at the first question: When did you divest Alamo Assets of the subsidiary Hearts Unlimited? "Do you have any children, Mr. Ruffner?" she heard herself say.

He held up a hand. "Otis, please." He shook his head sadly. "'Fraid not. Doctor told Velda she had this tipped uterus," he illustrated an inclined plane with one palm. "Biggest disappointment of her life. Made her, well, changed her nature, I'm convinced. No woman should be deprived of the experience of maternity, do you think, Miss Estes?"

She fixed her eyes on the yellow pad. "I suppose it depends on whether it's an experience the woman cares to have." She gave him a chilled glance and saw his expression gradually slide toward alarm.

"Guess I put my big hoof in my mouth." He grimaced and whacked his palms on his thighs. "I'm used to coming at lawyers like they was tough old birds—like Hoot. Just goes to show how outa touch I am. This is the first time I ever had a lady lawyer. No offense meant."

"No problem," she said stiffly, and read the question Arlene had typed.

"Lordy, lordy," he replied, leaning back with his hands behind his head and staring off into one of the room's dim corners, ruminating. "That goes back a ways. Velda changed the name of the outfit, you understand. I had a couple-a small planes, most of the time just sitting around taking up space, so I come up with the notion of putting refrigerated compartments on board and flying body parts into Houston. Accident victims, you know. For transplants. But it was just called, let's see, Med Express then, I believe. When Velda took over, she thought it should sound more"—he shrugged—"humanitarian, I guess."

"But Alamo Assets was still the parent corporation?"

"Well, you have to understand. I first started getting together my stake back in, musta been, sixty-three. I's just a youngster then, but I had this idea for a new way to sell oil, straight from the wellhead. You could do that kind of thing then, you know. Come up with a new idea. Get the right folks to back it. Make a fortune almost overnight." His eyes, crinkling with delight, moved to her face now, as if for approval.

The year I was born, she thought. He's old enough to be my father.

"Course, it wasn't Alamo Assets then either. I think I called it Wildcat Wellhead. Something like that. But it was with the money I made off of it that I eventually set up Alamo. By then I could see what a boom-and-bust proposition oil was. I knew I'd have to diversify. So I bought up a couple little outfits I thought might turn into something some day. Tortilla factory. Sold that to Frito-Lay up in Dallas. Mex'can import business. Cellular phones. Customized fishing boats. That one went belly-up. Like I say, you win some, you lose some. You know how it is."

"But Hearts Unlimited. You turned that over to your wife—when?"

He rubbed his chin as though he hadn't considered the point previously. "That musta been, let me see, eighty-five."

"And that's when your wife became head of the company?" She frowned, trying to concentrate on the list of questions instead of her growing nausea.

"Yep." He leaned forward again, clasping his hands together between his legs, rubbing the thumbs dryly against each other.

"So what was your involvement with the company after that?"

His eyes widened, stretching the skin so she could see the white inside the deep lines of weathering. He shook his head ever so slightly. "Why none a-tall, sweetheart. I had not one iota of authority. Oh, I retained a little of the stock, but not a controlling interest."

She swallowed hard and pushed at the corner of her legal pad. She wasn't going to make it. "Maybe so, Mr. Ruffner. But the court's going to consider, you know, that as her husband you were still—"

"Darlin', darlin'," he said, holding up one hand and waggling it to interrupt her. "You don't understand. Velda, like I say, her nature had got sort of soured, not that I'm blaming her, you understand, but she'd grown a bit fractious about life. And I—well, I guess she couldn't help it, but I was the one she blamed. Not that—" and here he splayed his stubby fingers across his chest—"well, I had the doctor check me out and it weren't my fault. Not that it was a fault. Not a-tall."

Deborah clamped her lips between her teeth, then covered her mouth with one hand, trying to look thoughtful. It was a moment before she could speak. "And that's why you—" She drooped the pen in his direction.

"That's when I give her Med Express—or Hearts Unlimited or whatever she wanted to call it. More or less so she'd have something to do, you understand? Occupy her mind. She needed an outside interest." He stopped and peered at her closely. "Sweetheart, you sure you feeling all right?"

"I'm sorry," she whispered. "I'm afraid you'll have to excuse me."

"Yes ma'am. You betcha!" He jumped to his feet and scrambled around the desk. "Here, let me help you." He was reaching out to her, helping her to her feet, then hurrying across the room to open the door for her.

Deborah stumbled once as the rejected Coke and crackers spurted from her mouth and nose onto the carpet and her beige skirt. Otis held the office door open, making little whimpers of lamentation on her behalf, then shut it gently behind her.

Deborah fled into the restroom and retched into the toilet bowl. After nothing else would come up, she moved to the sink and turned on the water to wash the gummy mucus from her chin and cheeks. Her hands were trembling so badly she could hardly twist the faucet handle.

She washed out her mouth, splashed the back of her neck with cold water, and straightened to survey the damage. There were splatters on her pale coral blouse as well as her skirt. She wet the corner of a paper towel and dabbed at them.

There was a knock at the restroom door. "You all right in there?" Arlene called.

Deborah opened the door.

"Don't worry. You can come out. He's gone. Said to tell you to give him a call whenever you felt better. No rush. He'd be at home."

Deborah followed Arlene back into their office and slumped into her chair. "At least Hoot wasn't here. Do you think he'll tell Hoot what happened? Are they buddies?"

"They go back a ways. Hard to say." Arlene paused, raising one eyebrow. "You musta smiled a lot. Before you upchucked, I mean. He seemed real troubled about you."

Deborah snorted. She was feeling better now, though a little lightheaded. "Sure. Me and old Velda. He's a real knight in shining armor."

Arlene shrugged. "I'm no expert on white guys. That's your department. One white guy I know though is going to want some notes from that interview when he gets back."

"I know, I know." Deborah dropped her head into her hands and sighed.

Arlene scribbled something on a notecard and laid it on Deborah's desk with a snap. "Here's old Otis' address and phone number. Now make yourself scarce before Hoot gets back and starts asking questions. You'll feel better this afternoon. Maybe you can wrap it up then."

Deborah looked at the card dully. The address was way out on the Southwest Freeway, almost to Katy. "I have an appointment this afternoon."

Arlene popped a disk into her computer and didn't say anything.

"I don't know how much longer I can keep this from Mom. I need to get it over with."

Arlene turned to look at her closely, her arms crossed. Then she swivelled around to her terminal. "I can't help you there. That's your call, sister."

Deborah fumbled in her handbag for her sunglasses; the glare off the hood was giving her a headache. Maybe she should stop and get a cup of coffee. She swung the car onto the next off-ramp, slowed for a stop sign, and turned into the parking lot of a McDonalds. The place was deserted except for one booth where a dark woman in a long, loose dress was dividing two Happy Meals between three children. Her head was covered with a white cloth that hung below her shoulders, its straight horizontal fold across her forehead lowering her brow in a way that looked intentionally unattractive.

"For here or to go?" the dark-eyed man behind the counter asked after Deborah had ordered, keeping his eyes carefully on the keypad.

Saudi? Iraqi? Afghan? Who would have guessed, years ago when she was growing up sixty miles south of here, that one day this section of Houston would be a Muslim enclave? Who could figure anything anymore?

She carried the styrofoam cup to the booth next to the woman and her brood and sat down, fumbling in a side pocket of her handbag for aspirin. The man at the counter said something to the woman in a language Deborah took to be Arabic. One of the children, a boy, reached across the table and grabbed the toy that had come from his sister's cardboard box. The man spoke again sharply. The boy looked up, looked at his mother, then withdrew his hand.

That, she thought, mentally addressing Arlene, is what you want with a man. So you don't have to spend your refund check on your son's bail. You want someone to pay the bills and make the kids behave. So when you say "just like your dad," it means something.

She blew on the coffee, placed the two tablets well back on her tongue and took a large gulp, casting a furtive glance sideways at the woman in the next booth. The woman looked up, caught Deborah's eyes on her, and looked away again.

She took several more sips from the cup. The little boy climbed down off the bench and, one hand still anchored to the table, stared at Deborah with eyes like wet charcoal. His mother spoke one sharp syllable—maybe his name—tugged at his shirt, and pointed him back into the booth.

Deborah stood up and slung her handbag over her shoulder. The woman turned toward the window, bending over the smallest child as if to shield it from her.

8

"Mrs. McMichaels," Hannah said again. "We lived in her house till you were four years old." The disappointment in her voice, weak though it was, came through.

"I remember the oyster-shell driveway," Miriam said. "I used to try to find whole shells the cars hadn't crushed so I could pretend they were dishes."

"She was like a second mother to me," Hannah said. Really, the landlady had been more than her own mother ever was, but she didn't add that. When Hannah had left home after high school to get a job at the new naval air station in Corpus Christi, her parents had watched her go as if resigned to her certain ruin, reproach already in their eyes. She had been determined to prove their fears unfounded. For one thing, she'd never felt even slightly tempted by the men she'd met. Either they were like her brothers, rough and inarticulate, or, if they spoke with an easy smoothness, she quickly spotted the predatory purpose in their eyes.

Hannah could never understand how some of the girls at the laundry where she got her first job could be so willing to take chances with men. What was the point? What did they get out of it? Now that she was off the farm, for the first time in her life she was beginning to feel as if she could lift up her head and look around her, get her bearings. She didn't intend to spoil it all now—certainly not for any man.

Then she'd met Sam.

Mrs. McMichaels, who was just her supervisor at the time, had invited all the girls at the laundry to an ice-cream social at her church. Lucille, a city girl from up north who worked alongside Hannah at the mangle, had badgered her into going. "Lotta opportunity at those church socials." She winked at Hannah. "G.I.s flock to Baptist girls and ice cream. Must be the contrast they like. Hot and cold." Lucille cracked her gum like a pistol shot and laughed, open-mouthed. "Come on, honey. You can go with me. I'll look after you."

That was a laugh, the idea of Lucille looking after her. Nevertheless, it was good to have someone to go with, despite the fact that Lucille soon disappeared into a cluster of khaki uniforms. Left alone, Hannah gravitated toward the oilcloth-covered tables on the church lawn and offered to help, preferring to work rather than stand around looking awkward. The soldier turning the crank on a wooden freezer straightened and grinned at her. "How about wrapping this one in that old quilt? It's ready to set up, I think." He tipped the wooden bucket to drain the melted ice water into a metal dishpan on the grass, then lifted the freezer onto the table. He cocked a fist on one hip and looked at her. "And how about I walk you home afterwards?" He jerked his head toward the growing crowd on the lawn. "A girl like you, I figure I better get my bid in early."

Sam's quick, half-anxious grin had intrigued her. His dark eyes reflected the lights strung around the church yard. She noticed the cleft in his chin, his height, and that he wore no wedding band—a detail Lucille had instructed her to watch for especially. She shrugged. "I guess so."

On the walk home she learned that he was only two years older than her, yet he seemed to know so much more about the world and had been places that seemed exotic to her then. Kansas City, St. Louis, even Chicago. Though never to Texas before, he told her, not until he'd been sent to Kelley

Field in San Antonio for basic training. Now he was stationed in Corpus Christi temporarily.

During the following weeks, under the pressure of loneliness and an uncertain future, Sam had poured out his short history to her. His parents—good Lutherans he assured her, not Italian Catholics as she'd feared because of his brown eyes and dark hair—had expected him to follow in the footsteps of his older brother, studying to be a doctor now in Boston. But to their dismay, Sam had rushed to enlist when Hitler invaded France in May, just as he was nearing the end of his freshman year at the University of Minnesota.

"I would have been drafted anyway. Everybody's having to register already," he told her one afternoon, leaning back on his elbows in the sand of a little stretch of beach he'd discovered up the coast. "Won't be long till we're in the thick of things."

Hannah had borrowed a pair of shorts and a halter top from Lucille. She'd never worn such an outfit before. She kept making minor little adjustments to the straps and rearranging the shirt he'd pulled off and tossed into her lap when he stretched out beside her. It was late September and still in the nineties in the afternoons. He was disappointed there hadn't been a hurricane hit the coast yet.

"If I'd hung around, waiting till they drafted me, I'd never have gotten into the Air Corps."

Hannah smiled faintly, focusing on the flat Gulf horizon. "I think you were very brave, not waiting. I would never have the courage to enlist. And if they drafted me, I'd probably just burn the letter and pretend I never got it."

Sam snorted and glanced up over his shoulder at her. "Women!" Then he laughed and put his sandy palm on her knee, shaking it gently.

She felt her heart lurch. She'd never been called a woman before or had a man's hand on her bare knee.

Sam rolled over onto his side and squinted up at her. "That's all right," he said, his voice growing softer. He scooped up a handful of sand and dribbled it into a cone beside her knee. "It's women we do it for, right? While you keep the home fires burning."

Hannah gave a little shrug, keeping her eyes on the grains of sand spilling down the sides of the cone. She wasn't really sure why men liked the service. If her brothers enlisted, it would be to get away from home.

"Let's not talk about the war," she said, lifting her eyes from the sand to his face.

"No," he said. And before she knew what was happening, he had raised himself on one arm and put the other around her back, pulling her against him.

She remembered exactly how he had done it, because that night she reconstructed the scene over and over again in her mind in order to experience the feeling that had gone with it. She remembered how the sand on his hands had gritted against her bare back. How surprising it had been to feel the hardness of his teeth beneath the soft flesh of his lips. She had never been kissed by a man before. And when she reproduced the scene in her mind, it was "man" she thought, not "boy."

But then he was leaning heavily against her, pressing her backward onto the sand, and she knew instantly this wasn't what was supposed to happen next. She didn't want to be like Lucille. She gave him a little shove and twisted her head away. "No," she said. "That's enough."

He pulled back, looking slightly dazed, as though he were trying to refocus his eyes. His chest, growing pink from the sun beneath its curling dark hair, labored up and down. Sam swallowed and looked away.

Without thinking, she ran her fingers across her lips and then touched her nose. "Silly," she said, but in a mock-serious way. She ventured a little laugh—surely he wouldn't take that as encouragement—and gave him another little push on the shoulder. "You better take me home now. You're going to be red as a lobster."

After that they began to see one another every weekend he wasn't on duty. Sam's outgoing nature seemed to make up for her own shyness. When they were alone they developed a kind of game between them where he kept up a mild kidding at which she would pretend to take offense. She also allowed Sam to kiss her when they were alone, though never long nor often. The sight of couples kissing in the park, their bodies pressed publicly together, still filled her with a vague dismay. Growing up on a farm, Hannah was familiar with the mechanics of reproduction, though she found nothing particularly appealing in the often brutal, cumbersome process. The only girl in a family of sons, she had heard her older brothers laughing and talking among themselves about women much the way they talked about livestock. As she had grown older, her mother began to caution her obscurely against men. Her father forbade her to wear makeup. They both seemed afraid for her, though their fear appeared mixed with suspicion that Hannah might conspire in her own downfall.

Their distrust had pained her. It wasn't that Hannah had grand ambitions. All she wanted was a little breathing room. And strangely enough, she'd found it. While everyone was saying the country was about to go to war, her life had achieved a level of cleanliness and order she'd never known on the farm. Polished shoes instead of muddy boots tracking across bare wooden floors. White blouses she starched, then sprinkled and rolled into tidy packets she stored in the refrigerator before pressing them with an electric iron instead of sad irons heated on the woodstove. A chance to sit down at the table, stirring her coffee with a spoon she could lay on the tablecloth beside a china cup while she talked, easily and about nothing in particular, to another human being. For Hannah, this was accomplishment enough.

If she began to think about marriage that fall, it was in those terms. A decent, respectable home, where the floors would be polished, the meals ample and hot, children's clothes clean and ironed crisp. It was a job she was sure she could do creditably, one she would take pride in.

She and Sam had been walking home from a movie one autumn evening, Sam's arm sheltering her against the damp chill off the Gulf, when the subject of marriage came up for the first time. Sam had seemed unusually somber all evening. By then the Battle of Britain was in its third month and she thought perhaps the newsreels had depressed him.

"I've got something to tell you," he finally said.

There was a city park across the street with benches facing the seawall. He steered her towards them, their steps crunching through the broken oyster shell as they crossed the road. Then he took her by the shoulders and sat her down on one of the benches so that the moonlight fell on her face. He didn't sit down himself but stood there before her, his fists on his hips.

"I've been saving it all evening because I don't know how to say it."

Hannah knew right away what it was. "What?"

He took a deep breath before answering and let it out slowly. "We got orders today." Then he dropped onto the bench beside her and leaned forward, his elbows on his knees, staring out at the moonlit breakers.

She made some muffled response and waited for him to go on. This was a moment she had been expecting day by day, ever since she'd met him.

"I don't even know where, of course. They won't tell us, not before we leave, not till we're almost there. I don't know why, but I have a hunch it'll be the Caribbean."

Hannah rifled quickly through her memories of the war maps she'd seen recently in the newspapers. She didn't care so much about the place as the time though. Gone was gone—it wouldn't matter where. She'd be alone again. "When, Sam?" She tugged gently at his sleeve. "When are you leaving?" She pulled the collar of her jacket close around her neck. The breeze coming off the water was colder.

"Hey, kiddo." He moved closer to her, curving his arm in around her shoulders. "This doesn't mean you're gonna miss me, does it?" he said in his old, teasing way.

"Of course, I'll miss you." She spoke soberly, refusing to fall in with her part in the game.

There was a long moment of silence. Then, before she knew what was happening, he was kissing her, only it was different this time. It was not just for the pleasure he usually seemed to get from it; there was more to it—a kind of desperation, an urgency. Feeling his breath against her neck, it struck her that his desire was tinged with fear.

The thought affected her strangely. It was almost as if their positions had been suddenly reversed. He, the confident one, the experienced one, all at once appeared to need her. And for her part, she felt, not her usual reluctance to return his affection, but, out of the startling plenitude of her heart, a desire to console him. She even let him, for the first time, run one hand roughly over the front of her blouse while the other cradled her head. But then she felt his tongue, prodding wetly against her lips, and she couldn't help turning her head away. She'd only let him do that once, and the sense of intrusion had almost sickened her.

"Sam," she said, "don't."

He drew a long, shuddering breath and pulled her head down against his chest. Hannah could hear his heart thudding beneath the khaki. She smiled to herself and lifted one of his large, square hands to her lips. "I love you, Sam," she said simply.

He pushed her upright suddenly, staring into her face, now in the deeper shadow of a palm tree, then pulled her forward so that the moonlight fell on it again. His own expression seemed to hover between delight and suspicion.

"What's wrong?"

Sam shook his head, then stood up abruptly and paced to the edge of the seawall. The moonlight, the breakers beating the seawall, Sam's figure silhouetted against the bridge of light across the water—it all suddenly seemed too dramatic a scene for a girl like her to be caught up in. She felt out of her element. In over her head.

"I don't want to sound melodramatic about this, but this could be a dangerous assignment. Even if it's the Caribbean, well, anything could happen. And if we get in any further, who knows where I might end up?" Sam turned suddenly and walked back to the bench. He stood there towering over her, eclipsing the moon's light, his face a dark shadow. He put his hands on his hips. "I promised myself I wouldn't do this. It's not fair to you, but I can't help it. I need somebody to come back to, Hannah, or it's not worth it." He paused, then finished in a rush. "Let's get married."

She hadn't said anything, not then. Finally he reached down and pulled her to her feet, wrapping his arms around her. This time she let him kiss her however he wanted to, without protest.

They had been married three weeks later in Mrs. McMichaels' church on Thanksgiving Day. Lucille and one of his crew buddies stood up with them. His parents hadn't come.

When she'd asked Sam what they said when he called to tell them, he pretended at first not to hear, then when she prodded, said with an angry edge to his voice, "What do I care what they think? I know how fine you are. You're a real lady. Good enough for them any day." He had kissed her gently. "Too good for me."

In December Sam had been posted back to Randolph Air Base in San Antonio for further training. "The West Point of the air, that's what the newspapers are calling it," he told her excitedly.

But by early March, with the dogwood and redbud already blooming, Sam was gone, shipped out, someplace he wasn't even allowed to tell her. She had come to the same park bench on her lunch hour. She wasn't hungry. At work she'd told Lucille she had a stomach bug.

"Honey, who do you think you're kidding? A 'stomach bug'!" She poked a finger at Hannah's navel and made a large, expanding arc with her hands in front of her own stomach.

That morning, as Hannah got out of bed, the floor had suddenly listed to one side. Knowing she'd never make it to the bathroom down the hall, she ran to the little kitchenette and threw up in the sink. The cool porcelain against her cheek had felt good.

She sat on the bench the entire lunch hour, watching the low, lazy Gulf waves roll in. She could hardly believe it.

She wanted to be by herself for a while and let the reality sink in. When Sam heard, he would turn it into his own accomplishment. She wouldn't mind, or only a little bit. He needed some kind of success to make up for not making bombadier, especially since he'd already told his parents he'd been recruited for a B-17 squadron.

Carefully placing her palm on her stomach, she planned how she would tell him. What word should she use? Expecting? Pregnant? Lucille abbreviated it to "p.g." The word wouldn't matter to Sam though; whatever she called it, he'd be proud. And relieved that her condition would make her less accessible to other men now that he was gone.

She took a long, deep breath, feeling the heavy Gulf air swell her chest and lift her shoulders. She raised her head and looked around the little park. She felt—what? Valuable. Important. Seriously important. For the first time in her life as if she had a certain claim to dignity. She cupped both palms over her abdomen. And it's mine.

I know what I'll do this weekend, she thought. Lucille's got a camera. We'll go on a picnic and take pictures. That way, I'll always remember.

Hannah opened her eyes, unsure if she'd fallen asleep. "That was a happy time," she said with a sigh.

Miriam, staring across the bed at the blank, hot sky outside, leaned forward as if to hear better. "During the war, Mother?"

"Well, the war. But I had you." Hannah's eyes closed, but the smile lingered another moment before her lips parted slightly and her rough but even breathing indicated she'd fallen asleep again.

Miriam sat back and closed her eyes too. Happy. Had she been happy when Deborah was born? She hadn't so much as hinted to Gordon before the wedding that she might be pregnant. Later she told him she'd kept it a secret because she didn't want him marrying her out of a sense of obligation—something she knew she had no reason to fear. Her real motive had been the desire to sustain as long as possible her romantic vision of living lawlessly, beyond the bounds, flouting respectability. This would be a love-child, she told herself, conceived in passion, at the very moment she was plummeting from the precipice, not within the stultifying confines of marriage.

But after Deborah's birth, Miriam had found Gordon's intensity, so romantic that first summer together, increasingly bothersome. Even before the stitches from her episiotomy healed, he was wanting her again.

"Can't you wait a little longer?" she complained. She was lying on her side, facing away from him, as far on her side of the bed as she could get after he'd slid his hand between her thighs and started stroking her, waiting tensely for her to respond. "Can't you tell I'm not ready?"

"How am I supposed to know?" he muttered angrily, pulling his hand away. "You don't have that pad thing on anymore. And it's been three months now. When are you going to be normal again?"

He must have been figuring in those last long weeks of her pregnancy when she hadn't wanted to be touched at all; her skin had felt like it was cracking open. Tears had leaked onto the pillow, but she hadn't answered him. Normal. What was normal now anyway? The body whose power had amazed and gratified her only a year ago had first swelled to unthinkable proportions, splitting her very skin, then deflated again, though not as quickly or as easily as she had hoped. Milk leaked constantly from her nipples now, leaving her smelling overheated and sour.

She hadn't intended to nurse the baby. Certainly neither her obstetrician nor the pediatrician had encouraged it. The hospital had supplied her with complimentary cartons of formula, assuming that, like most of their maternity patients, she would be in the market. But Hannah, who'd taken her vacation to care for Miriam and the baby during that first week at home, had allied herself with Gordon when, to her surprise, he insisted that breast-fed babies were healthier than bottle-fed ones. Gordon didn't often concede the superiority of nature to modern chemistry.

Touched by what she hoped was the dawning of a new tenderness in her husband, brought about by the birth of his first child, Miriam had submitted to the indignity of breast pumps and nursing bras. In the end, she was glad she did. For one thing, when the baby suckled, it was as though tendons attached directly from her breasts to her uterus contracted. It hurt, especially at first, and she had a strange squeamishness about the sheer animalism of the procedure. But when she read that the baby's nursing triggered contractions that pulled her stretched insides taut again, she resigned herself to both the discomfort and the indignity. She didn't intend to go all flabby just because she'd had a baby.

Then she discovered that, along with the tightening of her uterus, something in her chest also contracted when she looked down at the round curves of her baby's face, the flesh so new and flawless it broke her heart to look at it. The reaction amazed and puzzled her. Why should the mere sight of this delicate flesh newly introduced into the world move her so? All Hannah's descriptive clichés seemed impossibly accurate. Rose-petals, dew-kissed, fresh from the hand of God. On the other hand, how could such a disarming wonder come from the agony she'd been through?

A nurse who only spoke in monosyllables had shaved her pubic hair and administered an enema. Then Miriam had been left alone on a gurney in a bare cubicle to sweat and thrash in pain she hadn't imagined it was possible to endure. As the hours dragged on, she'd been reduced to a terrified animal. The doctor had arrived only after the baby's head had ripped her stretched, distended vulva.

Miriam had intended to enroll in school again as soon as Gordon graduated and Deborah was out of diapers. Other than looking at her baby, she didn't exactly enjoy the infant stage, sometimes thinking that, despite the discomfort of pregnancy, life had been a good bit easier when the baby was inside her and she hadn't had to worry about feeding and cleaning it, nor listen to it cry. So in July, after Dow offered Gordon a job in their Freeport plant in Texas, Miriam had started poring over undergraduate catalogues for colleges along the Gulf Coast.

She was feeding Deborah strained apricots and wondering if they should move her crib out of the bedroom and into the only other room in their student apartment—a living room with a kitchenette hidden behind folding doors—when Gordon had suddenly burst through the door. All week long he had been talking about North Vietnamese torpedo boats attacking a couple of U.S. destroyers. With every new report on the *Maddox* and the *Turner Joy* she could feel the volcano inside him building up steam.

"What's up?" she asked, wiping the baby's glistening pink lips. "Don't you have a lab this afternoon?"

"Didn't you hear?" he said, dropping his books onto the table.

Miriam had heard actually; she always listened to the news on the radio at noon, a habit she'd acquired during that first year. "Hear what?" she said.

"About the vote. It was overwhelming. 'All necessary measures.' Now maybe we can get somewhere." His eyes were shining. He scraped the high chair back out of his way and bent down to grip her shoulders. Deborah began to whimper.

"Watch out, Gordon. Look what you've done now." Miriam shrugged her shoulder from beneath his hand and pulled Deborah out of the high chair. The baby's knee caught on the tray and she began to cry in earnest.

Gordon frowned at them both, looking slightly dazed. "Doesn't she take a nap or something? The vote was overwhelming, Mir," he repeated. "Four hundred and fourteen to nothing in the House. Eighty-eight to two in the Senate."

Miriam looked at the baby, who was in fact rubbing her eyes sleepily, and thought about how she needed to go to the grocery store. They were out of milk. And she wanted to get some cup hooks. If she hung the cups from the underside of the cabinet over the sink, that would clear a whole shelf for her spices which were now just lined up on the back ledge of the stove where they got coated with grease splatters. Could she induce Gordon to stay with Deborah while she went to the store, if she promised the baby would sleep the whole time?

"Here. Let me put her in the crib. She needs a nap," he said, taking the baby out of her arms. Deborah reached over his shoulder for her mother and began to howl.

"No, give her here," Miriam said with a sigh. "She'll just scream unless I put her down."

In the spring before they were married, she thought as she lowered the baby into the crib, she would have asked him about the details of the vote, just how far the President was authorized to go now, which senators had voted against it. Now she was trying to remember if her car keys were in her handbag so she could slip out the door quickly without having to look for them. She patted Deborah's diaper, making crooning noises. If only Gordon were like Geri MacIntyre's husband who—so Geri said—got it over with during the commercial breaks in "Days of Our Lives." Besides, she'd forgotten to take her pills for the last three days.

Her handbag was on the window sill by the front door. She could, in practically one motion, step into her sandals, pick up the handbag, and open the door, calling over her shoulder that she'd be back in thirty minutes at the most. But when she tiptoed the two steps from the crib to the bedroom door, shut it behind her, then turned to raise her finger to her lips in warning, she found Gordon had already lowered the living room blinds and was waiting for her, smoking a cigarette.

She made for the sink and started running water into a glass, stalling for time.

"Come on, Mir. While the kid's asleep." He stepped behind her, pinning her against the counter, reaching under her shirt to squeeze her breasts with both hands.

"Come on yourself, Gordon. I've got things to do."

"This could be war, you know," he said, turning her around to face him and bending her back over the sink. "Real war. No more of this advisor crap."

"Please, Gordon. I need to—" She barely got the words out before he covered her mouth with his, pried her lips open with his tongue, and thrust it up across the hard palate. He knew her weaknesses. She put a hand on his shoulder, meaning to push him away. Her fingers gripped instead.

By the time they'd moved to Texas and rented a house with five large rooms, the fall semester was starting. Miriam was so sick every morning, though, she could barely get out of bed to take care of Deborah, much less find a sitter and show up for classes.

Discovering she was pregnant again, she felt suddenly and desperately unhinged. This time there was no thrill of desperado daring to sustain her during those first months of adjusting to the idea of another child. Now she was just a middle-class housewife. What was happening to her life? What had she allowed to happen to her life?

She took out her old college textbooks and began to look through them again, smelling the pages, trying to recall her teachers' names. She started reading her intermediate French text, *Le Petit Prince*, to Deborah. She also began attending St. Andrew Presbyterian Church. It had none of the soft, frayed edges of her mother's Baptist congregation. It was all starch and social responsibility. It ran voter registration drives and tutored black students newly integrated into the white school system.

At St. Andrew's the congregation sat on molded plastic chairs that hooked together with chrome bars on each side.

The minister had silvery hair, though he wasn't old. Every Sunday they said the Apostles' Creed, its elegant assertions unfamiliar but welcome to her ears, then stood to sing a rousing Gloria. It suited her exactly.

She went alone, of course. Gordon liked to work undisturbed in the lab on Sunday mornings.

In her adult Sunday School class they studied *Honest to God*. The teacher loaned her a copy of Betty Friedan. Then one Sunday—Miriam was about six months along—the teacher used Priscilla as an example of a woman leader in the early church. Miriam hadn't intentionally established a pattern of using biblical names when she'd called her first child Deborah. In fact, the baby was almost a year old before Miriam made the connection with the Old Testament warrior-judge. But the Greek woman's name lodged in Miriam's mind that Sunday, its short vowels and sibilants toughening over the next few weeks to the shape of someone at once lithe and muscled. Why not? she thought. If nothing else it would make Hannah happy.

And Miriam still had a vague sense of liability when she thought of her mother. When Hannah had come to help out after Deborah was born, she had never mentioned the fact that it was only a little over seven months since the wedding. Miriam had prepared herself to confess, say, a single indiscretion. Her mother, she figured, could handle that much truth. But Hannah had never asked for an explanation.

She had looked at Miriam searchingly a time or two, but instead of speaking, had scooped the baby up and nestled its head under her neck, rocking her shoulders slightly back and forth, closing her eyes and crooning a kind of keening consolation. To the baby? To Miriam? To herself? Miriam never had the courage to ask, but that inarticulate sound, somewhere between a hum and a moan, had chafed like judgment. Later, when things began to go wrong between her and Gordon, the echo of Hannah's stifled lament had risen up like an invisible wall, muffling her own confused mourning.

9

There was a tap at the hospital room door before it slowly swung open. Priscilla tiptoed in. "How is she?"

"Sleeping."

"You get any?" Pris asked, giving her a quick hug, then crossed to the bed.

"I died. What about you?"

"Fine. Just fine." The words came out vaguely, as though to underscore the insignificance of sleep at such a time.

Pris' preference for her grandmother had always pained and pleased Miriam simultaneously. On the one hand, it was the only tribute her mother's obscure endurance was likely to receive. On the other hand, it underscored Miriam's own failure to live up to Hannah's mark. At times Pris' conspicuous veneration of her grandmother made Miriam feel like pleading with her—Okay. So I failed you. But have a little mercy, for God's sake. This God you say is so good to you.

"How're the kids?" she asked.

Pris had gone around to the far side of the bed and was straightening the clutter on the nightstand. She glanced up now and smiled briefly. "Josh wants to know if you brought back any bones."

"Bones?" she repeated, realizing too late she'd said it almost angrily. *Infant bones are extremely delicate; they often come apart or disintegrate when they're moved. Thus I would assume . . .*

Pris paused with Hannah's glasses in one hand. "Remember? You took him to that dinosaur museum—"

"Sure." She forced a laugh. "I'm still a little befuddled from the trip. Sorry." But an injured look had already closed over her daughter's face.

Pris turned back to the nightstand. "So. What do you think?"

"About Gram?"

Pris gave a single nod, not even looking at her, and began to cull the used tissues from among the clutter on the stand with deliberate little snatches.

Miriam raised her eyebrows. "It's hard to say. I haven't talked to the doctor yet. He hasn't been in this morning."

Pris glanced at her watch. "No. It's usually around ten-thirty before he gets here." Her tone was still stiff.

"But you did the right thing, I want you to know. I'm glad you called. She's not—definitely not—in good shape."

Pris looked at her then, the cloud lifting a little from her face in provisional pardon. Then, in a sudden reversal of their roles, becoming the suppliant, she said, "I did the best I knew how, Mom."

"I know, darling. Of course. You did exactly the right thing." Automatically Miriam came around the bed to put her arms around her daughter and press her head onto her shoulder. They stood there a moment, rocking from side to side, as Pris took a long shaky breath. "Sweetheart, sweetheart," Miriam murmured, "I don't know what we'd do without you. Who would have found her? Who would have gotten her to the hospital in time? If you hadn't been there..."

"It was awful, Mom. I was so afraid. You should have seen her—"

Miriam smoothed her daughter's stubborn hair back from her temple and made small consoling sounds halfway between a hum and a moan.

Miriam had often wondered if it was the divorce that had caused Pris to be so needy. At first, the separation had appeared to affect her hardly at all. Strangely enough, it was Deborah, usually the stoic, who had reacted immediately, going into a frenzy of destruction for several months, defacing table tops, pasting pictures on her bedroom wall with Elmer's glue, then ripping them off the next week along with hunks of paint and plaster. She'd even scratched up her grandmother's vintage white walls that summer.

Priscilla, the impulsive, the spontaneous one, had seemed oblivious to the widening crack in their lives. Miriam had taken the girls to stay with Hannah that summer, leaving the house to Gordon who, she knew, had no place to go. She'd already explained to the girls about the fellowship she was taking at a university in a state where they'd never lived before. "That'll be interesting, don't you think, living some place new and different? There's mountains and snow."

Priscilla nodded gamely. Deborah's perpetually dour face turned instantly stormy.

"No. I hate it!"

"How can you hate it? You've never even been there, silly." Miriam laughed and tried to draw her onto her lap.

Deborah jerked away. "That's why I hate it."

Priscilla looked at them both anxiously. "Can we go outside now, Mom?"

Miriam stood up and shrugged.

Priscilla, a head shorter than Deborah, looped an arm over her older sister's shoulder. "Come on," she said, and awkwardly guided Deborah out the back door of Hannah's little white frame house and down the back steps to the carport.

Watching them, Miriam gave a faint snort of annoyed amusement. Hannah, sitting at the table behind her hemming a skirt for Deborah, inspected the aperture of her needle with a raised eyebrow.

"I would have expected this behavior from Pris, not Deborah," Miriam said.

"Don't be deceived, Miriam," Hannah told her. "Priscilla feels this more than you know. It'll come out sooner or later." That had rankled, although two years later Priscilla was still doing fine, despite their move from Freeport, the only home she had ever known, despite Miriam's preoccupation with graduate studies and graduate students. Fourth grade, in fact, had proved to be the height of Priscilla's academic achievement. She made only one C— social studies—and was captain of the girls' soccer team.

It took another year before the effects of the divorce kicked in. By then Deborah had adjusted to their new gypsy life by over-achieving and keeping her half of the room she shared with her sister rigorously organized.

After the two years spent in Denver for Miriam's master's degree, the three of them had moved to Austin. She'd accepted a part-time position there gratefully; the girls could see their grandmother frequently while she worked on her doctorate. Gordon too was only sixty miles away in San Antonio, though he was seldom sober enough to make the trip to visit his daughters.

Then suddenly, during their first year in Austin, Priscilla came "unstuck." That's what Deborah had called it when she phoned her mother at her office to tell her Pris hadn't shown up on the bus after school. "Now don't get hysterical, Mom. I don't think she's kidnapped or anything. I think—well, try Melinda Frazier's house."

Miriam had to call three different Fraziers before she finally got the right one. A snickering girl's voice answered, and, when Miriam asked for Priscilla Estes, she broke into shrieks of laughter. Miriam hung up, wrote down the address from the phone book with a shaking hand, and drove to the house in a south Austin suburb, praying all the way for protection, for forgiveness, for Priscilla.

It was much the kind of house they had left in Freeport. She banged on the front door, but no one came. She could hear Fleetwood Mac blasting away inside. Making her way to the rear of the house, she found a nervous Weimaraner pacing in front of the patio door.

"Get out of my way, dog," she said grimly, and it retreated to an aluminum utility shed with a dent in one side. The patio door, unlocked, slid back easily, and she batted her way through the closed drapes. A boy with pale hair and red eyes looked up at her from where he squatted by a sideboard, examining the stock of bottles. Two empty ones stood in the sink.

A girl squawked from the sofa. "Oh my God! We've been invaded!"

Another girl, quickly crushing a cigarette into a boot-shaped ashtray, stared at Miriam, wide-eyed.

Miriam found Pris curled up behind the sofa, asleep. She could hardly get her to her feet and practically had to carry her to the car. Pris threw up out the car window on the way home.

Melinda Frazier's father called Miriam that evening. "I hope you're not too hard on—Priscilla, isn't it? You know how kids are. I don't think they meant any harm."

She said she knew how kids were. She said she was aware they hadn't meant anything, that meaning requires mental processes and her daughter's had been severely impaired by a combination of alcohol and marijuana.

Deborah, sitting beside the phone, pressed her palms together as if in prayer, pleading with her mother not to say any more. "Pris has to live with those people, Mom. Try to understand. I'll see that she doesn't do it again. I'll keep an eye on her. She's only eleven, Mom."

Miriam put the phone down and stood there a long time, staring at Deborah, feeling each season of their history sift through her and settle into strata. She opened her mouth several times to speak. Once to say she was sorry for the divorce. Then to say she was sorry they didn't have a regular family. Then, remembering Mr. Frazier, that she was afraid alcoholism might be something you inherited.

"Sweetheart," she finally said, stroking the lank, streaky blond hair back from Deborah's solemn face, "it's not up to you to keep bad things from happening." She put her arms around the child's bony shoulders and rocked her against herself. "Don't worry. I'll think of something."

The next morning, fortunately a Saturday, she made Pris wash the car with a bucket of soapy water in the apartment parking lot. Deborah hovered by the kitchen window, volunteering to help, but Miriam insisted she stay inside. They both watched Pris from behind the ruffled curtains.

"She looks sorry, Mom."

"She looks sulky and hung over."

"Don't you think she's suffered enough?"

Miriam had smiled at the melodramatic phrase. "How much suffering is enough, Deb?"

It was a question that, during the past few years, Miriam had often put to herself, the kind of question she used to put to God, only she found she could no longer imagine him listening, much less answering.

Deborah had answered that day, though. "Enough to make you change?" she'd said hopefully.

Hannah gave a muffled moan. Pris pulled away. "Gram?"

"Is that Priscilla?" The last syllables whistled through Hannah's dry lips.

Miriam filled the water glass and this time put a straw in it. "Here, Mother." Hannah's hand fluttered toward the glass, then dropped. Pris lifted her head a few inches from the pillow while Miriam guided the straw between her lips. "Drink a little water," she said. "Wet your whistle."

Pris recognized that half-teasing, half-pleading tone in her mother's voice that she'd noticed in her own. Well, she should have stayed put, she thought.

Hannah sipped briefly from the straw, then pulled her lips away and turned her head to the side. "Enough," she said.

Pris lowered her grandmother's head carefully to the pillow and pushed the hair back from her face. "That better?"

Hannah lowered her eyelids to indicate a nod and smiled up at her. "How's my girl?" Her voice sounded stronger.

Pris glanced at her mother. "We're fine, Gram. It's you we're worried about."

"Tim?"

"He's fine too. He just got a promotion, in fact."

"Promotion? What is he now? Sergeant?"

"No, Gram. I meant at work. He's just in the reserves. He's been back a good while now—" She stopped herself just before adding, "remember?"

Hannah gave a short grunt and closed her eyes. Pris and Miriam looked at one another. Then Pris added, to fill the silence quickly, "How long was your husband gone, Gram?" She'd never thought of her dead grandfather as anything but Hannah's husband.

"A long time, honey. Years. After your mother was born the neighbor lady looked after her. Drove her to the base so I could slip out and nurse her during my lunch hour." Hannah inhaled deeply but the breath seemed to be coming easier now. "I even managed to put a little bit aside every month from the allotment check I got from the army every month. Fifty-five dollars." She closed her eyes and her lips twitched slightly. "Once in a while I even bought myself a new pair of stockings—when I could find them. Nylon was rationed, you know. But even with rationing, I had more of this world's goods than I'd ever had before."

Still, she'd had to practice thinking the words—"at war"—to make it seem real. She would get up in the dark, pick up the baby from her crib, and put her in bed beside her, telling herself this was what was real—this solid chunk of soft flesh and fragrant warmth. The world that invaded the house through the radio and newspapers was only a story someone had made up.

Nevertheless, as the days went by, Hannah found herself frightened by the very names of battle locations filtering through the radio's little fabric screen and appearing in newspaper headlines. Rangoon, Bataan, Guadalcanal, Corregidor—the strange names sounded like threats in her ears. With defeat after defeat, the stories began to take on more substance. Though he was not even allowed to say where he was, letters from Sam strengthened the war's reality. Reading between the lines, she could make out that he was not yet in the thick of things, though he longed to be.

Stories of Americans, both military and civilian, mistreated in Japanese prison camps began to appear in the newspapers, troubling her dreams. What if Sam were captured? Would he be able to stand up under torture? She realized she didn't really know him well enough to predict.

She pored over photographs from the front in *Look* and *Colliers*, studying scenes so bizarre it was hard to believe they were real. In one a Japanese officer brandished a sword over a blindfolded Australian soldier kneeling in the sand. The picture's caption reported that the soldier had been beheaded only moments later. The sword, the frozen moment, the alien face of the Japanese officer, all reinforced Hannah's sense that the war was a phantasm.

Pictures from the European front affected her differently, however. In those, the civilians looked like any you might see on the street in Corpus Christi. The American G.I.s were dressed in the same khaki uniforms.

One photograph in particular—a young Belgian girl being led off to a firing squad for treason—haunted Hannah. The girl, her matted hair still holding its curl, looked at the camera dully, without emotion, accepting the futility of her plight. On her feet were what Hannah took to be wooden sandals, held on by a single strap across the arch. She wore a loose smock covered by a canvas coat that gaped open lopsidedly, as if she hadn't any spirit left to pull it closed for protection against either bullets or the camera. We're about the same age, me and that girl, Hannah thought. She could only guess at what her treason had been. She appeared to have already abandoned her body, to have yielded it up to its fate. Her eyes seemed to despise her very death.

Pictures from the Pacific showed a different kind of war going on there. The background in the pictures looked like scenery painted for the movies—palm trees, beaches, jungles. The soldiers, stripped to the waist with vines festooned on their battle helmets, grinned like pagan jungle gods. Some of the pictures showed G.I.s making a game of their deprivation, holding up messkits supposedly containing monkey stew or dressed in improvised grass skirts and coconut brassieres. Even the shots showing their corpses, half-buried in the sand by the receding tide, seemed like scenes from a game, some elaborate fantasy that boy-men like Sam had cooked up in order to keep on playing at cowboys-and-Indians, thriving on the very danger that threatened them.

The clowning soldiers made Hannah angry, especially when stories of Japanese concentration camps full of American civilians began to filter back to the States. When she pictured such camps, either waking or dreaming, she found herself imagining the women who hadn't escaped from Luzon or Borneo in time with their children, perhaps missionaries or just housewives, slowly wasting away from starvation behind the barbed wire. Then she would urge Miriam to eat, as though the same fate might befall them someday with Sam gone and no one to protect them, as if she had to fatten her child against the day of some vague disaster in their uncertain future.

Nevertheless, despite the war, her own life was easier, happier, than any she'd ever known. She went to church with Mrs. McMichaels regularly now. Hannah sat beside her in the pew, watching her voile-covered bosom swell and ebb in measured rhythms. It had the same calming effect on her as the Gulf waves rolling in, steady and constant.

Hannah forced herself to open her eyes again.

"More water, Mother?"

She nodded and, when Miriam held the straw to her lips, reached up and put her hand on her daughter's wrist. She breathed carefully between sips, then turned to look at Pris, sitting on the end of the bed. "Your mother was a cheerful baby. All she had to play with was some spools the neighbor-lady strung on shoelaces, or buttons threaded on string for rattlers. I had this routine—in the evenings I'd wash up my underwear in the bathroom sink and iron her little dresses. Then I'd spread out newspaper on the floor and polish her little high-topped shoes. Remember, Miriam? That white, chalky polish?" She let her fingers slide from her daughter's wrist. "Girls today would think it was pretty dull. Even my friends thought so then. Oh, I was lonely sometimes, of course."

But the loneliness hadn't been for Sam in particular. They'd had so little time together after they were married that he was still practically a stranger to her when he'd been sent overseas. His letters, filled with jeers against the enemy, repetitious longings for home, complaints about the food or the CO, all studded with exclamation points, didn't reveal much more of him than she already was familiar with.

Her own letters were just as predictable. Except for new details about Miriam's appetite or teething problems, she wrote much the same thing every week—her frayed hopes for his safe return, admonitions not to take unnecessary risks. In the spring, he sent word for her to meet him in San Diego. His unit would be en route to the Pacific. The two days they had together seemed like a dream afterward.

Each time she had looked at Sam's picture on her dresser after that trip to San Diego, she wondered how she could have married anyone so handsome. His extreme good looks, the garrison cap tilted slightly over his left eye, seemed irrelevant to her life there in Corpus with Miriam. In San Diego, he had told her he'd be back in the States within a year, but the seasons continued to roll undifferentiated through the Gulf Coast and still nothing changed, except that Miriam began to walk and talk.

Why don't you go live with my folks? Sam wrote. *They've got plenty. You wouldn't need to work. Mom could help you take care of the baby.*

Live in Minnesota? She stared at the letter as if he'd suggested Mars. She pictured mountains of ice and snow. Cold, disapproving looks from the woman who had written Hannah only once on a small sheet of heavy cream paper: *Sam's father joins me in sending our love. We trust you will both be happy and that you will be able to make a good home for our boy.*

Her own parents, too old and tired to make a living on the farm by themselves, had moved in with Hannah's oldest brother on a ranch in West Texas when their two younger sons were drafted. Hannah went once to see them, taking Miriam on the train to meet her grandparents. Her mother moved through the house like a sleepwalker; her father sat on the high front porch and stared off to the empty horizon. Hannah could hardly wait to get back to Corpus. She felt free there, freer than she'd ever been. And with Miriam, life was perfect.

Sam finally admitted in one of his letters that he didn't know when he'd be home. *The powers that be have decided they gotta wipe up the Huns before we can take on the Japs. That's why we never get anywhere over here. They expect us to hold out till they send us reinforcements and more equipment. Looks like most of us are going to be out here for the long haul. The only thing*—he had underlined "only" three times—*that keeps me going is knowing that the only woman I'll ever love is waiting for me. And the cutest little girl God ever made!* Hannah sent him snapshots every month of Miriam. Still, it seemed to her that he'd added the last sentence almost as an afterthought.

One morning as she was dressing for work, turning the tiny screws on the back of her pearl-button earbobs and looking at herself absently in the mirror, it occurred to her that the next day was their fourth anniversary. She stopped and counted on her fingers. In four years, she had spent less than four months with this man. Gradually the marriage itself had ceased to seem real to her, had grown less substantial with every passing year of the war. She had the license, of course, folded carefully among other papers he'd told her were important, in a little cedar box in the bottom drawer of her dresser. But as the months passed, Sam had become not much more than that piece of paper: a formality.

Then suddenly, late the next summer, it was over.

Of course she was glad that the war had ended. How could anyone not be? For years she'd been braced to receive a telegram telling her Sam's plane had crashed or been shot down in some place she couldn't even pronounce. Now it was over.

On the day he was to return, Hannah moved around the upstairs bedroom in Mrs. McMichaels' house, straightening, rearranging, tucking the chenille bedspread around the pillows a little tighter. The headline on this morning's paper had read 40,000 TEXAS WAR WORKERS LAID OFF. Sam's last letter had mentioned making a trip to Minnesota right away, maybe even living with his parents for a while until he got on his feet again. *Time the folks got to meet both my wife and my daughter. Too bad the gas rationing has made that impossible so far.*

Hannah wasn't fooled by that excuse. She sensed that the Sniders had continued to hope, even after Miriam was born, that their second son would somehow shake himself loose from this unsuitable marriage. Hannah sent Miriam to the bathroom one last time, and touched up her lipstick. The thought of the wintry Minnesotans, aloof and disdainful of her little family, stiffened her resolve. She'd live in a chicken coop before she moved in with them.

Looking at herself in the round mirror of the vanity, she could tell that she was not the same girl Sam had married. If someone called her a woman now, she wouldn't be surprised. She felt grown up, finally.

And how would he have altered?

She had snapped the top back on the lipstick and tucked it in her handbag. In the end, it wouldn't matter what changes had happened in either of them.

Hannah could feel Priscilla's hand on her shoulder. "It must have been rough, Gram. Being alone so long."

"We just had to make the best of it," Hannah said. "That was all we could do."

10

Otis Ruffner's house wasn't what Deborah had expected. A wrought iron fence, its filigree painted white, ran along the sidewalk in front. Behind the fence, rank stalks of Johnson grass, heads heavy with seed, stuck above the Bermuda grass that hadn't been cut in weeks. Venetian blinds covered arched Moorish windows. The place looked deserted. Maybe Ruffner had told Arlene he'd be here, but Deborah would be very surprised if anyone answered the carved door, unvarnished and grey from weathering.

Just as she started to touch the door-bell button, however, the door swung in. "Come right on in," a wheezy voice said from the shadowy entrance. "I been sitting here waiting for you."

Deborah smiled briefly and waited till she was inside to slide her sunglasses up on her head.

"Step right on in here to the living room if you wouldn't mind. I been working outa here ever since the Feds shut down my office in town. Hope it's not putting you out too much, driving all the way out here. You feeling better now, are you?"

She murmured something indefinite about a bug going around and followed him into a dim room full of heavy Mediterranean furniture. She hadn't noticed earlier, but he wasn't any taller than she was.

"Scuse the mess," he said, picking up an apricot afghan and clearing a space for her on a lime-flocked sofa next to a coffee-table littered with packets of papers circled with rubber bands. An open sack of tortilla chips sat beside a can of bean dip. "Since my wife died nothing seems to run smooth around here."

"Oh," Deborah said as she sank onto the flattened cushion. "I hadn't realized your wife had died." The sofa was so low her knees stuck up higher than her waist. She shifted so that she was sitting sideways and placed her briefcase beside her on the floor. The smell of the bean dip reached her and she tightened her throat and coughed once, carefully. Arlene was right. She shouldn't have had any coffee. "Recently? Perhaps you'd like to wait—"

"That's real thoughtful of you, sweetheart, but I'm afraid the government don't have your kind heart." He grinned at her across the coffee table and shook his head. "Heart don't come into it these days, you know? Any kind of human consideration—sickness, a death in the family—anymore we're just so many numbers to the government." He shook his head and sighed heavily. "Anyhow. I'd just as soon go ahead and get my name cleared, you know? So I can—what do you young folks say these days?—get on with my life."

She smiled noncommittally and pulled the list of questions they'd started on earlier from her briefcase.

"Say. While you're getting set up there, let me get you something to drink. How 'bout some tea?" Before she could answer he had vanished down the hall to the kitchen.

As soon as he was gone, she picked up the can of bean dip, holding her breath, and carried it quickly across the room where she deposited it on a dusty étagère shelf beside a stack of *American Quarterhorse Journals*. In the distance she heard a microwave ding, and in another moment he was back, carrying a pink enamel tray.

"Here we go, young lady. Toast and tea. What my mama always give me for a upset stomach." He set the tray down beside her, the two pieces of toast skidding off the saucer onto the tray. A tea-bag string hung damply over the lip of an Oilers mug. His look scanned the coffee table for the bean dip. Noting its absence, he picked up the sack of tortilla chips, rolled the top quickly shut, and stuck it on the TV console.

"You shouldn't have gone to such trouble, Mr. Ruffner. I'm fine, really," Deborah protested, embarrassed by the reference to the scene in Hoot's office.

He handed her the mug, smiling at her encouragingly from under the lank strips of black hair. "No trouble. No trouble a-tall."

She held the mug between her palms. The surprising scent of mingled summer plants—roses, blackberries, hibiscus—rose against her face on the current of steam. This is what she'd needed. Not some styrofoam container of black coffee. Comfort, she thought, and reached for a piece of toast.

As she nibbled away at the toast, Otis sorted through his logs of rolled paper, arranging them in an order that appeared to have some meaning, all the while whistling "San Antonio Rose" between his teeth. She watched his cheeks move in and out. What was it with men like him? They could be as blunt and exuberant as eight-year-old boys, yet they had the guile necessary to transform a little venture capital into profitable businesses. Alamo Assets or Wellhead Whatever—Otis Ruffner's company must have been substantial at some point or Hoot Jasper wouldn't be wasting his time on him. The man was a type she generally avoided whenever possible, the kind that never got over the fact that you were a woman. A paradoxical combination of practical and sentimental, uncouth and fanciful. A dying breed. In fact, she frowned, his type ought to be extinct already. He seemed to come from Gram's era, though he looked like—what?—not much over fifty? Still, old enough to be her father.

He glanced up at her now, grinning and bobbing his head at the saucer. "Looks like you polished that off pretty well. You still hungry?"

"Hungry?" She looked down at the crumbs on the saucer, startled at the toast's disappearance.

"You know," he nodded toward an enameled clock on the mantle with a speculative squint, "I'm thinking what you need is some real food. Why don't we go find us some, Miss Estes? I've about exhausted my cooking repertoire with the toast and tea. And I don't imagine you're in the mood for bean dip and tortilla chips. What say we run down to the cafeteria and I can answer the rest of your questions while we eat. How 'bout it?"

Deborah started to make the obligatory noises of declining, but Otis was already getting to his feet, slapping his back pocket for his wallet. She thought, Why not? She was on a roll with the guy. "I think you better start calling me Deborah then," she said and stood up, straightening her skirt. After all, isn't that what Hoot had sent her to do—charm Otis Ruffner?

He drove them in what he explained was Velda's last car, a cream-colored Lincoln Towncar, to a Wyatt's cafeteria about six blocks away. He took the liver-and-onions and a piece of mud pie. She had fruit salad, fried chicken, mashed potatoes and gravy, black-eyed peas, macaroni and cheese, eggplant casserole, jalapeno cornbread, and strawberry shortcake. Food had never looked so good. They clinked their iced tea glasses together before they started eating.

"So," she said, stacking one of her small empty bowls into another, "the suit is being filed against Hearts Unlimited. And you say you had no controlling interest in the company after 1985 when your wife took over?"

He wiped his mouth carefully with a big green napkin, nodding sorrowfully at the little cardboard stand by the salt and pepper shakers advertising the Senior Specials. "I hate to say it, but Velda never was a judge of character. She hired on some guy supposed to computerize everything for her. Stole her blind."

Deborah picked the lemon wedge out of her iced tea and sucked on it. She could feel his pursed green eyes moving over to rest on her. "And you're sure you had no more say about the operation of the company?"

"If I had, you think that skunk woulda got away with what he did? Had to use all the profits that year off the imports just to keep Velda afloat."

"Wait, wait, wait. I thought you said you were out of the company altogether."

The thin skin below his eyebrows stretched upward, signalling his baffled simplicity. "That's the gospel truth. I left everything up to Velda. She was on a real tear about then. Didn't want me meddling in her affairs. Said she didn't want me sticking my oar in, she'd take care of it." He frowned down at his plate, then shoved it to the side of the table. "I had to think of all kinds of crazy ways to funnel money into that account so's she wouldn't know where it was coming from."

Deborah sensed a buried mine lurking there. She'd let Hoot defuse that one. "I suppose you have the documentation to show your wife's company no longer had any legal connection to Alamo Assets?" Hadn't Will Rogers had little spikes of hair that fell across his forehead?

"Yes, ma'am. Sure do. Right here." He reached in his back pocket and pulled out one of the packets that had been lying on the coffee table. He snapped the rubber band off, folded back the wrinkled sheets, and handed them to her, holding his elbow carefully above her melting pats of butter.

Deborah looked at the first page, frowning, then flipped through the remaining sheets. "What about the board of directors?"

"I give that up too."

"So you're saying there was absolutely no connection between Alamo Assets and Hearts Unlimited? Did you get your wife to fire this fellow, the one computerizing the company?"

"No ma'am. Whatever mistakes Velda made, well, they was hers. Course I made up the difference for what the computer nut cost her, just to keep her afloat. But I sure didn't let her know I was doing it. And after that," he looked down, "well, that was the end of it." He sat back in the Naugahyde booth and frowned in concentration, as though explaining a difficult philosophical point. "It woulda spoiled the whole thing for her, you see, if she'd ever found out. She'd think I was stepping in, trying to second-guess her." He shook his head sadly.

Deborah pushed the last strawberry around the dessert plate to scrape up the remaining streaks of the whipped cream. Her waistband was painfully tight. "Can you believe I've eaten all this?" she asked in amazement, fingering the button on the waistband. "I've made a complete pig of myself." Would her belt cover the gap if she undid the button?

Otis looked over at her, his eyes still confiding gentle melancholy. "Somehow I think you musta needed a good hearty meal, Miss Deborah Estes."

The button popped into her hand. She blinked at him, then down quickly at the little assemblage of bowls stacked at angles before her.

"You feeling okay?" His words came across the table's wreckage so softly and so tenderly that before she knew it, Deborah had clenched her eyes shut and crushed the dark green napkin to her reddening nose. She gave little bridled shakes of her head, trying to choke off the tears before they could spill over.

Otis closed a stub-fingered hand over her long one, drawn into a fist now beside her glass of iced tea. "Sweetheart, sweetheart. There now. Ain't nothing so bad it can't be fixed." He slid across the naugahyde and came around to her side of the booth, slipping in beside her and turning his back so that he shielded her from the lady in thick-soled sneakers who kept wheeling the coffee cart past their table. "You not in some kind of trouble, are you?"

She turned her head away and drew in a deep shuddering breath.

"This ain't just a bug, is it now?" He let his breath out in a whistle. "Well, I'll be."

Deborah brought the napkin down so that it was just covering her mouth and stared out across the dining room, blinking rapidly.

"Tell you what. Let's just—yes. Come on now. I'll get your handbag here." And before she could stop him he'd scrambled out of the booth, picked up the damp little paper tickets from the table and tucked up her handbag high under his arm, its strap hanging almost down to his knees. Extracting a twenty-dollar bill from his wallet, he dropped it along with the tickets on the counter as he hurried her past the cash register.

Making encouraging, inarticulate murmurs, he opened the door of the Lincoln for her, then hurried around the car, fumbling with the keys, and clucking at the traffic in order to give a cover for her embarrassment.

By the time they'd pulled into his weedy driveway again, Deborah had more or less composed herself, though the skirt button was still clutched in her damp palm.

"Really, Mr. Ruffner," she said, trying to restore the decorum between them as he switched off the motor, "I appreciate your concern, but—"

He waved a hand and jerked open his door, hurrying once more around the Lincoln's long body. "Don't mention it,

Miss Estes," he said with judicious matter-of-factness, at the same time gripping her elbow as if to leverage her out of the automobile. "Don't say another word about it." He pushed open the front door for her. "And here I was just going on about my own misfortunes," he muttered, as if to himself. Then scurrying ahead of her, he whipped the afghan from the back of the sofa. "Not that it's a misfortune. Oh goodness no. Not at all. In fact, well, there now. You just sit there." He gave her just enough of a nudge to get her onto the sofa again. Then he stood frowning at the afghan as if he might tuck her up with it.

"Please. I'm fine," Deborah said. "And I should probably go now. Maybe we can finish—I don't know. Maybe—"

He looked at her over the afghan, his eyes wide. "This business? Oh, honey. You don't need to be worrying about... I mean, maybe later. I'll check with Hoot and—"

"No!" Deborah bolted halfway up from the sofa. "Please. I'd rather you didn't."

He sank onto the end of the sofa, the swag of afghan falling between his knees. "No, no. Well, of course not. You're right. I can see. Knowing Hoot, I mean. Well. Let me think here a minute."

She started to protest again while she shovelled her things back into her briefcase, but he put out an arm to stop her.

"You're not going? Not now? Oh, you can't do that. Just a minute here—" He stood up, looking around in agitation. "We'll figure this out. I promise you. But you can't go, Miss Estes. Don't you see? I mean how all this is fitting together? Poor Velda. And now you. And this little problem of mine. Well, all I need is just a little while to think here. Don't you see this is all meant for a reason?" He pinched his bottom lip into a V and studied his boot toe. "It's almost like—well, I won't say that." He stood there holding the absurd apricot afghan, his face turning pink under the brown of his oilfield sunburn, the little diagonal points of black hair plastered to his forehead.

"Really, Otis, you're very kind, but I don't see how—"

"I know you don't," he said earnestly. "But I do. Or at least I nearly do. I'm closing in on it." He gave a single sober shake of his head. "Please. I beg you, Deborah. This is real important." Then, suddenly brightening, he added, "Why don't you just take a little nap here? Give old Otis a little time to think." He shook the afghan. "You just lay back there now and let me cover you up. You could use some rest."

Deborah took a deep breath and sat back. She wasn't sure what the man might be up to, but at this point she figured she had very little to lose by humoring him a while longer. "Okay," she said finally. "But no more than an hour. I'll need to get back to the office."

He bent down, drew off her shoes, and lifted her feet up onto the sofa. Then, beaming down at her, he spread the afghan gently over her and tucked it around her feet.

It had been Deb, Pris reminded herself on the way to the hospital, who offered her the most consolation when Tim had been called up for the Gulf War. She needed to remind herself of that whenever she began to lose patience with her sister. Deb had dropped by on her way back to Dallas one weekend and found her crying in the bedroom with the door shut.

Priscilla had been watching a reporter interview the pregnant wife of a Navy pilot in California. The woman had told him, giggling, that she was going to name the baby Desert Storm. Suddenly Pris had erupted from the sofa, dumping the bowl of popcorn she and the boys had between them onto the floor.

"You stupid bitch," she'd screamed at the woman. "This isn't a joke!"

Barton sucked in his breath and drew back against Joshua. "Go to your room and play," she shouted at them.

Deb had found the boys in Josh's bedroom, eating peanut butter out of the jar with a spoon. "Mommy cussed," Barton told her, his eyes gummy with spent tears.

Pris was face-down on her own unmade bed. As face-down as she could get, six-and-a-half months pregnant.

"It's the pits, isn't it?" Deb said, dropping down beside her on the bed and beginning to rub her back the way Mom used to when either of them was upset.

Pris could hear Deb's bangle bracelets clicking together as her arm moved back and forth. She didn't answer. Deb had been against the war from the first. "Oil," she'd announced at Christmas dinner. "If we go to war, it'll be over oil." Deb never held back from expressing her political opinions. She watched the Macneil-Lehrer Newshour every evening.

Pris, on the other hand, had had to look up Kuwait on the map back in October when Tim got his orders. Of course Deb had known where it was without looking, plus the names of all those Arab rulers who looked like they were dressed up for a Christmas play.

Deb had finally coaxed her out of the bedroom and back into the den where CNN was still on. She'd already cleaned up the popcorn and made a fresh pot of coffee. "I needed some for the drive back," Deb said, making light of the help.

They sat on the sofa together, their feet up on the coffee table, watching the coverage and making sarcastic remarks to the television set. A pilot, lifting his sunglasses to his forehead, swaggered across the screen and jerked a thumb up. The camera cut to the message chalked on the ordnance hanging, gonad-like, under his jet's fuselage: "Up yours, Saddam."

"What a jerk!" Pris found herself saying. "Just like some dumb jock, getting pumped up for the big game. It's all hormones, the whole bloody mess."

"That's what put the H in H bomb," Deb said. "You notice they don't say 'Make love, not war' anymore. That's because men can't tell the difference."

"Yeah. Look at me!" And Pris jumped up and did a little dance in her sweats and wool socks, displaying her engorged middle. Then she stopped and threw her arms out wide. "And where, I ask you, is the guy who did this to me? Over in that goddamned desert playing cowboys and Indians with his friends!" She collapsed onto the sofa again.

"Make eunuchs, not war," Deb said. "Let them put that on their bumper sticker and smoke it."

Pris looked at her quizzically. The catharsis of crying had left her feeling clarified. "Do you think God is really a man, Deb?"

Her sister blinked, sensing the shift in mood uneasily. "What do you mean?"

"A man. God. Well, Jesus, of course. But otherwise."

"What are you getting at?"

Pris threw herself back against the sofa and folded her arms behind her head. Her stomach made a nice distinct bulge already, but not enough to be miserable yet. "Sometimes when I get mad at God it feels like being mad at a man. Like he's used me or something."

"Used you?" Deb's echo was cautious. "I thought that was supposed to be the point. Like Saint Francis. 'Make me an instrument of thy peace.' "

"Yeah, but an instrument. That's different. Instrument sounds like a scalpel. Or a pen or something. Instruments act. They do things—cut or write or dig. They make a dent. I'm the one that got dented. I feel more like a—" She flung her arms open again, wordlessly.

"Vessel."

"Yeah. That. Vessels aren't instruments."

"Come on, Pris. You love being a vessel and you know it." Deb tossed a sofa pillow at her. "Look at you rubbing that belly of yours. You'll probably end up having a dozen."

"Yeah, well, maybe I'd like to try being an instrument for a change, you know, instead of just sitting around waiting for either Tim or God to screw me." Out of the corner of her eye she could see Deb's eyes widen momentarily. "Maybe I'd like to drop a few bombs myself." She sobered suddenly and let the pillow fall to the floor. "I get mad at God, Deb. Seriously. It scares me sometimes. I'm always having to wait and see what he's going to do with my life."

Deborah leaned over, hooked an arm around her neck, and pulled her sister's head against her side. "Doofus. You sound like Mother."

"Mother?" Her protest was muffled under Deborah's arm.

"Sure. You know that. Mom's mad at God too. Why else do you think she's on this goddess kick?"

Priscilla let her head rest there inside the crook of her sister's arm, consoled by contrast between the slatted ribs and the soft swell of her breast.

"Of course, if you Protestants hadn't thrown out Mary, you wouldn't have this problem, you know," Deb went on, her tone changing to teasing. "You wouldn't feel so driven all the time."

Pris twisted her head to look up at her sister's face. "Oh right. Look who's talking about being driven."

Deb shrugged. "At least I don't feel like I have to do it all."

Pris sat up. "And what's Mary got to do with it anyway?"

Deb smiled in that infuriating, smug way of hers. "She made passivity a virtue. She's the only icon of placid inactivity in all of western civilization. All you Protestants have to dash around doing things. It's the only way you can take yourself seriously. That's why you want to drop bombs." She switched off the TV with the remote and pulled Pris' head into her lap. "We're all waiting, you know. You're not the only one. I'm waiting for a job. Tim's waiting to come home."

Pris closed her eyes and yawned, then drew her feet up onto the sofa. Maybe she'd just go to sleep here with her head in Deb's lap, and when she woke up, it would all be over.

It made a certain kind of sense, Pris thought as she pulled into the parking lot. And if you knew what it was you were waiting for, that made it easier. Even Gram must be waiting for it to be over with.

But her mother. What was she waiting for? Not Dad. She'd given up on him long ago. Not even another man, not for a long time now. And certainly not God. She still remembered her mother explaining her dissertation to Gram whose face had been set in a disapproving pucker.

"Goddesses?" Hannah said.

"Like in the Bible, Mother. You remember—Asherah? That was a goddess."

Gram's shoulders contracted in small shudder. "It makes my skin crawl, Miriam."

"It's history, Mother. Older even than the Jews."

"Exactly. People learned better after that."

"Oh really? You think it's better to have a god who wipes out firstborn children in a fit of rage?"

Pris stared at Gram, waiting for her to defend God. But she'd turned back to her cutting board, her lips still pinched together.

Mother had pushed it though. "You've got to admit, Mother, a woman wouldn't do that. Especially not to her own children."

149

Gram had turned around then, her right hand still holding the knife. She stared at her daughter for a long time. Then she said, "You may have had a good deal of a certain kind of experience, my dear, but you have no earthly idea what a woman might or might not do, given the right circumstances."

Pris' eyes swiveled to her mother. Miriam opened her mouth, then shook her head and started setting the table, her hands moving swiftly with the chilling efficiency they had when she was angry.

When they sat down to eat, Gram had asked Deborah to "return thanks." During dinner, Deb kept glancing at Pris, bunching her eyebrows in a silent question. Pris kept her own eyes on her plate, frightened as she hadn't been since those last years with Dad. She'd never seen her mother and grandmother intentionally hurt one another before. Later, after the dishes were done, Miriam had come in off the back stoop where she'd been smoking a cigarette, her eyes red-rimmed.

When Priscilla had tried to recount the dispute to Deborah that night in Gram's tiny extra bedroom, her sister had been impatient, even peeved. "It's because of Dad," she said. "Mom gets him confused with God."

"Dad?"

"You're too young to understand," Deb sighed wearily, flopping over to face the wall. She was in junior high then and said that a lot. "Besides," she smiled to herself, "who wouldn't like to be worshipped?"

Pris thought about it, then shivered. "Me is who."

"Oh, you're too young," Deb repeated, rubbing her calf with an instep. She'd started secretly shaving her legs with Mom's razor in the shower. "Go to sleep."

One night, not long after Sarah was born, Pris had recalled the conversation. They'd already gone to bed when she asked Tim: "Do you ever feel like you want to be worshipped?"

"What?" Tim jerked as though he'd been on the verge of sleep.

She rolled onto her side and repeated the question.

"What are you talking about? Go to sleep."

Several times lately she'd ended in tears when they made love. It upset Tim. He froze above her as she stiffened in his arms. "What's wrong?"

She could only wail and pitch upwards against him insistently till he descended into her again and she locked him between her thighs like a skittish horse.

He'd repeat the question afterwards as she lay spent, letting both her tears and his fluid dry on her body, feeling like a seashore, rimed with rubble and salt. Usually, she pretended to be asleep so she wouldn't have to answer him. She didn't know.

She raised her head and poked him. "Do you?"

He reached and put a hand on her hip. His chest lifted as he took a deep breath, held it, then let it out very slowly. "Pris, I have no idea what you're getting at. So I guess no. I can't say that I ever have."

"Do other guys? As a general rule, I mean."

"How would I know about other guys, Pris?"

"I just thought you might have some insight. You are one after all. I could tell you about women in general if you asked."

"Well, I didn't ask."

There was a long silence, but she could tell by the way his fingers twitched slightly that he was thinking.

"So do they?" he finally said.

"Do they what?"

He jogged her hip with his arm. "Want to be worshipped. You know what I meant."

She yawned, suddenly sleepy. "I don't know. It was all a long time ago." And she rolled away, tucked the pillow under her cheek, and fell instantly asleep.

11

Miriam was staring out the window of Hannah's hospital room, her mother's signature phrase still echoing in her head—*make the best of it*. Hannah was an expert at making the best of tribulation. Makeshift, piecemeal, hardship. All those words cobbled together from other words described her mother's life. Along with tribulation, affliction, misfortune, words as syllabically ornate and archaic as cast-iron fretwork on public buildings. Miriam, on the other hand, was sorely aware she had not made the best of much.

On good days, when she wasn't worrying her daughters, Miriam interpreted the failure of her marriage sociologically, the result of having grown up in a gap generation, during an interval in history when all the rules had changed. When she married Gordon, it had been tacitly understood that, once wed, you were on your own. The line between childhood and the adult world was clearly drawn. Hannah had asked if Gordon could support a wife. These days, that question too would sound archaic.

All the rules from Hannah's world seemed obsolete now, nothing more than artifacts. She had always been careful, for instance, not to meddle, not even to inquire, much less interrogate, not even when Gordon's drinking became painfully obvious. Now, even Pris, who consciously aimed at emulating her grandmother, had none of Hannah's sense of manners, deportment, protocol. Somewhere between Kennedy's assassination and Miriam's divorce ten years later, all the tacit agreements governing domestic life, the patterns that made it possible to predict what you could expect from people you lived with, had dissolved.

Miriam had first felt the sand shift beneath her feet the day the man came to fix the washer. It must have been the year after they'd bought the new house in Freeport—two bathrooms, four bedrooms—when the washing machine broke down. The repairman had eyed her with a kind of lazy insolence as he carried his tool box to the laundry room that afternoon.

At first she'd told herself she was imagining things. Barefoot in a pair of old cutoffs, hair straggling out of a ponytail, she balanced Pris on her outthrust hip as she explained to him how she'd come home from the grocery store to a tubful of sodden clothes sitting in gray water, refusing to spin. Deborah, suddenly shy, sucked her thumb and pulled on the long tail of Miriam's chambray shirt. As she described the sound the machine made when she turned it on, she was suddenly aware that Deborah's tugging had popped the top two buttons loose. Miriam blushed furiously, slapped behind her at Deborah's hand, and jerked the front of the shirt together.

The man smiled. Not a companionable smile as if sharing her embarrassment, but an indolent, sardonic smile. Later, when he was showing her the machine's failed relay switch, he'd stepped behind her and let his hand brush against her bare leg. A little more than a brush maybe. When she looked around quickly, the smile had come back.

"He leered," she told Gordon that night. "Positively leered."

Gordon was frowning at the diagram of the barbecue grill he was trying to assemble on the patio. He looked up, still frowning, but not in a proprietary way. "Well." He shrugged and looked at the diagram again.

"Well, what?"

"Just be more careful. You could start wearing a bra for one thing."

On the face of it, it was a small thing. But she had felt at least momentarily frightened, and the man, who said he'd have to get another switch from the warehouse, was coming back the next day. She suspected him of inventing the excuse.

"Maybe I should call and tell him not to come till the weekend when you'll be here. That is, unless you could get off tomorrow afternoon."

Gordon crackled the instruction sheet between his hands and looked up at her, squinting into the sun setting over the cherry laurels beyond the chain link fence. "Are you crazy? Leave the lab to have a washing machine repaired? My God, Miriam, I can't be dropping everything to come home and make sure some repairman doesn't rape my wife. I'm in the middle of a very—" He stopped and batted a hand in her direction, as though he were swatting away a persistent fly. A moment later he added grudgingly and almost under his breath, "All right. Tell him to come this weekend."

His response had been like cold water dashed in her face. She'd been hesitant to tell him about the incident at first, fearing he might make too much of it, want to confront the guy. But he hadn't even seemed mildly alarmed. What had happened to his sense of proprietorship? Had her value dropped?

She lay in bed that night, half hoping the man would come back the next day and actually try something. She would run out of the house, clutching her two small children, find a blue-coated policeman who would later admonish Gordon, when he arrived with his lab coat flapping, that he should be more mindful of his wife's safety. He might even say "her honor." Then he would add that Gordon was to love her as Christ loved the church and gave himself for her (the policeman would be a Baptist and familiar with scripture).

After which a chastened Gordon would—But here the fantasy broke down. She couldn't imagine what Gordon would do next.

She didn't call the repair shop and tell them not to send the man back till the weekend. When he arrived the next day, she was wearing jeans and a sweatshirt when she let him in. Then she took the children into the backyard where she stayed, giving them alternating pushes on the new swing set, until he called from the back door that he was finished. She had handled it herself.

The stack of newly laundered underwear she put on top of Gordon's chest of drawers didn't trigger the conclusion that the washer had been successfully repaired. He paid the repair bill when it came, never asking her what arrangements she had made or what had happened. He appeared to have forgotten all about the incident. She didn't mention it herself. Not then anyway.

It must have been that December, not long after the Pentagon announced the number of combat deaths in Vietnam had reached nearly seven thousand, that she decided to make her own Christmas cards. She cut out the pictures of napalmed villages from Time and Newsweek and pasted them on construction paper with the lines from a poem by Robert Lowell inked below—

Still
the world out-Herods Herod.

Actually, "The Holy Innocents" had been written during World War II which she thought of as her mother's war. And after that had come Korea. Now her brother Barton was draft-age. She didn't send one of her homemade cards to Hannah. This war was hers.

She had been ignorant, as she smeared glue on the slick picture and stuck it, already wrinkling, onto the construction paper, of the irony of her project. She was soon to learn, however.

Gordon wasn't home that Christmas—Pris' first—announcing vaguely that he had to go to San Francisco "on business" a few days after B-52s bombed Hanoi in mid-December. She'd waited to start the cards until she was out of school for the holidays. He got back the day after New Year's.

"What's this?" he asked, picking up one of her spoiled attempts she'd left on the sideboard. Paste had smeared across the ink. "Somebody sending you hate mail?"

She took it from him and stuck it inside her psychology text. "No. It's something I did."

"You?" He frowned.

She turned away and started gathering up her mess. "This stupid war. Yes."

He caught her arm. "What do you mean? What do you know?"

That's when it had come out.

"You never told me you were working for the government," she said. Had she been accusing him or justifying herself? "I thought you were working for Dow."

"Dow. The government. What's the difference? I'm a chemist. I make stuff."

"What kind of stuff?"

He shrugged. "Pesticides. Herbicides. Chemical stuff. The government's our biggest client."

"Napalm?"

He laughed. "That's old stuff. World War II."

"So what kind of chemical stuff is Dow making?"

"It's classified, Mir."

"But it's Dow. Not you."

He laughed again. "That's splitting a pretty fine hair. Besides, the government gives incentives."

"I didn't know."

"Well, now you know."

"I didn't know," she repeated, sinking onto a chair.

"Come on. If you didn't know, it's because you didn't want to. How'd you think I was paying for all this"—he flung his arms at the walls—"plus your tuition and babysitters?"

"How was I supposed to know?"

He took a step back and looked at her, mimicking perplexity. "Let me get this straight. You don't have any idea how much an entry-level chemist gets paid but you feel sufficiently well-informed about world affairs to criticize American foreign policy?" It was a rare burst of irony for Gordon.

She didn't enroll in school the next semester. How could she justify profiting from money made on weapons? It seemed her only avenue of protest.

The next fall, however, restless and bored, she went back to school when Gordon left again unexpectedly. Not long after he returned, Johnson announced he was sending 50,000 more troops to Vietnam. She considered joining Students for a Democratic Society.

This time Gordon had brought home as a souvenir some kind of weapon and was showing it to Deborah in the kitchen, taking it apart piece by piece as if it were made of Legos.

"I don't want that gun at home around the girls," she told him that night.

It was the first time in all their life together, in all their disagreements, that she'd seen his eyes move sideways, make a little diagonal stutter of uncertainty. She pressed her advantage. "Deborah only listens to all that to please you anyway. You're home so seldom."

When he left the next time, right after the new year began, telling her Seattle, she understood for the first time that this was only his first stop, his jumping off point. He was actually headed for Vietnam, for field trials of a new pesticide. Mosquitoes in the central highlands had proved resistant to the standard issue sprays. He was gone three weeks that time, and when he came back, he no longer made any pretense of disguising his destination or his mission, only cautioning her against telling her friends about his classified work for the army.

He needn't have worried.

She did go to SDS meetings that spring, though she never joined. The young guys with greasy hair running the meetings made her impatient. Maybe they had endless hours to debate Maoist politics, but she was paying a babysitter. With money made from finding better ways to burn babies.

It seemed she was always angry now. Angry with the war, with the National Guardsmen who stopped her to search the car for weapons the night after Martin Luther King was shot, with Nixon's hanging jowls, with Johnson's flabby earlobes, with Wallace's low and puckered forehead, with Gordon—why couldn't he make connections, see implications? With herself. How had she gotten into such a labyrinth of contradictions? How was she ever going to find her way out?

She watched her daughters for signs of anxiety or stress. But though Pris was still in her terrible twos and Deborah's kindergarten teacher reported she had hit another kid with a toy telephone, they seemed happily absorbed in their own child-world which existed in another dimension from the adult sphere of war and marriage.

She'd already stopped going to St. Andrew's. She'd helped them pack canned goods for the striking farm workers in the Valley but, because of the children, she hadn't been able to drive down in the van that delivered them. After that, the interminable discussions on Bonhoeffer had begun to bore her. The man had tried to kill Hitler, for crying out loud. It was hard to imagine any of the members of St. Andrew's plotting an assassination. Instead, they made a sacrament of talking, as though their collective verbalization was itself a vicarious participation in some larger reality.

But for her, talk wasn't enough; she wanted to act, to do something. Something gutsy and dangerous. She was as impatient with St. Andrew's talk as she was with Hannah's "strength and shield" religion. She could feel her own strength, fueled by anger, rising within her. And she didn't want to be shielded. Not any longer.

Meanwhile, she and Gordon lived almost as strangers, he absorbed in his work but never talking about it at home, she sponging up classes and the heady campus camaraderie. She was not particularly unhappy with this arrangement. She liked having a life secret and apart, and the less she knew about his the better. Once in a while she would go with him to an obligatory company party where her only social protest was a rather extreme miniskirt and black fishnet stockings.

At the same time, she began to sense a good deal of give to the world that had, until then, always seemed dense and compacted around her. Now, it seemed to be loosening, like a baby tooth. She wasn't sure whether this give was in the world itself or if her own perception of reality was escaping its former confines.

Not till after the My Lai massacre, however, did the tooth loosen enough to come out.

Gordon had just returned from another trip. During the past year he'd begun to drink heavily, something he'd never done before. Even in graduate school he'd never allowed weekend bashes to interfere with his work. At first it was only out in the garage tinkering with the car. Then in the evenings in front of the TV in his recliner. She hadn't thought much about it, except to make sure no bottles were sitting out when her mother came to see them.

When she'd picked him up at the airport this time though, he was noticeably drunk, the first time she'd ever seen him unsteady on his feet. The sight unnerved her. Whatever Gordon's deficiencies, his strength had always been cool reason. To see him with his rumpled raincoat sagging crookedly from his shoulders, his lids slack over eyes like boiled onions, gave her a jolt.

"Free drinks all the way back," he told her as she unlocked the trunk. "Couple of Tigers made their year and a day." He fell asleep in the car on the way home. Her palms were damp on the steering wheel.

As she was helping him into bed, he reached for her, but she took a step back, avoiding his grasp. He was asleep almost immediately.

She picked up the raincoat he'd dropped on the floor and took it to the hall closet, feeling in the pockets for the ticket stubs he had to turn in with his expense accounting. With them was a paper napkin from a Saigon Hotel. "Amber Angel" it said on one side in Gordon's large square printing, followed by a phone number. She made up a bed on the sofa. During the night she thought she heard him moving around, but after a while all was quiet again.

The next morning, after he'd had a shower and shaved, he looked in somewhat better shape. The children were still sleeping, but she'd made coffee and fixed him an omelet. He thanked her as he sat down at the bar where she'd put the plate, something he never did. She handed him the newspaper without responding. There was a picture of Calley on the front page, the lieutenant in charge at My Lai.

"Poor devil," she heard him say.

"What?" she asked sharply.

"This guy—they're crucifying him."

She took a deep breath, bracing her stiffened arms against the bar. "And you don't think he—"

"It could have been anybody." He said this abruptly, as though to cut her off.

"And that makes it better? That this war turns everyone into monsters?"

He looked up then, as if to answer. But then his gaze contracted, and his eyes sank onto the page. "You don't know," he muttered, picking up his cup.

"That's what you always say, Gordon. I don't know how much houses cost. I don't know about running a war. You're right. I only know how to take care of kids, not kill them."

She saw his jaw clench and his hand tighten on the paper. He didn't look up.

"Don't you ever consider the consequences of what you're doing, Gordon? Those children at My Lai, they could have been Pris and Deborah."

"Lay off, Mir. I'm not Calley, okay? I haven't killed anybody." His voice, incredibly, was shaky and hoarse.

She pushed herself away from the counter. "Have you ever heard of Nuremberg, Gordon?" She was already in the laundry room before he could answer.

"I don't recall them trying any chemists there, sweetheart," he called after her.

She cursed in a whisper, pulling out the dial on the washer, letting the noise of the gushing water cover the words. She could hear him, however, opening the cabinet where he kept a bottle of scotch.

Later, when the girls got up, he got the cereal boxes out and put their bowls on the table. While she was emptying the hamper in the bathroom, she heard the doorbell ring. He went to answer it. On her way back through the kitchen, she saw a large carton on the counter, evidently something left behind at the airport the night before. Pris was still dawdling at the table, but Deborah was insisting on seeing what was inside. Gordon laughed and boosted her up onto the stool by the counter.

Miriam went back and forth through the house, straightening, picking up, pointedly ignoring him. She took the clothes out of the washer and put them in the dryer, setting the timer with a deft jab.

She could hear Gordon's voice in a low monotone, describing to Deborah whatever it was that had been in the carton. She stepped to the door of the laundry room to look. At the table, Pris made a whooshing sound and shot her hand in an arc across her bowl. It took Miriam a moment to realize that the pointed metal tube lying on the counter was a rocket.

He looked up and saw her in the doorway. Instantly the elation drained from his face. That's when she'd started shrieking at him.

The girls' eyes darted back and forth between them. She knew they shouldn't be hearing this, but she couldn't stop. After a few minutes he left, almost splintering the front door as he slammed it. She stood in the laundry room door, still hearing the echo of her shrill impotence.

That night after the girls were in bed, she heard him come in. She was in the guest room, making up the twin bed. Silence and distance, she had decided, were her only weapons.

She was shaking the pillow into its case when Gordon appeared in the doorway.

"What's this?"

"What does it look like?" she said, refusing to look at him.

He hesitated, then said in a unusually softened way, almost wheedling, "Come on, Mir. Let's forget it, okay? I've been gone for weeks. It's been a long time."

"Oh?" she said, her eyes snapping suddenly to his face, "has it?" At the same time, somewhere on the underside of her consciousness, she registered gratification at his plaintive tone.

His look wavered, then he took a step into the room, sliding his hands into the back pockets of his jeans. "You know how much I need you."

"I don't know anything, Gordon. Remember? As far as you're concerned, I'm just this dumb broad you keep around to screw and take care of your kids."

He swayed a little, maybe surprised by the language, maybe startled by her accusation, maybe just drunk again. She went around to the other side of the bed and whipped the spread up over the sheets. Before she could straighten it, he sat down heavily on the foot of the bed and dropped his head into his hands.

"Look," he said, "I know we don't see eye to eye on this, but—"

She straightened and put her hands on her hips. "You don't get it, do you, Gordon?" Her voice had begun to rise again, and she forced it down almost to a whisper, the pressure causing it to quaver. "I'm not even talking about the stupid war. Whatever rationalization you can dream up to justify your macho fantasies is your business."

He raised his head from his hands and stared at her, his eyes narrowing. "Fantasies? My God, woman, it's no fantasy. I don't know what kind of bullshit your little friends at school put in your head, but I saw Khe San. We turned the woods there into a fucking moonscape. Craters as big as swimming pools."

He got to his feet, his hands drawn up into fists. "And I was glad! Five thousand Marines penned down there for seventy-seven days. And I bet you couldn't even find the place on a map, you stupid bitch!"

He was shouting now, spittle flying from his lips. "Hundreds of Cong blown to bits in their tunnels—and I was glad! Do you understand me?—glad!"

He stopped then, his chest heaving. She had backed against the wall. He swept his gaze away from her now in disgust. "You and your faggoty little school pals. You're right. You don't know shit. Believe me, sweetheart, being a lamb in the middle of a herd of sheep is one thing. But being a lamb in a world of wolves is something else."

She leaned against the wall, feeling it slide along her arm. "Maybe so, Gordon," she managed to stammer. "Be a wolf if you want to. But I don't, all right? And I don't want my children to either. I'm not going to have you filling their heads with your garbage."

He turned his head away with a desolate laugh. "Don't forget that what you call my garbage is feeding those little lambs of yours—and their mama too."

She drew in a shuddering breath. "Fine," she finally said. "Feed us or not, just as you please. But you're not getting what you pay for any more. Not from me anyway. You can pay Amber Angel or whatever her name is."

His shoulders stiffened at that, his whole body seeming to expand as he took in her meaning. He raised his right hand a few inches, and she thought for a moment he might strike her. But then it dropped, and, after another long moment when she could hear the blood pounding in her ears, she saw his mouth harden, and he turned away and left the room.

A couple of days later she switched their double bed with the twin beds in the guest room. Gordon ignored both her and the change of furniture. The girls moved almost noiselessly through the heavy tension in the divided house.

Later that summer, Nixon started pulling troops out of Vietnam. In September Gordon and the Marines he'd met on the plane had a party at a bar along the beachfront to celebrate the death of Ho Chi Minh. He didn't come home for three days.

Fine, she thought. It's better when he's gone, wherever that is.

She'd been stringing out her classes at the university, taking only a couple a semester. But in the spring of 1970 she enrolled as a fulltime student. Since the girls were both in school now, she didn't need a sitter except for one required course offered only at night, when Gordon was usually home.

Still, she was nervous about leaving the girls with him. He was often asleep in the living room by seven.

Nevertheless, on those evenings when her class met, she escaped from the house tingling with a sense of release. The murky region of her home was like a prison now. But as soon as she headed up the freeway to her seminar on the Southern Hemisphere, she felt transformed, like Cinderella starting for the ball.

The class was taught by a professor who'd spent three years on a tributary of the Amazon, studying initiation rituals. He had a heavy mane of grey-streaked hair, wore cowboy boots, and smoked small black cigars in class. He would teeter back on the rear legs of his chair, stroking his moustache thoughtfully, then suddenly slam the chair forward and lunge across the seminar table, making them all jump. It had not escaped Miriam's notice that the girls in the class jumped every time, even after they'd learned to expect the move, while the guys braced themselves warily, determined not to react. Miriam refused to flinch. She wasn't a girl, after all, but a grown woman. A mother.

After class, the students usually adjourned to a bar tricked out as an Irish pub on the edge of campus. Sometimes they cajoled her into joining them. The extra hour meant she sometimes didn't get home till midnight. Gordon never knew when she came in anyway.

She was careful on these occasions to stick close to Nelson, a thin fellow with a pompadour and sideburns who had confided to her on the second night of class that he was gay. He had to explain to her what the term meant. They seemed to find one another's company mutually comfortable, and when the film series on campus ran Bergman movies, they went together. Miriam thought wryly of Gordon's comment about her student friends.

Gordon went to Vietnam only one more time, in April, right before U.S. troops invaded Cambodia. Looking back, she could see that even then his work for the military was being phased out, his usefulness ended, though neither of them were aware of that at the time. The previous year the Air Force had, from low-flying C-123s, sprayed ten million gallons of the defoliant 2,4,5-T in the central highlands of Vietnam. Gordon's job was to monitor the effects.

That same year, however, the American Academy for the Advancement of Science had released its report on the chemical, one at variance with the National Academy of Science report commissioned by the government. The disparity had been so great even the administration could not ignore it. Now the defoliant was being phased out. Troop levels were also dropping. But war protests on college campuses were only beginning to peak.

Along the Gulf Coast, the April days were already warm. The roadsides were a riot of Indian paintbrush and yellow cosmos which glowed in the evening light as she drove to class the evening after he left. Something's got to happen, she told herself. Something's got to change. And whether she meant in her own life or in that half-mythical world of war and politics, she couldn't have said.

As the students were gathering up their books to leave after class, the professor told her he needed to speak to her about her term paper. Waiting till the others had drifted from the room and left them alone, he pulled her paper from his briefcase and spun it onto the table between them.

"You know what the penalty for plagiarism is, don't you, Mrs. Estes?"

"What?" She blinked, open-mouthed.

"Plagiarism. Using other people's work. Having someone else write your paper." His own mouth, beneath the moustache, was a frozen line.

"I don't know what you mean. I wrote this paper." She could feel the blood creeping up her throat.

He stared at her a long moment, as though he were waiting for her gaze to falter. She frowned, angry now.

"I suppose you can supply me with copies of your sources?"

She glanced down at the paper. "Well, yes. Of course."

"Fine. Why don't you do that. Then we'll talk. In my office. Thursday afternoon."

She drove straight home, badly shaken, not wanting to see the other students. The next day she made a special trip to the library and checked out the half-dozen books she'd used for her paper. That night she pored over them, trying to spot anything that might have slipped into her paper unacknowledged. By the time she arrived at his office the following afternoon, she was angry, determined to stand her ground.

"Sit down," he said, surprisingly genial as soon as she stepped into his office. It was narrow, every available surface crammed with books and papers, the blinds drawn and dusty.

She lowered herself to the front edge of the chair across from his desk. He settled on the end of the desk, folding his hands around one knee and leaning back.

"Mrs. Estes, isn't it?" he asked. Then without waiting for her to reply, "Miriam."

"Yes," she said stiffly.

He raised an eyebrow, avoiding her look, and picked up the folder with the paper. "I have to apologize. I checked out your sources. You were absolutely right. It's just that I don't often get a student with your insights. Maturity, I guess." He looked at her now, smiling wryly. "Forgive me."

She felt the rush of relief flushing away her anger, all the energy she'd marshalled to defend herself dissipating like breath from a balloon. She put her hand to her heart and inhaled deeply, then closed her eyes and whistled out a long, slow sigh.

"Hey." He reached over and shook her gently by the shoulder. "You didn't let this get to you, did you?"

She kept her eyes on the floor and shook her head. His hand on her shoulder had started her heart pounding again, replacing her momentary relief with confusion.

He stood up abruptly. "You've got a long hard climb in front of you, Miriam. Maybe it's lucky this happened early on"—he touched her shoulder again lightly—"not that I'm reneging on my apology."

She raised her eyes. "What do you mean?"

He folded his arms across his chest and jerked his shoulders once, brusquely. "You're bright, Miriam. The best I've seen since I've been in this godforsaken place. For a woman in academics right now, especially someone with your abilities, well, it won't be long till you can write your own ticket. Graduate fellowships. Research grants. All you've got to do is learn how the academic game is played. How to take the heat. Stick with it. Persevere."

It wasn't until years later after she'd even forgotten his name that, fingering through a card catalogue drawer at the library, it suddenly struck her that he couldn't possibly have checked her sources. The books he would have needed had been sitting on her dining table at home.

She hadn't thought of that then—or hadn't let herself think of it. She hadn't yet discerned the pattern she had already begun weaving into her life. Of course, with Gordon she had felt daring and free, hurling herself off that precipice. But with the professor—and all the others that followed—it wasn't adventure she was seeking but mere confirmation of her existence. You only got to jump off the precipice once.

She did not initiate the affair. Nevertheless, standing at the card catalogue twenty years later, she knew she must have been radiating little pheromones of need as she sat there in his dusty office that afternoon. And he had picked them up on his antenna. Someone always did.

He had slowly extended his hand and, placing one finger under her chin, had, with the gentlest pressure, lifted it, forcing her to look up at him from where she was already lying at the bottom of the precipice, bruised and waiting.

12

Without her glasses, Hannah could just make out that Miriam was standing at the window, her back turned toward the bed. Was she crying? Was she angry? Hannah couldn't tell. The edges of everything looked worn as if they'd been rubbed to a soft, furry nap.

Hannah was very tired, perilously close, she knew, to not caring, not having the energy for that tremendous effort any more. She wasn't afraid of dying—not even if it meant judgment or oblivion—since there wasn't anything she could do about it anyway. She was only afraid of not having sufficient strength to care any longer. The fire which had fueled her core all those long years since Sam had first ignited it required physical energy as surely as running a race. Once that was used up, she knew there'd be nothing left of her. They'd all be on their own.

For a couple of years now, ever since her heart had developed this problem of not pumping hard enough so that her body's juices collected in stagnant pools, Hannah had been teaching herself to turn them loose. The girls would do all right—Priscilla and Deborah. They'd make mistakes and suffer for them. But that was just on the surface. They were tied to something deep down, something that would keep them from drifting aimlessly over the edge of the world. It was Miriam she was worried about, as much as she still had the energy to be. That terrible night still stood between them. They'd never found a way to get back to the place they'd been before that.

It hadn't come as a complete surprise when Miriam had appeared at her door one summer night, transfigured by a kind of grim rage. Hannah had seen Gordon drunk on more than one occasion, and the children got tense whenever she mentioned his name. She'd seen less of Miriam in the past year too, and her excuse of schoolwork didn't account for all the change. Hannah knew, of course, when it got bad enough, her daughter would tell her about it. Meanwhile, Hannah sewed matching outfits for her granddaughters, took them to have their picture taken with Santa Claus, baked their birthday cakes, doing her best to assuage their growing sense of uncertainty.

"I'm afraid I've got bad news, Mother," Miriam had said as she collapsed into a chair at Hannah's formica kitchen table and drew her hair tightly back from her face on either side so that her eyelids pulled up at the corners. She was wearing those awful cut-off blue jeans, strings ravelling around her thighs. You could tell that under the thin t-shirt she had no bra on.

Hannah sat down across from her and folded her hands carefully on the table. "You're pregnant?" It was the first thing that had popped into her head.

Miriam laughed raggedly. "Fat chance."

Hannah lifted her hands and moved them to her lap, ignoring the implication. "Tell me."

"I'm leaving Gordon."

Maybe she should have asked why next, made a space for her daughter to air her grievances against her husband, an opening for sympathizing. Instead she said, "The girls— what about them?"

Miriam was leaning on her elbows, her lowered head thrust forward so that her shoulder blades stuck out as she traced the pattern in the formica with a fingernail. The long loop of her hair was coming loose from the affair she had fastened it with, a leather strip and wooden stick contraption. She glanced up at Hannah. "What about them?"

"How will it affect them?" Hannah tried to make her voice gentle.

"I don't see how it'll be any worse for them than it is now. Pris wets the bed every night. Deb's not eating. Surely you've noticed how uptight they are. They'll probably do better, in fact, once the pressure's off." She said this rapidly, with a kind of desperation for it to be true.

Hannah lifted her eyebrows in a kind of provisional agreement. "Miriam," she said carefully as she tried to frame the question in her mind.

Across the table, Miriam stiffened.

You're not—" Hannah broke off, substituting a vague gesture for the words she couldn't bring herself to say.

"Not what? I'm not what, Mother?" Miriam said, as if challenging her.

Hannah shifted her gaze to the blank square of the window and tightened her lips.

"Oh, I see," Miriam said after the moment's silence. Her voice had a scraped edge to it now. "You think it's my fault. Of course."

It would be a while—months—before Hannah could admit the moment of unexpected relief this outright affront had brought her. It had made Hannah, abruptly, the injured party in a situation where she hadn't known what her part was.

Already, Miriam was drawing the line between them plainer, darker. "I ought to be willing to put up with anything," she said, "any kind of humiliation. Anything's better than a divorce. Is that it?"

Hannah got up and started running water into the tea kettle, trying to clear her own mind. "Things never work out the way you expect them to, Miriam," she said after she set the kettle on the stove. "Sometimes you just have to make the best of things."

"I've been doing the best I know how, Mother."

The wounded tone must have sounded forced, even to Miriam. It was the same wail she'd used as a child to protest her unlikely innocence. Hannah cast about in her mind while she waited till the gas jet popped and caught, then adjusted the blue flame under the kettle. "You're absolutely sure you have nothing to reproach yourself with?" It had been the best she could come up with.

"Reproach myself?" Miriam echoed. "Why don't you just ask me outright—'Miriam, are you having an affair?' "

"An 'affair'? Is that what you call it?"

There was a moment of frozen silence. Then Miriam pushed the chair back from the table and got to her feet. "Fine, Mother. If that's what you think—that this is my fault."

"Miriam, I only asked. I had to," Hannah pleaded, suddenly frightened. "Listen to me." She put her hand on her daughter's bare forearm. "I know Gordon has this drinking problem. But two wrongs don't make a right. Don't make things worse. Think of the children."

Miriam's eyes wavered uncertainly.

"This war—all this," Hannah went on rapidly, "it'll be over some day. It won't last forever. Just because you're angry with him now, don't—" she shook her head and ended lamely, "make a mistake."

Miriam was panting in the effort to keep back tears. "If all I do is worry about making mistakes, Mother, I'll never—" her eyes flew wildly about the room, "—live!"

"Live?" Hannah had jerked her head back at the sheer folly of this. "What do you call what you've been doing?"

Miriam expelled the air in her lungs as if she'd been hit in the stomach. "If that's living..."

Hannah shook her head. "You think only the good parts

174

count? The easy parts?" She heard the bitterness in her own voice now.

Miriam turned away, muttering something under her breath.

"Sweetheart. Your children. Your family. Don't you think they're worth—"

Miriam turned back to cut her off. "I don't seem to know what's worth what any more. I don't know how to make everything come out even, like you do, Mother. You go to church. You don't make mistakes. You follow the rules. You believe in them. And I guess they've worked for you. But they don't seem to work for me. All I know is, things can't go on like this. You don't know what it's like." She bent swiftly and retrieved the limp handbag she had left beside her chair.

And that had been it. She'd left, waving a vague hand at Hannah's equally vague offer—"Let me know if I can help." The next time Miriam had brought the girls over, she'd told Hannah very matter-of-factly that she'd filed for divorce. Later she'd asked if they could stay with her when school was out till time to leave for Denver and her fellowship there. Her asking had been matter-of-fact as well, if stiff and bruised, as though she half expected Hannah to refuse. It had broken Hannah's heart. Losing Barton had brought her pain, but this was a whole new kind of loss.

Alongside the pain, rubbing it raw, was the anger. She couldn't sleep at night for making up speeches to Miriam. *No marriage is perfect. Your father and I had problems too, you know. You can't just give up.* It wasn't fair. What she'd gone through the year Sam came home from the war was every bit as bad as what Miriam faced now.

The first thing Hannah had noticed when Sam stepped off the train was how he wasn't smiling. The last time she'd seen him three years ago en route to the Pacific Theater from the Caribbean, he'd still had his old grin. Now it was gone. He stepped onto the platform, shading his eyes with one hand, his mouth straight and set. The old Sam would have been beaming and waving. He smiled when he spotted her, but briefly, as though it used energy he felt he had to ration. When he reached them, he crushed her against him as if he'd staggered and was struggling for balance. Then he stepped back, still gripping Hannah's waist, and inspected his child. Miriam was squinting against the summer sun and staring at him, her index finger in her mouth.

"Say hello to Daddy," Hannah urged, bending down and pulling the finger from Miriam's mouth.

Miriam blinked and her lips moved but she spoke too low to be heard.

Sam squatted down before the child. "Hello, sweetheart," he said. "You're going to have to learn to speak up." He glanced up at Hannah. "She doesn't suck her thumb, does she?"

"No. No, she doesn't. Just that finger once in a while."

Sam stood up. "She'll have to stop that," he said. He looked around, keeping his gaze just above the heads of the other soldiers and their families. "All right. Let's go." He glanced down at Miriam. "Hold Daddy's hand," he said.

Miriam shifted her gaze to her mother as if referring the request to her. Hannah smiled and nodded encouragingly. Her face was aching from smiling. Please, she pleaded inwardly, please take his hand. Slowly Miriam raised her hand to her ear, then extended it a few inches in Sam's direction.

The corner of his mouth drew up in the old way and he gave a shallow snort. "Not too sure there, are you, kid? Well, we'll see."

The provisional tone of the remark had made Hannah nervous then, and after a week, Sam and his daughter had still only made a conditional truce. Hannah tried to keep volatile situations under control so that the two of them avoided outright duels of will, but she could feel that control slipping away, the brushes becoming unpredictable. She lurched between the two, steadying each of them so they wouldn't blunder against the other.

One evening after putting Miriam to bed, Hannah tiptoed down the stairs, taking care to avoid the creaks she had learned in the long months in Mrs. McMichael's house. Sam was on the porch, smoking, one foot propped up on the railing, staring out into the darkness.

"I got the tickets today," he said. "We leave on Monday." Then he looked around quickly, as though to surprise her response.

"Oh," she said. "Fine."

He turned back to his survey of Mrs. Michaels' Saint Augustine grass. Even in the dark, the oyster-shell road in front of the house gleamed whitely. He slipped an arm around her waist and casually pulled her against his side. "Don't worry. You'll love it. Mom's good with kids."

Hannah stiffened. Was that a cloaked complaint about her own mothering?

"Miriam needs a little brother," Sam said, flipping the butt of his cigarette beyond the rail. His tone had been grim.

It had taken all of Sam's separation pay—$100—to get them to Minnesota. They rode the train to Minneapolis, then took a bus for half a day to a little town where his father owned a hardware store. Great expanses of careful fields stretched in square directions along the road, the farm houses tidy and tended, never ramshackle or reckless. Again she thought how strange it was that Sam should have sprung from such a landscape. The war had given him a reason for marrying recklessly. But now the war was over. And all they had was a ramshackle marriage.

Miriam had slept, her head resting in Hannah's lap. Hannah smoothed back the fine hair falling across the round forehead. As long as she had Miriam she could survive anything. This wouldn't be as bad as a concentration camp, after all. But no more children. Not now. She couldn't get pregnant again until things were sorted out, till Sam had a job and they were in their own home.

If she'd found it difficult maintaining equilibrium between three people, the balance among five was definitely more than Hannah could manage. Henry Snider—Hannah could hardly get used to the idea that they all shared the same last name—was as silent and close-mouthed as her own father, yet she felt his silence did not signify resignation so much as distaste. He had repeated her name as he shook her hand at the bus station. Other than that, he scarcely said two words at a time to her. Since he was at the store most of the day, he saw little of Miriam, whom Hannah had counted on to melt her in-laws' icy hearts.

Greta Snider—Hannah choked on "Mom," the unfamiliar word Sam called his mother, yet couldn't bring herself to call the older woman by her first name—was almost as difficult to read as her husband. Most of her comments were in the form of instructions. *The towels are in the closet in the hall. Close the window so the dust doesn't blow in off the street. Get me two jars of beets off the top pantry shelf under the stairs.* There was no casual chatter, no family stories of what Sam had been like as a child, no tracing of kin to orient Hannah to her new relations. Hannah had to save up all her questions till she and Sam went to bed at night.

At meals the Sniders addressed most of their remarks to their son. Did he know that his brother Gene, a doctor now in Duluth, was engaged to the county judge's daughter? Lena, his sister, was expecting again. Sam's high school basketball team had won the state championship. His grandmother had given up the farm last year when she had a stroke. He needed to go see her. She was living with her youngest daughter now. And Millie Ilfeld had been asking about him. This last was followed by a stealthy glance at Hannah; she supposed Millie Ilfeld must have been a high-school sweetheart.

Hannah spent much of her time at the table keeping a close eye on Miriam, watching to see that her elbow didn't upset the glass of milk or that she didn't pick up peas with her fingers. She had often fed Miriam from her own plate at home, holding the child on her lap at Mrs. McMichaels' kitchen table, while she recounted stories from the office that day or listened while the older woman filled her in on the latest news about the girls at the laundry. When they first came to the Sniders', Hannah had offered to feed Miriam in the kitchen before the adults ate, but Mrs. Snider wouldn't hear of it.

"No, no. We're used to children. Lena's eat at the table with us when they come. They have to learn to behave sometime."

Sam took to spending most of the day either visiting his old friends in town or helping out his father at the store. At night, he crawled beneath the sheet, dressed in pajamas, and touched her only lightly and furtively. It astonished her, how this once grinning, now often grim husband of hers had lapsed into childhood as soon as he crossed his parents' threshold. But being home seemed to rest him somehow, as if the stress of war had worn out the adult in him. Maybe he needed to loaf around in adolescence a while to recover his strength. The stiff silences of his family didn't seem to bother him. She suspected he even found his own subsiding need of her a comfort. Hannah felt abandoned, adrift in a sea of strangeness. She remembered, almost enviously, the women she'd dreamed of, struggling to protect their children in the Japanese concentration camps.

They'd been at the Sniders' two weeks when her mother-in-law invited her to the Lutheran women's circle. Hannah dressed carefully, wearing her new six-gored gabardine navy skirt and a white blouse with a Peter Pan collar and spectator pumps. Before she went downstairs she looked at herself in the bureau mirror, turning to one side then the other, admitting to herself that she was proud of the way she looked. She'd even put on the pearl-button earrings and the gold bracelet Sam had sent her from overseas. She was determined to please Greta by pleasing her friends.

"My goodness," the woman had said, raising her eyebrows when Hannah came downstairs, "it's only a circle meeting, dear."

Though the women at the house where they went were politely pleasant, Hannah wondered if maybe they found it easier to be congenial with strangers than their own daughters-in-law. Throughout the meeting she felt Mrs. Snider watching her, the way she kept an eye on Miriam at the dinner table.

The pastor came in halfway through the refreshments, apologizing that he'd made an emergency hospital visit. She hadn't gone to church with the Sniders the first Sunday because of Miriam's sore throat. Now he pumped Hannah's hand enthusiastically when they were introduced and asked a series of questions about where she was from, what Sam was doing, if Miriam's throat was better. She felt like a shriveling plant soaking up a sudden shower.

She went home glowing with hope. That night she sat on the side of the bed brushing her hair till Sam came back from the bathroom. She had put on the crepe nightgown he'd bought her when they were newly-weds. For the first time since Sam returned, she felt existence begin to swell again with possibilities. After all, they were starting a new life together. As he closed the hall door behind him, he looked at her and stopped with his hand on the knob. Hannah smiled at him, half shy, half pleased. Miriam was asleep in the next room. His parents had already gone to bed.

She moved to make room for him beside her. "We could be very quiet," she said, surprised at her own boldness.

He looked at her, a smile starting to tug at his mouth.

Just then his mother called down the hall. "Sam? Did you remember to lock the front door?"

The smile drained away. He snatched up a pack of Luckies from the dresser and went clomping down the stairs and out onto the front porch, for all the world like a petulant teenager. He was gone a long time, and she pretended she was asleep when he tiptoed into the room again.

The anticipation she felt that night had faded altogether by the next day. However, on Saturday Sam asked his mother at breakfast if she'd mind watching Miriam that evening while he and Hannah went to a party some of his old friends were throwing for several returning soldiers. It was the first Hannah had heard of the party, but she didn't object, though she hated being caught off guard in front of her in-laws.

The party was at the lake, and they went in the Sniders' Buick—the first time she'd ridden in such a nice car. She could sense Sam's anticipation growing the further they drove. Sunset was turning the lake's surface pink and gold when they arrived at the pavilion. Lights had been strung around the hexagonal log structure and a three-piece combo was sending out tag-ends of "I'll Never Smile Again" over the water.

The evening was like something out of a book for Hannah. She had never been to a party like this before. The lights, the music, festoons of laughter wreathed the revolving couples. She and Sam danced a couple of times to the slower music— "Dancing in the Dark" and "I'll Get By." She was stiff and awkward at first, till he lifted her elbows, placing her arms around his neck, then wrapped his own arms around her waist, pressing her against him so she could feel the muscles of his thighs and anticipate his movements.

Mostly they sat at a picnic table though, where Sam was frequently interrupted by greetings from friends. "Say, old buddy! You made it back. You look great. Say, congratulations! I hear you're married." And turning their eyes to Hannah, "Don't tell me you fell for this big ape's line. You look too swell for him!"

Once a fellow climbed over the bench to join them, pulled out a flat bottle encased in a brown paper sack, and passed it around the table. She shook her head when it reached her.

"Hannah's a Baptist," Sam grinned to his friend. But then he squeezed her against his side as if he'd only called attention to some appealing quirk. Sam himself, she noticed with relief, more often than not let the bottle pass him by.

Still, she could catch the alien scent of whiskey on his breath as they left the pavilion a little earlier than she'd expected. "I have something I want to show you," he said as he shut her car door. He climbed in and started the motor. The pavilion lights fell on his face as he backed the Buick, and she could see the old teasing grin, his face more mobile than it had been in weeks. He was humming the last tune the band had been playing as he turned the car into a rutted trail instead of the road home.

"Where're you taking me, Sam Snider?" she asked, falling into her part in their old courting pattern.

A chuckle came from deep in his chest as he peered ahead along the grassy track. As they came out into a pine-ringed clearing he cut the headlights. Beyond the clearing, a pier ran out into the lake. She had expected him to turn toward her as soon as he turned off the engine, but instead he got out, came around, and opened her door.

"Come on," he said. "Here. Hold onto my hand."

Gingerly she swung her feet out into the tall grass. "Where are we?" she asked again.

"Just come on," he said, and she could hear the rising urgency in his voice.

"Is it safe?" she whispered as she followed him onto the dark planks over the water. "What are we doing?"

"Curiosity killed the cat," he said, staring around into the darkness.

"Satisfaction brought him back," she answered smartly, repeating without thinking the line from childhood.

"Really?" he said, spinning her against him. "All right then."

Hannah had been terrified that someone's headlights might suddenly swing through the darkness and find them sprawled there on the wooden pier. Sam moaned and panted so heavily against her ear that the whiskey smell gradually dissipated on the night air. Afterwards she lay with her blouse undone and her skirt hiked up around her waist and stared up at the stars, wondering if this was the way life was for most people. This easy, this unguarded. Here she was in strange country, doing outlandish things. For a second time she felt her existence lift as if its thirsty tissues were swelling with rain.

Then she heard Sam jump to his feet, take two steps, and leap into the lake. "What in the world do you think you're doing?" she called in a shouted whisper toward the dark water, not sure whether she was speaking to him or to herself. He laughed, splashing water with the flat of his hand up onto the pier. He sounded thoroughly pleased with himself.

It was the last time, as she remembered it, that they'd ever been pleased with one another. They'd been happy that night, the both of them. She'd marked the feeling in her memory, it was so rare for her. Maybe things are changing now, she'd told herself. Maybe this is what life is supposed to be like. And that was why she'd never, afterwards, trusted happiness any more.

13

Deborah lay still, breathing deep and slow, wondering where she was. For a moment she felt the way she used to in her grandmother's house, waking from a nap on summer afternoons, her cheeks flushed and the pillow under her mouth damp from saliva. That twilight area between sleep and waking had felt luxurious then, a warm, easy drift into the slow, steady current of ordinary life.

Then she lifted her head abruptly from the sofa pillow and stared around the room. Otis was sitting at the table by the window, a pair of reading glasses on the end of his nose. He tilted his head down at a sheaf of papers, then raised it again as he punched numbers into a calculator. She pushed back the afghan and sat up.

"Had a good nap?" he asked, laying the glasses on the table and swivelling around to face her.

She glanced at her watch. "Good Lord. I've got to get back."

"You feeling better then?"

"Yes, fine." Her voice was husky from sleep. She cleared her throat as she slipped on her shoes.

He was smiling indulgently, the way Gram used to when Deborah woke up cross. "You got some color back anyways. If you want to—you know—" he pointed down the hall toward the bathroom.

She started to refuse, then put a hand to her hair. She must be a mess. She picked up her handbag and went down the hall. Looking in the bathroom mirror, she didn't know whether to laugh or cry. Her hair was tousled, her skirt twisted to the side, and the middle button of her blouse had come undone. The lace on her slip showed through the gap.

She stood staring into the mirror for a long time. For some reason her brain was having a hard time sending the message to her muscles to move. Finally she bent down and splashed cold water over her face. It struck her that, for the first time in days, she was actually feeling pretty good. Relaxed even. The nausea had completely disappeared. Despite the languor, she felt stronger, less jittery. She looked in the mirror again. Otis was right. Her color had come back. She rubbed her hand dreamily over her stomach before she straightened her skirt. Then she shook her head sharply and began making repairs to her makeup.

Little bottles of nail polish lined the back of the counter below the gold-rimmed mirror. A dusty tissue leaned from a lavender crocheted cover. So this must have been Velda's bathroom, preserved like a shrine. Poor old Velda.

When she came back in the living room, Otis had collected her papers and put the briefcase on a table by the front door. "I'm not rushing you off, you understand. But since you gotta get back to the office—"

"Thanks," she said, smiling at him. "You've been very kind, Mr. Ruffner."

"Otis. Remember?"

"Otis. And I'll see what I can put together from our talk. After I show it to Mr. Jasper, I'll send you a copy. I suppose he'll take it from there."

He gave a preoccupied nod and opened the door for her. He was rubbing his chin as he walked her to her car, and when she waved a quick good-bye, he had merely lifted a hand before turning to go back inside.

As she drove back into the city, Deborah could feel the muscles between her shoulders begin to tighten again. She'd have to tell Hoot something about the deposition. Arlene would have covered for her, but he'd want a report as soon as she got back. She needed to pull herself together again. This bucolic interlude with this Bubba had been pleasant in a weird kind of way, but it was time to get serious. She tried shaking the muzziness from her head and decided to stop for coffee.

As it happened, the next exit led to the same McDonald's she'd stopped at that morning. She started to turn into the drive-through lane, then parked instead and went inside. She was beginning to feel in control again, that things were going to work out after all. She'd gotten most of the information she needed for her report to Hoot, and she felt she could count on Otis not to mention the fiasco at the office. The next step was to reschedule her appointment at the clinic.

The swarthy man was still at the cash register. His eyes flicked up from the Arabic newspaper he was reading with no hint of recognizing her.

She ordered a large diet Coke, and as he turned to pick up the paper cup, she noticed him glance across the parking lot, then down at his watch. His shift must almost be over.

Shading her eyes, Deborah blinked into the afternoon glare at two dark shapes moving across the expanse of strip-center parking lot stretching between them. Sixties apartment units, the city's new slums, were arranged at right angles like Monopoly buildings just beyond the shopping center. The figures undulated within the shimmering waves of heat like seaweed stirred on the ocean floor. As they came closer, she could make out the woman from this morning—the man's wife. She was holding one child by the hand and had the other one, the little boy, hoisted onto her hip.

Deborah turned back to the counter as the man set the tall paper cup down and caught his look of unguarded pride. The man jerked one shoulder and raised an eyebrow as if to discount the look. He handed her the cup, sweating cold moisture. "One dollar three."

Deborah fumbled in her handbag for the change, thanked him, and left, noticing as she pulled out her keys that the woman had stopped to set the boy down to walk on his own. The kid must weigh a ton, she thought. Then she lost sight of the little group as they passed behind a delivery truck parked in the middle of the lot.

She remembered later having felt glad that the heat would not seem especially oppressive to them; wherever they were from, they were probably used to this kind of weather. "Come on, Deb, get a grip," she muttered to herself. "It's just hormones making you sentimental."

She opened the car door and slid gingerly onto the seat, now blisteringly hot. She took a long pull at the straw in the cup before setting it into the holder by the gearshift. After all, it couldn't be any picnic being married to that autocratic bastard behind the counter in there and holed up with those two kids in a ratty little apartment all day long.

She started the car, then flipped down the mirror over the window to check her makeup one last time before she got back to the office. She was conscious of not allowing her eyes to wander from her own reflection in case she should catch a glimpse of the mother and her children again.

She'd been right not to tell anyone about her decision, not even Pris, not till she'd acted on it. She hadn't bothered Mother with it either. She was just going to have to tough this one out alone.

She shifted into reverse and picked up the cup again, in one determined motion. As she swung the steering wheel down with her left hand, giving the accelerator a resolute little nudge with her toe, she simultaneously reached to set the paper cup back in the holder, missed it, and glanced down.

She heard a woman's shrill cry and then a child's scream as her right rear tire lifted and bumped over something soft and giving.

Deborah jammed on the brake so hard the small car skidded sideways. The cup tipped and fell, its dark contents shooting across the floorboard on the passenger side.

Everything stopped then. The engine had died; she couldn't breathe. The moment froze, her mind refusing to move forward, to take in any more information. Then she saw the stain on the floor still seeping into the carpet, smelled the odor of burnt rubber penetrating through the air-conditioning vents.

She could hear more crying somewhere behind her. She tried to lift her hand to the door handle. The dark man, shorter than she'd thought him to be, burst through the glass door of the building. He ran toward the car, striking the fender with his open palm as he passed. The impact reverberated through her, the sudden noise restarting her lungs. She dropped her head onto the steering wheel. "Please, God, let him be all right. Let me die. Anything."

At last the muscles in her hand gathered themselves and gripped the door handle. She pushed herself out of the car and took a half step. From the corner of her eye she saw the woman crouched over the child on the pavement several yards away, the man standing above her waving his arms to the heavens. She reached out to steady herself on the hood. I can't, she thought, and felt herself sway. How could I?

Then the woman looked up at her husband, shouting something Deborah couldn't understand, but angry. The woman swung her left arm out and struck him just above the knees so that he dropped his arms and stared down at her, too astonished to move. The other child, the little girl, her hand clamped tightly across her mouth, shifted her eyes from one parent to the other without moving her head.

Deborah came on around the front of her car. How could she have knocked him so far? The man, his mouth still open in amazement, watched as his wife half-stood, still bent at the waist, and raised the little boy to his feet.

The child looked dazed. One elbow was bloody where it had scraped the gravel. The mother gathered him in her arms and rocked him back and forth for a moment, making crooning noises, while the father puffed out his sallow cheeks and scrubbed one hand back and forth through his hair.

"Is he all right?" Deborah asked. She had to repeat the question twice before she could make herself heard over the child's sobbing and the mother's comfort.

The man swivelled toward her, one hand still grasping his thick, heavy hair, his eyes opened so wide she could see the startling white all around them.

"I'm sorry," she stammered. "I didn't see."

The man dropped his hand and glared at her. The mother, her arms still wrapped around the boy, turned to look at them both. Then she began speaking swiftly to her husband, her words punctuated rhythmically with bursts of emphasis. The man turned toward her and first shook his head vigorously, but his wife closed her eyes, a torrent pouring from her, until he shook it again, more tentatively this time and stared down at the pavement. Finally the woman's rush of words slowed. Deborah had crept closer, near enough to see the teardrops matting the child's eyelashes. He stared at her over his mother's shoulder and then, jerking his head away from her gaze, hid it in the folds of cloth covering his mother's head.

Deborah leaned against the car and began to shake, then to cry, biting her lower lip. The man took a step toward her and said, his voice unsteady, "Lady. Lady? You all right?"

"It doesn't matter. I'm sorry. Yes."

His wife spoke to him again, abrupt, preemptory.

"I'm sorry," Deborah repeated.

"She says the boy threw off her hand, ran away from her. He did the wrong."

"No, no," Deborah protested. "I should have been watching."

"I tell her this already," he said stiffly. "All the time, people drive bad in this parking lot."

"Yes, yes."

"She is saying is not your fault. Maybe you mother too. You understand how it happen. Calamity with children."

Deborah raised her eyes now and saw that the woman was looking at her, searching her face. The woman's eyes were dark but perfectly clear and steady, her nostrils still distended by adrenalin.

"She is saying," the man continued, "she is feeling sorry for you. All women fear, she say, the extreme harm coming to children. I have no need to tell you." He muttered the last only grudgingly, as though he doubted his wife's judgment.

Deborah nodded dully, watching the little girl who had wandered over to where a stuffed purple dinosaur lay flattened. It must have been that she felt.

The woman spoke again. This time her voice lilted upward at the end.

"She ask if you are in fact mother." The man looked around him. He was obviously tiring of his role as interpreter. He began murmuring something that sounded at once like censure and reassurance to the boy. Without waiting to hear her reply, the man lifted him from his mother's arms.

Deborah said, "Yes. Yes," nodding so that the woman could understand the answer.

The man was already walking away, back into the building, carrying his son. The woman dipped her head once toward Deborah and took the stuffed animal, dirty and torn, from the little girl's hand.

Deborah pointed at it and then at her own chest. "I'll bring him a new one," she said, pointing again at the dinosaur and nodding.

The woman lowered her eyes and, taking her daughter's hand, followed her husband inside.

Deborah stayed on the frontage road till she came to the next service station that looked as if the restroom would be relatively clean. Locking the steel door behind her, she washed her face, scrubbing at the smudges of mascara and splashing water over the back of her neck. Her hands were still shaking when she handed the attendant back the key, but she hadn't cried anymore. She had said yes. She couldn't believe she had said yes.

Arlene shook her head as Deborah came in. "What you been up to, girl? Hoot wanted to see you."

"Fine," she said.

"No. It ain't fine. He left already and was he ever on the warpath. He got a call a while ago sent him into orbit."

Deborah shrugged. "Well, I got this Ruffner business just about sewed up so he should be happy."

Arlene looked at her, shaking her head again. "If you say so." She turned back to her terminal. "Just don't say I didn't warn you."

Hannah had been sleeping most of the day, but her breathing had settled into a pattern of exhaling in two ragged bursts, then dragging in air again with a small whistling whoop. The doctor had explained this was because the labor of breathing had constricted her throat muscles. He warned Miriam that Hannah might start picking at the oxygen canula. "They do that sometimes," he said. "Your mother told me she didn't want a respirator." He looked at Miriam, checking her response. She hadn't said anything.

Miriam and Pris had only left the room once—to have lunch in the hospital cafeteria. When they came back, the afternoon light in the room was softer and Hannah's breathing seemed easier. She opened her eyes as they tiptoed in and set their tote bags behind the chair in the corner.

"She looks better, don't you think?" Pris asked her mother in a low voice.

"No need to whisper," Hannah said. "I'm awake." She took another breath and added, "Hand me my glasses, if you would, Priscilla."

Pris picked up the glasses from the nightstand and started to slip them over her grandmother's ears, but Hannah pulled away, frowning, and gave her head an impatient shake. "Just let me have them, honey. I'm not dead yet."

Pris stepped back and dropped into the chair, feeling scalded but trying to swallow the hurt. Her mother turned from the window and gave her an uneven smile, one meant to console while excusing. The same kind of look she'd used to get them to overlook some failure of Dad's, when Pris had been little. Sometimes Pris felt, even now, as if she were only masquerading as a grown-up; underneath that frightened three-year-old still had no clue why all the people she loved were always angry.

After she got suspended from middle school in Austin and Mom, out of desperation, enrolled her in Westwood Christian Academy, Pris had suddenly sensed she was starting life fresh. For one thing, no one at Westwood knew anything yet about her or her family. When the teachers talked about being "born again," Pris had known instantly what they meant—she felt as if she'd just been invented. She settled into the new regimen and began to flourish immediately. After two weeks she was saying a lengthy impromptu grace at every meal instead of their standard "God-is-great." She began greeting her mother and sister at breakfast every morning with a Bible verse.

"This is the day that the Lord hath made; Let us rejoice and be glad in it," she'd sing out as she burst from the bathroom. It was as though she'd found a way back to her old breezy optimism.

Even Deborah, who'd done nothing but mutter at her for weeks, began to feel safe enough to tease her about her newfound piety, though her mother, Pris could tell, still didn't feel she could afford that luxury. The school, after all, had been her mother's idea. She couldn't risk disparaging its tactics, now that it had worked. Now that Pris was a mother herself, she understood how Miriam must have considered her daughter's devout onslaughts a small price to pay for her stability.

Pris had looked up churches in the Yellow Pages, trying to find one within walking distance of their apartment—she didn't want to impose, she said gravely—but Miriam had outflanked her by taking them all to a little neogothic Episcopal church close to campus. Deborah had rolled her eyes in conspiratorial resignation at her mother's scheme, but once there, she was the one who relished the stained glass, the procession, the sonorous prayerbook language. Priscilla herself could only frown moodily, uncertain where St. Christopher's fitted into the categories of Westwood Christian Academy.

It wasn't until the following year, however, that Priscilla broached the subject of divorce. Miriam had given her the choice of returning to public school in the fall. Westwood had by then served its purpose by getting Pris "stuck" again, and keeping her in the private school would mean borrowing money for the tuition.

Pris had been shocked at the suggestion. "Mother, how can I go back to public school? Do you realize that soon the government won't even let you pray there anymore?"

"I guess I was weighing that against other considerations," Miriam answered cautiously. She was wrapping the long strands of Deborah's off-blond hair around plastic permanent wave rollers.

"You could always pray silently, couldn't you?" Deborah said, her voice muffled by the towel she had wrapped around her shoulders and over her forehead to catch the drips.

"That's not the point." The tiny muscles in Priscilla's nose began to flex.

"It says in the Bible you're supposed to enter into your closet to pray and not parade your piety before men," Deborah said, lifting her chin off her chest to make sure she was heard.

"It also says whosoever shall be ashamed of me and my words, then Jesus will be ashamed to confess you before the Father," Pris shot back.

"You and your words?" Deborah sneered. "You've got your grammar all screwed up. I mean if you're going to quote, do it right, for God's sake."

Miriam yanked back on the strand of hair she held between her fingers.

Pris' mouth flew open. "Mother," she breathed, "Deb took the Lord's name in vain."

Deborah jerked her head around to face her accuser. "What about you? Quoting the Bible wrong is taking the Lord's name in vain too, doofus."

"All right, all right," Miriam intervened.

"It's not the same thing and you know it. And calling your brother a fool is a sin, too."

"I said doofus, not fool, and besides you're not my brother."

"Girls, stop it!"

Priscilla, however, sensed her sister's defenses weakening. "You meant it in your heart though. And it puts you in danger of hellfire. It's just as bad as lying or murder or divorce."

They all froze. Then Deborah turned around in her chair and put the towel up to her forehead again. Priscilla felt her lower lip begin to tremble.

Miriam reached for a curler. After a long silence she said, keeping her eyes on the plastic rod, "You're misinformed about that, my dear. I suggest you look up divorce in one of those concordances at your school."

That evening, feeling miserable, Pris had gone into her mother's room and plopped onto the bed where Miriam was reading. She noticed she had on her pajama top wrong side out. Even Westwood had failed to make her neat.

"You're right, Mom," she said. "About divorce. But it does say drunkards."

"What, sweetheart? What are you talking about?" Her mother closed the book over her thumb.

"They can't inherit the kingdom of God. First Corinthians six ten."

Miriam took off her glasses and sighed.

"That means Dad's not going to heaven, doesn't it?"

"That's God's problem, not yours, Pris."

"But it bothers me, Mother. Sometimes I imagine him with these flames all around him in the lake of fire, and I just can't stand it." Pris' face had crumpled suddenly and she pressed her elbows inward against her stomach.

Miriam put the book down and pulled Pris up under her arm, smoothing back her wiry curls.

"It wasn't your fault, Mom. The divorce, I mean. I know that. Deborah said I should tell you that. It was because of Dad's drinking. It's not your fault."

Miriam took a deep breath and let it out slowly, pressing her daughter's face against her bosom. She didn't say anything.

Priscilla listened, waiting for a confirmation. Her mother opened her mouth to answer—Pris could see their reflections in the mirror across the room—and shut it again. Then she looked off toward a corner of the room, and shook her head.

The anthropology professor Miriam had allowed to seduce her had been followed the next semester by a visiting linguist from Brussels, then a naval officer attached briefly to Dow Chem. She had made love to him in his office just down the hall from Gordon's. Later, in Denver, there'd been a couple of graduate students as well as an intense interlude with the head of the SDS Chapter at the university. Miriam shuddered now when she considered what might have happened if the washing machine repairman had showed up during those years. She would have gone to bed with him just to prove to the ghost of D.H. Lawrence that intellectual women were indeed a match for blue-collar workers.

Gordon had his Vietnam, the terrain upon which he tested himself against life. She had sexual intrigue. It was her jungle, her playing field, her laboratory, her stock market, her battleground and church.

She'd been in love with only a few of the men she slept with, though she maintained a friendly feeling for most. Once or twice there'd been an encounter with a virtual stranger out of sheer carnal curiosity. Yet despite her upbringing, Miriam felt little guilt about any of these episodes. Her one point of honor was a steadfast refusal ever to count the number. Quantifying would have made it seem crass.

She did worry about the effect on the girls, but none of her entanglements lasted long—a few months at most—and generally she managed to keep the men isolated from her life at home. Though she stuck to her resolution not to sleep with anyone on her dissertation committee, there had been two affairs while she was finishing her doctorate—one with her divorce lawyer and the other with a Danish grad student. But the move to Austin and Pris' "unstuck" phase had frightened her into greater discretion. After enrolling Pris in Westwood Academy she never so much as mentioned her lovers around her children.

Still, she had no desire to "settle down" with anyone else. She was already settled. She had her children. What she wanted from men was unsettling. Something beyond the borders. An exploration of some towering unknown.

Even during those early days with Gordon, their two bodies had seemed to strain toward a realm just beyond their reach, a place attainable only by threading themselves through one another. In the throes of lovemaking, life could become suddenly elevated, more than mundane, raised above the tedium of the commonplace.

With Gordon too she had first discovered a certain kind of power. The Vietnam era politicized everything, including sex. Miriam sensed, however, that a force more mysterious than supply-and-demand fueled the engine of copulation, just as it fueled the war.

She wasn't above going to bed with someone just to be a good sport though, and it must have been the time she'd ended up consoling a student who'd flunked his orals that the question first formed itself in her mind: how could sex be so ecstatic, so transcendent one day—one hour—and so tiresome the next?

It was after her first tenure appointment, during a conference in Toronto, that these episodes she'd seen as metaphysical field trials began to lose their spiritual efficacy. One of the conference speakers—he'd studied Sherpas and been halfway up Everest—had asked her to have a drink with him, and as soon as she sank into the crushed velvet armchair in the hotel bar she heard the gears of biological destiny—Nature—grind to life. As if her body had a mind of its own.

She felt her pulse quicken, and in the mirror behind him, she caught sight of her reflection, leaning toward him, lips slightly parted. By the time the waitress set the second set of glasses down on the narrow table between them, everything was already committed. It was just a matter of playing out a script as inevitable as a mass.

Academic conferences, she told her naked image in his bathroom mirror, were simply modern versions of aboriginal fertility cults. Anthropologists might imagine themselves superior to—or at least remote from—the beliefs they studied, but the same erotic forces which had driven the Dionysian maenads still compelled these ritual academic couplings. Nor was it unusual, among the supposedly serene groves of academe, to come across remnants of wrecked careers, dismembered by frenzied passion. Some of her own colleagues had thrown over marriages of several decades, a brace of children, and their life's work while in the grip of irrational passion.

She took a step back and turned to either side, examining herself critically, feeling the adrenalin kick in. Dr. Everest-Climber, waiting for her on the other side of the door, probably didn't have a clue. It wasn't just the sense of power being desired gave her, but even more important, the heightened sense of her own reality. A greater, more substantial definition.

Maybe, just as most ancient cultures believed, they were serving some life force, some *élan vital* (the French stimulated her imagination more). Certainly her own passion was for something more than just the middle-aged man in the next room. She had observed—for professional purposes—whirling dervishes, Sioux peyote rites, and snake-handlers get completely free of the limitations of ordinary consciousness. But this was still the best, most universal path to transcendence she knew. With that hazy thought, she opened the door, determined to do her liturgical best.

He was lying on his side, a gray leer dragging at his face. As he lowered himself over her, she caught sight of the snarl of hairs escaping from his nostrils like broken sofa coils. Nevertheless, she arched herself upward to meet him, the way a missionary might resolve to face a crowd of cannibals. This wasn't about him, she told herself, hearing her own ritual gasps. This was about the act itself. They were the mere elements, the bread and wine that made corporeal divine substance. A convergence of duty and desire.

She forced herself to think of Gordon instead of the professor, Gordon that first summer, how splendid and supple he'd been. Seizing on a fleet image, she concentrated on reconstructing the peculiar quality of light in that upstairs room of his, irradiating the memory like a hologram till it was real enough to slip inside. And just as she sensed her mind sliding over the rounded rim of consciousness, finally free to catapult into some empyrion of ecstasy, the whole thing crashed. His weight rolled off her with the finality of a stone.

The Sherpa expert groaned, then mumbled, "Sorry. Can't," and turned face down. In an instant he was asleep.

Miriam sat up, forcing her lungs to inflate slowly, held her breath, then even more slowly exhaled. Her ears were ringing and she felt slightly dizzy. Her liturgical best obviously wasn't sufficient for them both. How much had the jerk had to drink anyway?

She got out of bed, crossed to the floor-to-ceiling window that overlooked the city, and stood there in the dark watching the lights till she began to shiver from the room's chill air and her own apostasy.

Gradually her head cleared—she could actually feel her liver absorbing the excess secretions of her glands as her pulse slowed. So it was only that and nothing more. Stripped down, demythologized, and deconstructed, the emperor was revealed as only biochemistry, not Eros. She sighed and turned away from the window to gather up her clothes from the floor. Another god shot to hell, she thought, and had suddenly longed to be fifty—an age she had assumed would at last provide amnesty from this oppression.

14

The one-night stand at the conference in Toronto hadn't been the last time—she hadn't expected it would be—but in some way it had been a turning point. Increasingly, Miriam found such encounters, once charged with mystery and passion, merely banal and redundant. She didn't deny that sometimes she had imagined herself an avatar of Aphrodite locked with an instrumentality of Eros. But as the ecstasy grew less frequent, the tangle of limbs and the smack of damp flesh came to seem faintly silly. She found she couldn't sustain her interest level at the necessary pitch for longer than, say, the average sitcom. Sex had become merely a matter of friction and sweat.

If she didn't want to end up like Gordon, she needed to make some kind of ultimate renunciation. So she had come to Israel a stoic, determined to repudiate her craving for transcendence. And of course, just as if there had been a God, the ironic sort who delighted in giving you just enough rope to hang yourself before he kicked the stool from beneath your feet, she had met Yigal. She knew as soon as she saw him that he would be the one to test her resolve.

In the desert climate, she discovered that her figurative drying out was accompanied by a physical one. The Israeli doctor she consulted—he wasn't much older than Deborah and wore denim shirts and deck shoes in the office—had in fact prescribed estrogen for the symptoms he described as "vaginal dryness." He announced this as one with no fundamental belief that his own body would some day give up its own juices irretrievably.

Every morning she looked in the small mirror hanging on the ridge pole of her tent at the dig site and eyed her face and throat appraisingly. Even though Ashkelon was on the coast, the air was parched, and the etchings on her face, which the Texas Gulf humidity had kept plumped up, grew deeper there. Why couldn't she just give it up instead of trying to console herself with the hope that the lines at least showed a certain amount of character? Not that she was Isak Dinesen yet. But someday... She shuddered and turned away from the mirror. When she was convinced she was completely cured she might take it down. Till then she would keep it there to strengthen her resolution. The one thing she couldn't have borne was catching a glimpse of furtive pity in the appraising eyes of someone watching her dress.

That had been at the end of last summer. When she'd returned to Israel this year toward the end of May, Yigal had not disguised his pleasure at seeing her again. He had met the plane himself and crushed her in a bear hug before kissing her on both cheeks and then the mouth. His open delight had been so unexpected Miriam was taken completely off guard, and, inundated by the flood of his pleasure, she felt her knees go weak. Then he seized her bag and, with a hand on her elbow, propelled her toward the rank of taxis. Fortunately, when he came back from accumulating the rest of her luggage, she had checked her body chemistry sufficiently to have her defenses in place. By the time they reached her apartment in Jerusalem, she had reestablished the previous year's protocols between them. She could tell, however, that this time he had made up his mind to breach them.

Nevertheless, it had not been until mid-June that Yigal showed up at the small camper trailer that served as the project's office one morning, as she had known he eventually would. She had agreed to straighten out the team's financial records—a rat's nest of invoices and purchase orders.

"All right," he said, pressing the thumb latch on the door behind him. "We've wasted enough time. I want you."

She looked at him and pushed her reading glasses further up her nose. He was, she thought, the only man in her current acquaintance who might have caused her to reconsider her renunciation. And his forthright approach would have worked once too.

She shook her head and added a number to the debit column. "Maybe so," she said. "But not as much as a lateral move to Harvard with tenure."

After that rebuff, he had pouted for a couple of days, treating her with chilly and exaggerated detachment. Then the team had discovered the villa next to Lady Stanhope's basilica, and a whirlwind of excitement had blown even the recollection of his crumpled pride away.

The crew had been working on what was commonly called Lady Stanhope's basilica for two years before they discovered the villa. Lady Stanhope was an almost legendary figure in Near Eastern archaeology who had in the late nineteenth century gone to Ashkelon, attempting to find a treasure reputed to have been buried there by an Italian monk. She had uncovered a second-century basilica, but never the treasure. A formidable woman, she had once smashed a statue of a Roman centurion, worth a small fortune, in order to convince the ruling Ottoman sultan that she had no intention of carrying antiquities out of the country.

The villa had been found in Grid 38, a distinctly patrician neighborhood. Its Roman inhabitants would have had a magnificent view to the north fifteen centuries ago. Yigal had insisted she come with him that evening to wander over this latest find. He made her sit beside him on an outcropping, pretending they were the middle-aged homeowners, enjoying their view of the terraced gardens below. She had been pleased to see him so happy. He still liked to take her places, even kiss her casually on the cheek in public, probably hoping to generate gossip about them. But Miriam had no doubt that their friendship was now more valuable to them both than what would have been an inevitably stormy affair.

The next day, however, he had come to the trailer again, frowning this time at something he cupped in his hand.

"What's that?" she asked as he slumped into a canvas chair and slid a bit of ceramic sherd onto her desk. It was a thin disk, one edge broken off, with a small circular aperture at one end.

"Fourth-century pornography. We've discovered a dozen of those already this morning." He crossed his legs and leaned back. "There's a scene inscribed in the clay. Go ahead. Look at it."

She adjusted her glasses and held the disk a few inches from her nose, frowning. She often had trouble making out indistinct figures that seemed plain to experts. The grooves and lines always took a few seconds to slide into some pattern that made sense to her.

Yigal waited silently. She caught her breath and then expelled it in a small, nervous laugh. "For heaven's sake."

She looked up at him, then back at the sherd. The incising showed a figure reclining on a couch, knees up, legs open. Another standing figure grasped the ankle of the first while thrusting himself between the raised knees. Yigal wasn't smiling. She put the clay fragment carefully back on the desk. "Quite an athletic performance."

He shrugged. "Not all are like this. Some have mythological figures—Europa and the bull, that kind of thing."

"A collection."

Yigal held out his hand for the disk and, when she handed it to him, turned it over, shaking his head. "Filth."

"Come on, Yigal. This is an urban site. You've dug up this kind of thing before."

He turned the disk over once more, then slipped it back in his shirt pocket. "Sometimes I wonder what is the point of all my efforts. When I started out, I wanted to find something—significant."

Miriam sat back and took off her glasses. She was familiar with Yigal's depressions by now. Once he began in this vein, he could descend into a three-day funk, bringing the team's work to a standstill. "Look at it this way," she said, keeping her tone light, "these little disks will make an entire article all in themselves. Whatever purpose they served then, that's their present value to you now."

"Ah yes. It's all simply grist for the academic mill, is it not, Miriam? Sexual predation. Pederasty. Pogroms. Death camps."

She started to protest, then stopped herself. The last time she'd tried to reason him out of his angst they'd ended up arguing about Palestinian refugee camps.

"Is there nothing that is precious in your life, Miriam? Or is it all one?" He heaved himself to his feet with a great sigh as he said this.

"Yigal, really—"

Pacing the two steps the length of the trailer allowed, he turned and tilted his head back as though composing himself. Then, as if something on the shelf at the other end of the trailer had suddenly caught his attention, his eyes widened. Pushing past her, he reached to the level above his head and lifted a glass jar off the shelf where he kept his private specimens. "Remember that public bath we found last year?" he asked, a kind of sad triumph in his voice that made her wary. "Probably fourth-century, possibly a brothel? Look at these."

She took the jar he was holding out to her. It was filled with what looked like small animal bones. Some of them were fragments but a surprising number were whole. She handed the jar back to him and looked up questioningly.

"The sewer under the bath was stuffed with debris, you remember. During the winter I sent a sample to a friend of mine at Hebrew University, an expert in bones." He unscrewed the jar lid and shook some of the contents onto her desk.

Miriam moved some of the calcified fragments apart with her finger, noticing a murex shell among them. "Rats?" she asked, looking up.

"Human," he said, springing the trap.

Involuntarily, she jerked her finger back.

"Infant skeletons." He set the jar down beside her. "Nearly a hundred." He replaced the lid on the jar but didn't screw it down. "Some animals too, of course. Rats, as you said, but rabbits as well, strangely enough. And the odd coin."

As she contined to stare at the chalky white arrangement before her, his voice took on the tone she'd heard him use in lectures. "Since infant bones are extremely delicate, they often come apart or disintegrate when they are moved. But most of these skeletons were intact. Thus my friend assumes the corpses—she says she can tell by the teethbuds—were no more than three days old. The ages are too uniform for plague or famine to explain these. I'll show you the letter."

Miriam flicked her hand impatiently at the desk. "Romans regularly disposed of unwanted babies—especially girls. You know that."

"Fourth century, remember. Constantine had outlawed infanticide."

"That didn't stop it from happening. Just like abortion."

"My friend thinks perhaps child sacrifice."

"Come on. You can't use Constantine to rule out infanticide and then fall back on something even more archaic."

"As you say, legal prohibition does not always achieve its intent. The fourth century was an age of frantically competing gods. Ashkelon was Tanit's stronghold in this area."

She couldn't keep from glancing up at him then, and he had smiled as if he had willed it. "Didn't that goddess of yours employ such rituals? Sacrificing children? But of course, you're the expert there." His smile faded and he raised his shoulders slightly. "I merely thought you might be interested. You were here when we found the bath but gone in the fall when we discovered these. Matter for an article perhaps."

Miriam sat there for a moment, frozen with anger, then abruptly raked the pile of tiny bones on the desk into her palm and dropped them back in the jar. She screwed the lid on carefully before she spoke. "I've almost got the totals done on the equipment we charged to the museum grant. I should be finished by noon—if I don't have any more interruptions." She closed her eyes and pinched the skin between them as if to hold back a headache.

Yigal made a noise deep in his chest and turned away.

She glanced up at his rigid back. *Her* goddess. She could see what he was doing all right—trying to cast her in the role of soulless goy. Was this his revenge for her rejection? A viperish symptom of his depression? Whichever, it certainly blinded him to the blight in his own moral landscape. But why should that surprise her? People, she'd long ago concluded, did what they wanted to and made up reasons afterward. Including world-class scholars and archaeologists. The only true morality, Miriam was convinced, lay in refusing to delude yourself about your own motives.

What really worried her was that she was coming dangerously close to domestic familiarity with this man's moods and shortcomings. Sometimes she felt almost married to Yigal these days; the contest between them had that quality about it. Here he was, insisting on making her his emotional surrogate when she was the one who'd managed to fend off their combined carnality. Well, all right. Let him get on his Hebraic high horse and ride right out of her life.

At least, that's what she'd thought that day, studying the uncompromising khaki stretched across Yigal's obdurate shoulders as he left the trailer. Hardly a week ago, though looking down at the weedy hospital parking lot now, she found that hard to believe. The two oceans and multiple time zones she'd crossed since then seemed to have stretched the time to match the distance between them. It seemed more like a year.

"Mom?" Miriam noted the same plaintive tone in Pris' voice she'd heard from Deb the night before. She looked at her younger daughter, collapsed like a rag doll in the vinyl chair. Her freckles stood out the way they always did when she was run down.

Miriam glanced at Hannah, her strange staccato snore making her lips puff slightly at regular intervals. "Try not to let it upset you, Pris. Gram didn't mean to be sharp with you. She can't help it. She's using all her strength for—other things." Immediately Miriam could tell she'd misjudged. Pris had turned her head sharply to the side and was staring out the window, leaning her compressed lips against her fist. "I'm sorry. What is it, Pris? Priscilla." She gave a self-disparaging little laugh at her inadequate imitation of Hannah's name for her daughter.

Priscilla closed her eyes, dropped her fist from her mouth, then, taking a deep breath, straightened her shoulders and stood up. "Nothing," she said.

Miriam let the silence run its course while Pris picked up a towel from the end of Hannah's bed and carried it to the hamper by the sink at the other end of the room, glancing as she passed the other bed at the woman in it, sleeping soundly on her side. Miriam watched her looking in the mirror, inspecting first one side of her face, then the other. "So what about Deb? Is she doing okay with those two old coots she works for?"

"Okay, I guess," Pris said, raising an eyebrow at her reflection in the mirror, "but you better not let her hear you say she works for them."

Miriam made a humming noise meant to indicate both acknowledgment and gratitude for this admonition. Then she asked, frowning slightly, "Is something wrong though? She seemed awfully tense last night. Distracted maybe."

Pris turned on the water in the basin and ran her fingers under the stream, studying them.

Miriam's frown deepened and she put one hand on her hip. "What about her love life? That guy she was seeing before I left—Scott, wasn't it? What about him?"

" 'Seeing' him? Mother, they were living together. You know that." Pris' mutter hardly carried above the splash of the water. "They broke up. A few weeks ago. He's in Mexico now."

"Oh. I didn't know. Is that what's bothering her?"

Pris didn't answer, but her face grew stiff. Miriam waited till she'd turned off the water, shook her hands, and looked around for another towel. Then she repeated, making her voice stern this time "What is it, Pris?"

As soon as Pris looked up again, she knew. The censure she'd seen on her daughter's face at first had cracked and

211

was collapsing in slow motion like a detonated building.

"Oh Mother," Pris cried suddenly. "Poor Deb."

First she thought: This was a mistake. I should never have come back. If I hadn't come back, I might never have known.

Miriam had sent Pris out to retrieve a magazine she'd left in the car, waiting till she heard the door close behind her before crossing to the window. She stood staring out at the pitiless noonday sun beating down on the ragged vegetation pushing up through the cracks in the hospital parking lot below—a visual metaphor of her discontent. The steamy fecundity of Nature was exactly what she'd gone to the desert to escape. Like the weed-choked drainage ditches bordering every road and boggy lot in this flat alluvial plain, maternal life was clammy with the vapor that continually rises from a river of mucus, blood, milk, semen, urine, strained apricots, dishwater, wet laundry, breath. She had felt smothered by the tumid dampness, hemmed in by fogged mirrors. By the everlasting humidity of women. A little distance and dry air—that was all she'd asked of Ashkelon.

Being around her daughters often gave Miriam a sense of severe dislocation. She never knew where she stood with them, now that they were adults. Her own memories of those years in Denver and Austin, when it had been just the three of them, she guarded like a cache of stolen goods, guilty pleasures she didn't deserve.

But Pris and Deb, she knew, were more ambivalent about that time. They still used the private language of that familiar world when they were together, a vocabulary invented and understood only by the three of them. They laughed when they retold stories from their schooldays. But then without warning they could suddenly turn impatient, both with their past and with her. Then a sense of betrayal—

not simply of her, but of time itself—left her dazed and dumbfounded. How could they repudiate the past so easily, throw whole years overboard like so much superfluous garbage?

Miriam still geared herself automatically to her daughters' needs when she was with them, instinctual reactions overpowering whatever or whoever she was when she wasn't being a mother. But their own unpredictable responses threw her off-balance, left her completely undone—a silly middle-aged woman snivelling like a teenager over being misunderstood.

She told herself it was only natural for them to pull away from her, but there wasn't much comfort in that thought. Nature, she'd discovered, usually had something on its mind besides human happiness. She herself had given no more thought to leaving home than a cat.

Next she thought: No. It wouldn't have made any difference. Even if I hadn't come back. It was already too late. There never is any escape.

Miriam adjusted the blinds to cut down the glare from outside, then circled the bed and sank into the chair beside Hannah. The bill was coming due. It always did, sooner or later. Simply knowing the truth about your mistakes wasn't the same as paying for them. Contrition didn't wipe out the damage they'd done.

After Yigal had left the trailer that day, she'd gone to her tent to lie down. The headache she'd improvized had become a reality. But the heat was oppressive, and a pair of flies circled her aimlessly. Finally, unable to keep still, she left the tent and made her way down the rutted track that led to a secluded stretch of beach below a stone seawall.

She walked north along the sand, the slow waves tumbling shoreward at her left, until she felt the edge of her agitation begin to wear itself away. As her pace slowed, she spotted a large log washed up at the base of a cliff. She angled towards it, and, when she reached the scoured trunk, sat down on it heavily. Leaning forward, she let her hands fall between her knees. After several minutes she turned her palms up and looked at them.

She lifted her eyes to gaze out at the long line of incoming waves. The noon sun glinted off the moving water. She squinted into the glare, shading her eyes with one hand. How dare that bastard use that jar of bones against her like that? They were fourth-century, for crying out loud. By then Tanit had become no more than an oddity in the cafeteria line of Palestinian deities. Why blame the bones on Tanit? And on her.

Miriam's shoulders twitched suddenly, an involuntary shudder. However the bodies had ended up in that sewer, she wished she hadn't touched that jumble of tiny bones. She stood up suddenly, wrapping her arms around her shoulders, staring out to sea. Then, stolidly, doggedly, she set out across the stretch of beach to the water's edge, the wet sand giving way beneath her shoes in cleanly defined scallops.

Out over the shallow limestone shelf that extended maybe fifty yards into the sea, the water was green, like copper oxidized by weather. Farther out, however, it became a darker, deeper blue. Beyond the line of low breakers, the sun's shimmer spangled across the broken surface of the sea.

Miriam waded in slowly, feeling the salt water sting the blisters on her heels. Salty water—her mother's universal cure for any infection, whether in throats or feet. She edged her way forward, feeling the push and suck of the sea on her calves and knees first, then around her thighs. A wave, higher than she'd expected, struck her chest, knocking her off balance. The spray ran down her face, and she licked the salt from her lips.

The next wave staggered her, heaving her feet off the sandy bottom. For a moment she felt fear grip her like an icy undertow. Then she leaned back and let the water bury her.

Her face breaking the water's surface startled her. She breathed, and blinked at the sun-whitened core of the azure sky. She didn't know, she didn't know, she just didn't know. Not anything, not even her own mind. How one thing was tangled in another in the world or what happened if you cut the threads. She only had a sense of herself, small, embedded in that immense, lapping question. Rocking. She closed her eyes.

For a long time she simply lay in the water, alternately rising and settling on the lift and skip of the waves, attentive to the patterns the light made penetrating her closed eyelids. This must be the way the world is for an infant, she thought. And then didn't think, only drifted, eyes still closed.

When she waded onto the beach, she stumbled once or twice on a narrow strand of pebbles. The salt water squished in her canvas shoes all the way along the shoreline back to trail up the stone seawall. She'd missed lunch. She went to her tent and slept the rest of the afternoon.

"You're wrong about me," she told Yigal that evening. They were outside under an awning set up to cover a table full of grid charts.

"Wrong?" he echoed.

"Here's the museum grant figures."

He lifted an eyebrow, shifting his attention to the sheet she'd handed him. When he'd scanned the figures, he snapped the page and dangled it toward her. His mouth had stiffened in a way she'd become familiar with. "So? I ask again. In what way am I wrong?"

"There are things that matter to me." She spread her hands to extend the scope of her meaning. "There is something..." She shook her head. Why wasn't he helping her with this?

"So."

She flinched at the single abrupt syllable. He looked down at her, and his frown deepened for a moment. Then he turned his head aside and nodded sharply once. When he walked away, she'd felt desolate, deserted.

The next morning he had suggested she go back to the city for a couple of days. It was almost the weekend. "Shopping," he said, pulling his shoulders inward to indicate perplexity, "or whatever women do."

She hadn't seen him again. She'd packed that morning, and he'd been at the dig when she left after lunch.

The call from home had come during her second night back at the apartment.

Miriam raised her head to look across the bed toward the window again and was startled to find Hannah's eyes open and watching.

"Mother?" Miriam scraped the chair closer and seized the limp hand with its blue knotted veins.

Hannah started to smile, then closed her eyes. Her fingers exerted a pressure so slight Miriam thought she might have imagined it. Then the strength ebbed as the muscles went slack again.

Miriam leaned her head against the edge of the mattress, resting her cheek on the hand. Their own early years together when the world had been at war, those had been her mother's only years of peace. Everything after that had been sacrifice and loss for Hannah. Had her mother also felt their past together betrayed that night in her kitchen, when something between them had broken? Even the small solace Hannah had come to count on from her she had lost. Sacrificed really, because her mother must have known what that confrontation would cost. But such extravagant expenditures, such sacrifices seemed to be what fueled the world, what kept it going. Maybe life cost life. Always.

Miriam lifted her head from the mattress and kissed the loose skin of the hand she held. Mother, she wanted to say, I've come back. Don't leave me now.

15

Finally Hannah was alone. Miriam had closed the blinds before she left, leaving the room dark, except for an irritating light somewhere just behind and slightly above the headboard. Its artificial glow kept her from ever fully resting, though. And she longed for rest, as if cessation of effort were something tangible, almost edible.

She'd waked once to find Deborah in the room and Priscilla gone. Home to take care of her babies, Hannah hoped. She was neglecting them too much on her account. It was hard for all of them, but especially for Priscilla. Hard for them to get used to the idea that she wouldn't need them anymore.

In fact, Hannah discovered, it was a relief to be left alone for a while. Even from the foot of the bed, which seemed a great way off now, the commotion of their lives buzzed like a swarm of bees, throbbed like some huge engine. There was nothing she could do for them anymore. How could she concentrate when they swarmed at her like that? She needed to sort things out. She needed to be ready.

Never had she left on a trip without making sure everything was clean, that buttons weren't missing or a hem ripped loose. Yet there was still so much to get ready. When she was done, the dresser drawers, even the rooms would be bare, a few hangers clicking together in the empty closet and maybe a handful of boxes left on the floor, labelled for whoever could use the contents. Everything had to go this time.

Not that there was much to leave. And such a pitiful little bit to take.

She and Sam had gone to church with his parents the Sunday after the party. She'd dressed Miriam in pink organdie and her black patent Mary Janes. Sam had worn his uniform one last time. Hannah had thought they must be the handsomest family in the state of Minnesota that morning. Miriam was used to sitting through Mrs. McMichaels' long services in Texas, but Hannah gave her a pencil and a program to make sure she kept quiet.

The psalm that day—she could never forget it—seemed specially chosen for them. *Except the Lord build the house, they labour in vain who build it.* Yes, she thought. We're starting fresh now. And the night on the pier had seemed suddenly confirmed when the pastor continued, " 'Lo, children are an heritage of the Lord: and the fruit of the womb is his reward. As arrows are in the hand of a mighty man; so are children of the youth. Happy is the man that hath his quiver full of them.' "

Hannah had blushed as Sam's hand, lying along the back of the pew, squeezed her shoulder. From the corner of her eye she saw Mrs. Snider's eyes slide sideways in her direction, her lips tightening. Hannah lifted her head and smiled directly at the pulpit. Let her scowl if she likes, she thought, but the Bible says it: the fruit of the womb is a reward. She closed her eyes and imagined her breasts engorged again.

The pastor had preached from Luke that day. *For which of you, intending to build a tower, sitteth not down first, and counteth the cost, whether he have sufficient to finish it?*

Surely Sam wouldn't want to go on living with his parents, she thought. After the army stopped sending the $100 check next month, what would they do? What kind of a job could Sam get? Would he want to go back to college on the G.I. Bill? That would mean she'd have to get a job. Hannah stroked at the fingers of her gloved hands. They'd better discuss the future before they started thinking about more family. Count the cost.

She'd broached the subject that afternoon while she and Sam lay reading the paper in their room, she in her slip and he in his boxer shorts. Sam dropped the sports page onto the floor with a sigh. She turned toward him on her side and propped her head on her elbow. "You've been thinking about it, haven't you?"

"Of course I've been thinking about it," he said.

She had been silent, waiting for him to go on.

"Look," he'd finally said. "I just got home, okay? We're all right so far, aren't we?"

"Well, yes, but—"

"Just give me time, all right? I'm looking around. I've got to see what the possibilities are. Every G.I. in the country is looking for a job right now. You know that." He'd twitched her hand from his arm when she touched him.

The silence between her and Sam had grown as heavy as the sultry afternoon air. She rolled over onto her back and stared at the ceiling. There was a faint yellowish water-mark along the west wall.

"You just take care of Miriam," he'd finally said, as if the response had been dredged from some interior marsh, "and I'll handle the rest."

After that night on the dock though, Sam seemed to have lost interest again. She happened to be checking her savings passbook sometime the next week and noticed the little calendar at the back where she kept count of her periods. It was a few days past time. She felt her breasts. Were they a little tender? She found it particularly difficult not to be irritable with Miriam that day, but that was all.

She said nothing to Sam, but the next week she began to get up feeling dizzy. She ate nothing for breakfast, only drank a cup of black coffee. Thirty minutes later she would hurry to the bathroom and run the water loudly in the sink so no one could hear her retching.

No, she said to her reflection in the mirror as she washed her face afterwards. Not this soon. Frantically, she tried to reconstruct the few times Sam had made mute love to her at Mrs. McMichaels' house. Suddenly she longed for the little upstairs bedroom, the curtains stirring with the damp Gulf breeze, the discreet kindness of her old landlady. Maybe it was just the tension, she told herself.

Still she said nothing to Sam. By the next week he had settled into a routine of leaving with his father for the store in the morning, returning for lunch, then going back and taking over while Mr. Snider came home in the afternoon for an extended nap. Both Sam's parents seemed, if not cheerful, at least satisfied with the arrangement. Mrs. Snider began to take Miriam along on her trips to the grocery store, and she cut out special small biscuits for the child's breakfast. Once she even rocked her to sleep when Hannah went to lie down, complaining of a headache.

After another week she was all but certain she was pregnant. The nausea wasn't quite as bad as it had been with Miriam, and she managed to conceal it from the others. She could tell, however, that her mother-in-law was watching her closely. Hannah tried to talk to Sam one more time about his future plans, determined this time to be more direct.

She had waited till the two of them were sitting in the front porch swing one evening, rocking gently back and forth in the gradually cooling dusk. "Sam," she'd begun, "have you been able to check out the possibilities any more?" She'd said "possibilities" purposely, remembering that had been the word he used before.

Sam took the pipe he'd started smoking out of his mouth. "What? What are you talking about?"

"You said you were looking around at the possibilities—for jobs or whatever."

He stuck the pipe back in his mouth and took a deep breath which he let out slowly.

She waited, determined not to upset the applecart by saying more.

"There's not a heck of lot in a little town like this," he said. "You know that."

Really? she commented to herself with mute irony. Then why has it taken you so long to check them out? Aloud she said, "No. I suppose not."

Her mildness seemed to work because he went on. "So far as I can see, my best bet is to go on helping Dad at the store. Actually, I'm lucky to have a father with an established business here. A lot of guys don't have that."

"The two of you have discussed it then?"

"Discussed what?"

"You working in the store. I mean hours and pay and all."

"How can I do that, Hannah? I mean we're living here free of charge, aren't we? That's worth a lot. You can't even find a decent place to live these days—not at any price. When he can spare it at the end of the week, Dad gives me a tenner. We get to use the car when we need it. And Mom's a great cook. I'd think you'd find it almost as good as living in a hotel."

At her sharp intake of breath, he glanced at her. Then he jammed the pipe back in his mouth, gripped it between his teeth, and after a moment jerked it out again. "What have you got to complain about anyway? From what you've told me about your family, this is probably the best you've ever had it."

The swing stopped. The world stopped. A high-pitched whirring started in her ears. Hannah stood up and went inside, surprised that she could still move, crossing carefully the living room to the stairs as if the room's tenuous reality might shatter at any moment. She tiptoed into the little dormer room where Miriam was sleeping, pulled the sheet up over her shoulders, then went into the bedroom she and Sam shared. She turned all the way around once, looking—she didn't know for what. Then she went out into the hall and down the back stairs. Pushing open the back screen, she stepped out into the night, shivering in the early autumn air, crossed the grass to the alley, and began to walk.

She walked until something in her frozen brain clicked and she felt it begin to stir again. All right, she told herself, maybe Sam doesn't have the gumption to look for a real job, but I do. Tomorrow, tomorrow I'll get dressed up and go downtown and apply at every business I can find. Somebody's bound to need a clerk or a typist or even a stock girl. Then I'll look for us a place to stay. Maybe a little garage apartment.

"'Best I've ever had it. Like living in a hotel'," she muttered to herself, jamming her hands into her pockets as she crossed Main Street. Anger made her feel stronger than she had in days.

Days. She stopped in the middle of the deserted sidewalk. And if she were in fact pregnant? Who would hire her then? During the war, things had been different. People overlooked a lot during a labor shortage. But not now. Not here.

Her steps slacked. She walked back to the Snider house more slowly than she'd left, opened the back door, and climbed the steps again. She undressed in the dark—Sam was still downstairs—and lay staring overhead into the darkness.

Mrs. McMichaels would have told her to pray. But this was something she didn't know how to pray about.

Her exile in Minnesota had seemed longer than it actually was. After Sam had a falling out with his father—she'd worked in the drugstore no more than three months—he'd found a job in St. Paul with an old Army buddy with a used car lot who hired him to take radiators off old cars for resale. Then an auto parts salesman had convinced Sam there was money to be made in seat covers; the salesman also had a deal on a storefront lease in Dallas.

By the next fall they'd been back in Texas. Hannah found herself pregnant again. This time, however, she told Sam as soon as she suspected. She hadn't resented the meagerness of their lives; she was used to dealing with that sort of adversity. But both children were tentative and watchful around Sam, uncertain of his swift moods. She became the pivot, the buffer, the hub through which every exchange between her husband and her children was routed. She grew sharp with the children, trying to squelch potential conflicts with their father. With Sam she was distant, exhausted by monitoring of his moods.

Then, only a couple of months before Barton's third birthday, the Eighth Army broke out of the Pusan perimeter in Korea and the government began calling up reserves. Sam suddenly brightened, grew resourceful and teasing again. She didn't protest when he began to talk of re-enlisting in the new Air Force. In late October, MacArthur had advanced to the Yalu River and Sam was gone.

Ten years before, Hannah had not followed the details of the war except as they related directly to her husband's own fortunes. This time she traced reports of both the political and military maneuverings, knowing they would affect her family more directly. While Sam was on a troop ship headed for Korea, the news grew worse. The UN troops had been pushed back across the 38th parallel. Hannah studied the newspaper maps and began to have misgivings. Sam's hopes for combat duty were dashed when he was assigned to a crew flying cargo planes out of

Okinawa to Seoul. As the summer wore on, however, the second Chinese offensive made his job more dangerous, and his spirits lifted.

Then peace talks began. Dependents of military personnel were allowed to join their husbands at Kadena Air Force Base where he was stationed. *Things have settled down*, he wrote in the same familiar hand she remembered from his former letters. *It probably won't be long till this thing is over. I've put in for base housing. You don't know how much I miss you. Everyone says the schools on base are good. The weather's a lot like Texas, along the coast. Remember Corpus?*

It seemed decided already. There was nothing to hold her back, no objection she could raise. And, as if making a final concession to clinch his case, he wrote that clerical jobs were plentiful on base. *The wife of a buddy of mine works as a cashier at the PX. Not that you need to work, you understand. I just know how you like having something to do. And everybody has maids here. Yard boys too. You may never get this chance to play Lady Astor again!*

Hannah was used to doing for herself. When she arrived at the house Sam insisted on calling "quarters," she felt uneasy with the maid he had already hired for her. The girl's eyes were so black you couldn't make out the pupils in the center. When a job at the base hospital opened up, she took it quickly, as much to escape the strange woman in her home as for the money.

Miriam, always a mystery to her father, was growing distant and aloof. "A bookworm," he complained. Sam marked a target with chalk on the back wall of the house for Barton to practice throwing a baseball at.

Hannah had been surprised at the children's guileless grief the day their father's plane went down.

The airman the captain had arranged to drive her home pulled up in front of the grey-green stucco house and opened the car door, glancing at her nervously. She thanked him, told him she was fine, and waited till he'd driven off again before she opened the door. Natsuko was playing the radio in the kitchen, that thin, whining oriental music, and didn't hear her come in. Hannah looked out the back window of the living room and saw Barton throwing a softball into the air and trying to hit it with a broom handle before it came down.

She went into the bathroom, turned on the water in the basin, and washed her face. Washed it with soap, then rinsed it thoroughly. She would be calm. Reassure them. Tell them to be brave. That Daddy would want that. That they would be going home.

She dried her face, folded the towel, turned it and folded it again. How could it be over so quickly? Without warning, Sam and his insatiable disappointments were gone, extinguished in the cold waters of the East China Sea. Years ago, when he was still a boy with no bitterness, only eagerness, she had thought she could satisfy his youthful pride and constant need for reassurance. On what field might he have won some essential victory he could believe in?

She'd never know how it actually had ended for him. Had he been afraid? Had he been brave, there at the last? She saw him again, silhouetted darkly on the beach at Corpus, the moon rising behind him. And suddenly she hid her face in the damp towel, mourning for all that might have been.

After a while she stood up and hung the towel over the shower rod, adjusting it carefully so that the folds were even. "I'm sorry, Sam," she said, and at the sound of her own voice almost started to cry again. But she steadied herself, took a deep breath, and opened the bathroom door. Then she went to Miriam's bedroom and stood in the doorway watching her daughter until she looked up from her book. One ankle was propped across an awkwardly angled knee. She was picking at a scab on the knee absentmindedly while she read.

"Go call your brother in," Hannah said. "There's something I have to tell you."

Miriam marked her place in the book with her finger and looked at Hannah anxiously, her eyes large and sensing trouble. By the time she came back in the living room with Barton, Hannah was sitting in one of the rattan chairs, her palms pressed together.

Hannah patted the sofa, indicating they should sit down, then leaned toward them, looking at the floor a moment before she spoke. She raised her eyes. Their faces were already solemn and round.

"I have some bad news." She took a deep breath. "Daddy's plane has been shot down."

The two children gave a startled jerk.

"It was out over the ocean. None of the crew survived."

Instantly their hands reached out to her as if they themselves were falling. Hannah spread her arms and drew them to her, Miriam against her side and Barton onto her lap. They were making small muffled moans. She contained their knobs of elbows and shoulders within her arms, letting the scent of their slightly sour sweat mark her memory. Then, even as she rocked the children against her, for the first time in a long while the memory returned of that dark pier out over the Minnesota lake, the wisps of music stretching toward them across the water. The one time she'd ever really felt free and easy.

Sitting back, she forced herself to loosen her grip and let her arms slide along the shoulders of the two children. She would never feel free and easy again.

That night she lay awake, trying not to picture the cargo plane spiralling downward, outlined in flames. Or Sam, plummeting terrified into the sea. It's already over, she whispered to herself in the dark room. Whatever pain or terror he suffered. It's over now. He doesn't feel it anymore.

And whatever they'd done to one another. That was over too.

No point in worrying about that now, Hannah, she heard Mrs. McMichaels say. What's done is done.

Hannah frowned. Why hadn't she found a way to tell them, to make them understand? All they could say was How're you feeling, Gram? You hungry? What would you like? All the words that needed saying still were stuck in her throat while the tide kept rising, lifting her. She could feel it gathering itself, pushing against the shore as it turned, the undertow sucking her out into an ocean she'd never seen, out beyond any life she'd ever known.

Even this knowledge came to her, not in words but in pictures—pictures she felt as much as saw. Every once in a while she felt herself tilt and rock, swinging around on the current like she'd seen the boats at anchor in Corpus. The pull, the tug of the tide thrummed along the anchor chain. Then her breath would catch, waiting for that first long glide out into the open water. She couldn't make the anchor hold much longer. Not even to tell them.

They were all, even Priscilla, better with words than she was. Life had always overwhelmed her, been bigger than the words she tried to match it with. And even if she could find the words, would they listen? How many times had she smiled at things Mrs. McMichaels tried to tell her? When she'd come back to Texas, alone with two children to raise, the old lady had written her: *Twelve years is not a very long time to have been married, Hannah. You still got a lot of years ahead of you. Believe me, I know. Don't rule out getting married again. Those children need a father, especially Barton.*

She'd tucked the letter away in her Bible, shaking her head. She had about as much inclination to marry again as she did to live in Minnesota. Sam's love had been more of a burden than a joy. A load she never wanted to shoulder again.

16

Deborah had picked Miriam up at the hospital, intending to take her to her favorite Italian place for dinner. Over linguini and fumé blanc, she'd tell her. Now that she'd made up her mind, Deborah was feeling a good deal better. She was certain her bloodstream, nutrient-laden from that immoderate meal with Otis Ruffner, was coursing through her veins, bathing her own cells as well as that little translucent clump inside with all the necessary vitamins and minerals. On the way to the hospital she noticed a little nervous flutteriness, but it wasn't nausea, just a sensation she couldn't place at first. Not till she'd puzzled over it, turning it over in her mind the way the tongue turns over unfamiliar food in the mouth, did she realize that what she was feeling was shy.

Not embarrassed. Her mother would be the last person to censure either her living arrangement with Scott or its unplanned results. And Mom would be the first one to applaud her decision. In fact, she'd dare Pris and Tim to criticize. Not that they would. In fact, if anything their relief would be all too palpable. And, she thought with a further jolt of release, now she could tell Father Botts. Being obstinately pregnant and single made you practically a martyr with Catholics these days.

Miriam looked bedraggled, wilted from her day's vigil at Hannah's bedside when Deborah found her waiting near the entrance in the lobby. "Gram's sleeping," she told Deborah.

"She seemed better this afternoon, at least her breathing was easier. Probably best to let her go on sleeping now."

When Deborah suggested the restaurant, though, Miriam shook her head. "I've got a splitting headache. I'd really just like to lie down a while and relax." Then she added quickly, "Unless of course you're hungry."

"I'm fine. We'll go home and I'll make you tea," Deborah said, though she thought later she should have sensed it coming then. She could feel her mother's eyes moving across her face as surely as if they'd been fingers. But she was still coasting on that sense of release.

Instead of heading for the bedroom when they got to the apartment, Miriam flopped down in a chair, slipped her shoes off, and propped her feet on the coffee table. "Come sit down and talk to me. We haven't really had a chance. Tell me what's been happening with you."

Deborah took off her jacket and folded it carefully across a chairback. Instantly she regretted it. The side of her waistband where the button had come off earlier was gaping. She sank onto the sofa and curled her legs under her so that her left side was hidden by the cushions. "Nothing much." She wasn't feeling shy now, only wary.

"How's work going?" Miriam had closed her eyes and dropped her head back.

"Oh." Deborah hesitated. "Okay." But her voice sounded a little too flutey, so she added quickly, "You know Hoot and Hank. They think of me mostly as decoration. Never give me anything really substantial to work on. It gets frustrating."

"What about your love life? Pris said you'd broken up with that Scott fellow."

"Yes." Deborah couldn't keep the stiffness out of her voice. "Would you like some tea? I've got herbal."

Miriam smiled, her eyes still closed. "So you don't want to talk about it."

"What's there to talk about, Mother? He dumped me." She expected that her mother would follow up on this with some little reassuring noises, but Miriam said nothing for another couple of minutes. Deborah got up, went into the kitchen, and put the tea kettle on.

When she came back with two mugs, Miriam sat up and leaned forward to take one of them. "I'm sorry," she said.

Deborah looked at her. "For what?"

"That he dumped you."

Deborah sat down again and held the mug under her nose. She shrugged.

Miriam leaned back and looked at her over the rim of the mug. "How did your Father Botts feel about it?"

Deborah looked up. "*My* Father Botts?"

Miriam dropped her gaze and gave a little shake of her head. "I'm sorry. All I meant was—" She broke off and hitched her shoulders up. "I guess I never understood why you—" The shoulders dropped.

Deborah twisted the ends of her hair while her thoughts raced ahead, tracing out the various paths this conversation might take.

"I'm surprised that your—that the priest let you go on living with Scott. I mean you have to go to confession, don't you? What did he say about that?"

"Really, Mother. The priest didn't let me do anything—or keep me from it. Since Vatican II there's this thing called the inner forum." Deborah made a frustrated wave with both hands to suspend her explanation. It wasn't theology her mother was interested in. "Anyway, what goes on in the confessional is privileged information." She struggled to lighten her tone. "Like lawyers."

Her mother was frowning now. The implied rebuke hadn't gone down well. "And what about abortion? Since Vatican II. That hasn't changed, has it?"

"What about it?"

Her mother gave her a long, level look. "Is it an option? For Catholics? I guess I'm wondering just how serious you are about," she paused and shrugged, "all this."

Deborah drew a deep breath. "I take it Pris has let you in on my little secret."

"She didn't intend to. It just came out. You know Pris."

"Sure. Good old Pris."

Miriam leaned forward now, her elbows on her knees. "You were always the one who took things so seriously, Deborah. I can't imagine you shrugging something like this off so lightly. I just don't want you doing something you'll regret, sweetheart."

Before she knew it, Deborah was on her feet, the unfairness of it all roaring in her ears. What right did Pris have to tell Mom, to tell anyone? She'd spoiled everything. And Mom, what right did she have to be giving her these little lectures? "Like you never had anything to regret, Mom?" she heard herself saying. "You weren't exactly a paragon of virtue after you left Dad. You were just better at it. You made sure you didn't get pregnant. You managed to avoid my embarrassing predicament. Is that what you mean?"

Miriam raised her head and stared at her daughter for a moment, then dropped her eyes to the mugs on the coffee table.

"Did you think I was stupid or something?" Deborah went on, her throat constricting but unable to stop the rush of words which seemed to come of their own accord. "Did you think I was blind? It wasn't enough to know my mother was sleeping around; I was the one who made up stories about your 'friends' so Pris could feel safe, so she wouldn't hate you."

She stood up and stared down at her mother's shoulders, rounded now as if to fend off physical blows. "Well, just for the record, I was planning to tell you myself. Not that it matters."

Miriam got up and walked to the large front window and stood looking down into the deserted street, scrunching up her toes inside her stockings. "You're right," she finally said. "I have plenty to regret."

Deborah waited, frozen, as the silence around them hardened. Then she picked up her jacket from the back of the chair and her handbag from the table by the door. "I'm going out for a while. There's aspirin in the bathroom," she said. "Don't wait up."

Miriam stood at the window, still staring down at the empty street, long after she heard the door close behind her daughter. What had she been trying to bring off here with Deborah anyway? What a line—*something you'll regret.* Maybe Hannah could have gotten away with that kind of ominous gentility, but not her. Women who threw themselves off cliffs like tragedy queens weren't allowed those kinds of lines. And she had to hand it to Deb. She knew how to hit where it hurt. Protecting Pris from her. Miriam cringed, remembering that one.

What had prompted her to make such a clumsy appeal to her daughter? For an hour after Pris had dumped the news on her so abruptly, Miriam had felt as if her body was an empty plain, passive under the onslaught of a storm. Emotions had moved through it like a series of conflicting high and low pressure cells. Anger at Deb for the untimeliness of this crisis, at Pris for the inopportune announcement. Even, for a moment, a flash of infantile anger at Hannah for being sick when she needed her. Interspersed with the anger was vicarious anguish for Deborah, worry that she would blame Pris for divulging the secret, anxiety that Hannah might have heard all this.

What she had wanted to feel—the one clean, clear emotion—was fury with the man who had abandoned her daughter, but that kept getting washed away by stronger currents. Finally though, simple fear had set in, cold and constant, and without her bidding. That was what had led her to her inept little speech to her daughter.

But what was she afraid of? Doing something you'll regret, she'd said to Deborah. But what would Deborah regret?—that was the question. Sitting there on the sofa, Miriam had known suddenly, as soon as she'd started speaking, what she wanted. Wanted, but, as Deb had made plain, had forfeited the right to advocate.

An hour after she'd fallen asleep, Priscilla waked up with a start, so furious she was panting. The muscles in her throat were clenched, as if she'd been screaming. She could almost hear the echo dying away as she lay next to Tim in the darkness. He hadn't moved though.

It was Deb she'd been screaming at. Her sister, looking sophisticated and cool in one of those short-skirted suits of hers, had come into the kitchen where Pris was cooking supper. The package Deb was carrying was about the size of a ham.

Here, Deb had said in the dream, use this instead. I don't need it. And she'd laid the package on the counter.

Pris slid the bundle over in front of her, still holding a knife. But when she pulled the paper back and started to cut, she suddenly saw it wasn't a ham at all, but a baby. Brown and dry and shriveled. It looked like jerky.

Then Deb had laughed.

That's when she'd begun to scream. And with every breath, she was whacking at the dried, shrunken baby with the knife.

Pris drew a shuddering breath. Tim stirred beside her. The hair around her face was damp, and her nightgown stuck to her chest. Easing out of bed, she crept down the hall to the kitchen.

She stood staring at the stagelit interior of the refrigerator, then took out an open carton of orange juice and carried it to the living room where she collapsed cross-legged on the floor in front of the sofa. The square red numbers on the VCR display showed only a little after midnight. She pulled open the mouth of the cardboard carton, fuzzy from use, and turned it up, spilling a little down her chin and using the shoulder of her nightgown to wipe at the dampness.

Across the street in front of the Jaworskis' she could see the dark, low hulk of an unfamiliar car, the kind with louvered slats in the rear like the plates on an insect's back. Strange cars often parked in front of the Jaworskis'. They had three kids, two of them teenagers.

The car's dome light came on, then went off again quickly as someone got out on the driver's side. Another figure followed. Illuminated by the green glow of the street light, Donna Jaworski was buttoning up the front of her denim halter and grinning at a tall boy who flicked a heavy swatch of hair back from his forehead, his hands jammed into his back pockets.

"Idiot," Pris muttered.

The girl started around the nose of the car, keeping her shoulder blades well back and angling her hips up and sideways with each step. A long topknot hung down along her right temple almost to her shoulder.

The boy followed her onto the lawn, then stopped. He jerked his head in the direction of the car and took a step back.

"Well, go on if you're going," Pris said.

Donna turned to face the boy, her head tilting to one side so that the topknot swayed a little. She shifted her weight to the other foot, hooked a thumb in her belt loop, and jounced one heel up and down. The boy flicked his hair back again and took a step toward her.

Just then the Jaworski porch light came on. The boy scuttled backward to the car. Donna stood on the lawn, putting just a bit more arch into her back—a final dare. The dome light glinted briefly again. The engine started and the tail light glowed red. The girl gave the swag of hair a final scornful sling as she went up the sidewalk and jerked open the front door. The porch light went out.

Pris leaned back against the sofa and closed her eyes. What was she going to do when Sarah got to be a teenager? Lock her up? She sighed and tilted the juice carton up again.

This thing with Deb—it was eating at her bad. Already the dream was fading from her memory, but it had left behind a lingering uneasiness. Okay, she confessed into the darkness, I admit it. I'm jealous. I know that already. How many times do you want me to say it?

She closed her eyes, squinting them tight. It wasn't really the jealousy that was bothering her, and she knew it. She'd been living with that a long time, as long as she could remember. It was like having some lifelong condition like diabetes. You just did what you could not to make it worse. But the other—she didn't know what to do about that.

She sighed, wishing forlornly that Tim would wake up, find her gone, and come to comfort her.

I could tell her I'd keep it, she thought.

Sure. Like Deb would thank her for that. If her sister decided to have this baby, she'd definitely keep it herself. She wouldn't believe anyone besides her could do a good enough job. The real question still was, was she going to have it?

So far, Pris hadn't thought of any new way to appeal to her sister. Threatening her with God's wrath would only get her back up. Even being a Catholic wasn't likely to change that. Ever since they were little, Deb had always dug in her heels when threatened with punishment. To her, a threat was the same as a dare.

Deb never talked about wanting children, but then she wouldn't. She never talked about what she couldn't have. She liked to think of herself as self-sufficient, independent, self-contained. Pris was almost certain, however, that her sister would have married Scott if he'd asked her. That was one disappointment she hadn't been able to conceal. She was still smarting from the way that had ended. But even so, even if she'd married the jerk, would she have wanted children?

Pris drew her knees up and propped her elbows on them, dangling the almost empty carton. Maybe a better way to put it was, more than what? More than being a lawyer? More than shopping at Nieman's? More than she hated being embarrassed and, even worse, pitied?

She shook the carton, drained the last of the orange juice, and crushed the tented top of the container into careful segments. There was the Catholic angle. That was a possibility. Maybe she could go talk to Deb's priest. Enlist his help. Yet even as she began to form images of walking into a musty office in some grey stone church and sitting down across the desk from some Father Dowling, she knew it was hopeless. Deb would never forgive her, would hate her for interfering. It wouldn't work. She never could stand for Deb to hate her.

She shivered suddenly. Even worse, could she stand to hate Deb?

She shut her eyes again and tried to picture that stubby glob stuck to the inner wall of her sister's uterus, still translucent as a minnow but already unfolding little nubbins of fingers and toes. So what if that spoiled son-of-a-bitch Scott had put it there, if half of it was him. It could overcome that. After all, the other half of it was them. Her and Deb. Uncle Barton. Mom. All they had left of Dad. And Gram. The only way they'd still keep Gram.

The carton collapsed with a sudden damp whoosh between her hands. That little glob contained within it all those years of hoping for first one thing and then another. All their wit, their grit. It was the fact that they were still here—an actual flesh-and-bone fact. And all that would go down a literal drain somewhere in scraps and tatters of tissue.

She pushed herself to her knees and then to her feet, stumbling over a plastic telephone as she made her way into the kitchen. Damn, she thought as she dropped the crushed carton into the garbage sack under the sink, why did she ever have to tell me?

Deborah opened her briefcase and took out the notes she'd made last night after she'd come back to the empty office. She'd worked steadily for over an hour, hoping, when she returned to the apartment that her mother would already be asleep. Whether or not Miriam was sleeping, Deborah had found the apartment dark except for the light over the sink. This morning she'd showered, dressed, and slipped out again before Miriam had appeared.

Now she gave Arlene a look that warned against any questions and crossed the waiting room to Hoot Jasper's office.

Hoot was leaning back in his chair facing the window with his feet propped on the sill. He didn't turn around when she tapped on the door and came in.

"I got what you wanted," she said.

He kept his gaze aimed past the scuffed toe of his boot, toward the bend in Buffalo Bayou where the sun glinted off a stretch of flat muddy water between the brick walls of a warehouse and a freeway arch. She could see his pink scalp through the white bristles of his half-inch hair. On the downward scroll of the oak chair arm his left hand flopped up and down a couple of times. "Did you now?" he said.

She sat down in the straightback chair across the desk from him and waited. Arlene had been right. He was still upset.

"How long you been working here, Debbie?" He shifted in the chair but still didn't turn around. "A year yet?"

She waited a moment, frowning, then opened her mouth, but before she could answer, he went on.

"Not yet a year. My, my." He took his feet from the sill and swung around to face her now in one motion. The bottom rims of his eyes were red and he looked at her balefully.

She frowned and opened her mouth again, but just as she started to speak, he intruded once more. "No, hasn't been a year yet, has it?" He leaned forward over the desk now and put his hands together, resting on his elbows. "And in that short span a time, Deborah, would you say you have attracted an appreciable number of new clients to this firm?"

"What do you mean? I don't see what you're getting at. Is something wrong?"

He raised one hand. "Something wrong? Why should anything be wrong?"

She sat back and crossed her arms. He was obviously determined to do this his way—whatever it was.

"Now I may be wrong," he went on in a tone of exaggerated deference, "but I don't seem to remember us being overburdened with new customers during these past months. Am I right?"

"What are you getting at, sir? It wasn't my impression you were interested in taking on new clients. I understood that you and Mr. Crawford had all the clients you wanted. You've both built up a large clientele over your careers."

Hoot shook his grizzled head dejectedly. "So we have, girl. So we have." His eyes swivelled up under his shaggy brows to lock onto her face. "You, however, seem to have a different notion. I just assumed that you must be planning on bringing in some new trade." He hesitated.

"New—why?" As soon as she said the word she saw he'd left that gap she would step into so he could zing a shot through the crack.

"Why?" He threw himself back in the chair as if his amazement at her question had blown him there. "Because why else would you be divesting us of our old clients?"

She uncrossed her arms and sat forward on the edge of her chair. "I think you better tell me what this is all about. I'm just not following—"

"What it's all about, girlie, is Otis Ruffner, a client the firm of Jasper and Crawford has been representing for thirty years, in good times and bad, through thick and thin. Now this client calls up to say he's withdrawing this case from us. In fact, all his dealings with us."

"But that's impossible. I was just there yesterday. He seemed—"

"I know you were there, goddammit! And 'seems' don't come into it. I'm telling you what happened just yesterday afternoon—when you had such a hard time finding your way back to the office." His voice had risen so high it cracked. He pointed to the telephone on his desk as if the object itself were evidence against her.

"But we had a—very amiable conversation. He took me to lunch. I brought my notes back." She shook the pages of yellow paper she'd been holding in her hand.

Hoot was mopping his face with a stained handkerchief. He stopped and stared at her. "Honey, buying a girl lunch, well—" He stuck the handkerchief back in his pocket, shaking his head.

"But he liked me. I know he did." She could hardly tell him about the tea and the nap and the afghan. "We talked about his wife. Who, by the way, no one bothered to tell me had just died."

"Velda?" For an instant Hoot looked genuinely shocked. "The woman died five years ago. That old galoot didn't pull that one on you, did he?"

She sat back. "Five years ago? But I thought—I assumed—"

Hoot laughed harshly. "In this business, darling, you don't assume nothing." His eyes narrowed. "What else he tell you?"

"Well. That he'd turned everything over to his wife to operate—"

Hoot slapped the desk top with the flat of one hand and gave a whoop which was followed by a series of hacking coughs. "Did he also tell you," he said between gasps, "that he 'turned it over to her' in a divorce settlement?"

"Divorce?" she repeated. "He didn't say anything about a divorce."

"No, I reckon not." Hoot was grinning broadly now. He took out the handkerchief again and spat into it, chuckling to himself. "I guess he musta been practicing on you, trying out the act he intends to pull on the feds."

"You mean—"

"I mean Velda Showacre divorced him back in eighty-three—back when ever'body in the oil patch was going belly up. Over the years he'd parlayed her daddy's money into a sizeable business, but like ever'body else he was working too much on margins. Lost just about ever'thing. She got out, taking what was left with her. Course there wasn't much by then."

Deborah creased the edge of her notes, keeping her eyes on the pages. "Did they have any children?"

"Children?" Hoot shook his head. "A merciful God kept that woman from reproducing. The world don't need no more

243

Veldas. I'd sooner sleep with a rattlesnake than her kind. She was one mean woman." He shook his head again. "I told Otis that wildcat company of his was a small price to pay for being shet of her."

Deborah folded her hands in her lap. "So, if he lost everything, then why—I mean how—"

He looked up at her sharply. "You mean why do I care about losing his business, or how come the feds are after him now?"

She lifted her shoulders slightly. "Both, I guess."

He leaned back in his chair. "Men like Otis always come back. You may not a learned that yet in your young life, but there's some people never quit. You learn to spot who they are and you stick with 'em. They don't forget who stuck with 'em when they come out on top again. And as for the rest—well, Velda couldn't a played a worse trick on old Otis if she'd planned it. Seems like after she divorced him, she never got around to writing a new will. Then when she took sick, she just couldn't bring herself to admit she might die. Her lawyer told me she just about turned the air blue right there in the hospital room when he brought up the subject of the will. So old Otis ended up getting ever'thing back she'd taken from him. And now he's saddled with straightening out all these back taxes with the feds. Hoo-boy!"

He began to laugh again, shaking his head. Then gradually the laughter faded and he stared at her, suddenly sober again. "But you still ain't explained why now, after thirty years of me'n Hank sticking with him, Otis Ruffner suddenly takes a notion to pull out. What you got to say for yourself on that score, missy?"

Deborah put her hand to her throat. "I don't know, sir. I swear. I just don't know. I'll call him myself if you like and try to straighten things out."

"Here," said Hoot gruffly, pushing the phone across the desk toward her. "Go right ahead. I want to hear this."

She dialed the number, unable to focus on what she would say, but the phone rang on, and no one, not even a machine, answered.

17

Deborah checked her watch in the eerie green light of the hospital parking lot, feeling her resolution falter. She had made a couple of calls to the hospital during the day to check on Gram and been assured by Pris, anxious to appease her, that Hannah was having another good day.

"I've got to work late," Deborah had lied. "Can you take Mom home?" She'd kept her voice as flat as possible, letting the ambiguity of "home"—whether her place or Pris'—hang there for her sister to struggle with.

"Sure," Pris agreed, over-eager, not even allowing herself that momentary pause that hinted reproach.

When Deborah had finally left the office about six after her last unsuccessful attempt to reach Otis Ruffner, she hadn't wanted to see either her mother or her sister. In hopes of avoiding them, she'd eaten at the Italian place she'd planned to take Miriam the evening before, then driven around the city till she thought they'd probably left the hospital for the night. By the time she'd scouted out all the rows in the parking lot, checking to make sure Pris' van wasn't there, regular visiting hours were over. Gram would probably be asleep by now.

Deborah considered leaving, forgetting the whole thing. Gram didn't need this. Then a car she was blocking honked behind her. The sudden noise startled her memory into replaying yesterday's parking lot scene, and her body responded once more with the physical effects of terror. Her heart was pounding in her throat as she pulled the car into one of the slanted slots and turned off the engine.

She sat there a moment till her pulse began to slow. Unfortunately, the memory of the euphoric release that had come later was proving harder to reconstruct. Of course, it didn't help any that Mom had squashed it. Now she wasn't sure about Father Botts' reaction either. "All right," she muttered to herself in the darkened car. "You know what's going to happen if you don't do this." She opened the car door and made her way toward the lighted entrance.

She had another moment of hesitation when the elevator doors opened on Gram's floor. But the aide at the nurses' station hardly glanced at her as she passed. Inside the room, the woman in the first bed, plainly vexed at this late-night intrusion, turned away heavily and jerked her coverlet up past her ears. The curtain had already been pulled between the two beds for the night.

Deborah tiptoed past the foot of the woman's bed and around to the far side of Hannah's. When she saw her grandmother's eyes were closed, Deborah felt her heart sink, realizing only then how desperate she was to talk to Gram, especially after what had passed between her and her mother the night before. In a detached way she knew that telling Gram would be selfish, even cruel. If her grandmother were in fact getting stronger, this might possibly set her back. But Deborah felt her own need crushing the breath out of her, like a heavy stone she'd never be able to lift by herself. And if she never had another chance—

Deborah pulled the plastic chair up close to the bed and eased into it. Hannah still showed no sign of waking. She looked withdrawn, far away, surrounded by an almost palpable wall of silence. Like God, Deborah thought.

Her grandmother had never admonished her about Scott— or any man, for that matter. She had never offered her opinion on any choices Deborah made, whether about law school or her conversion. Just as she'd never said anything—not to her granddaughters anyway—about their parents' divorce. Her silence was like the silence of God—ominous, swollen with its unpronounced meaning.

Beyond the curtain, the door was suddenly thrust open and the charge nurse swished toward them, a blood pressure cuff in her hand. "Visiting hours have been over for a good while," she said. "It's almost time for shift change."

Before Deborah could respond, Hannah opened her eyes. "This is my granddaughter," she said. "I want her with me."

Slipping the black cuff around Hannah's arm, the nurse looked uncertain. She held between her fingers Hannah's wrist, frowning silently while she studied her watch. Finally she said, glancing toward Deborah, "I don't want her tired out."

Hannah's eyes closed again before the nurse was gone. "She's right, Gram," Deborah said. "I should let you rest."

The orbs moved under the papery lids. "Deborah?" Gram said without opening her eyes.

"Yes. It's me."

The eyes blinked once and opened.

"Can you talk?" Deborah laid a hand gently on Hannah's shoulder.

Her grandmother's voice had been hoarse when she said her name. Now she cleared her throat carefully before she spoke. "I think it's you needs to talk." Her stare in the dim room was flat and depthless.

Deborah broke off the beginning of a weak laugh. She drew a deep breath to reply, but Hannah cut her off. "You don't need to tell me, honey," she said. "I know what it is you've got to say. I couldn't help hearing your mama and sister talking."

Deborah dropped her eyes and withdrew her hand. There was a long silence during which the woman in the other bed began to snore in long rough whistles.

"There's something I need to tell you, too," Hannah said. "And it won't be easy. You'll have to bear with me."

Deborah scooted the chair closer and bent her head toward her grandmother. Just then the latch to the heavy door clicked open from the hallway. Deborah looked over her shoulder and caught her breath, then frowned and turned back.

"Deb?" Pris' voice bent up on that pitiful pleading note she always used when someone was mad at her. With exaggerated care she tiptoed into the room and slid into the space between the curtain and Hannah's bed.

"I thought you'd be gone," Deb said, still not looking at her.

Pris started to say something, then shut her lips tightly, folding her hands in front of her.

Deborah felt her grandmother's fingers on her wrist, gripping. "Now, Deborah," Hannah said, low and warning. "Just you hold on. Priscilla may as well hear this too." She loosened her grip on Deborah's wrist, then gave it another little shake. "But not your mother. You hear?" She waited till they both nodded, her lips jerked impatiently. "You girls remember that time I took you to visit your great-grandmother up in Minnesota?"

"The only time we ever saw her," Pris said.

"The first time I'd seen her myself in over twenty years," Hannah said. "We weren't close." She closed her eyes, remembering how Miriam had stared when she'd asked to take the girls for a visit.

"I thought you never liked Grandma Snider," Miriam had said. Then she shrugged. "Sure. Why not. I've got orals coming up anyway. I could use the break."

So Hannah had driven fifteen hundred miles with Priscilla and Deborah in the back seat of the car and forced herself to sit in the chair next to her mother-in-law's knitting basket, still in the same spot Greta Snider had always kept it, though it was obvious she hadn't been able to knit for years.

Deborah leaned forward, her elbows on her knees. "I remember a dark, hot room."

"It was summer and she wouldn't open the windows."

"We sat on this hard, slippery sofa. Pris' legs were so short they stuck straight out."

"I took you there for a bad reason," Hannah said. "It wasn't, like I said, because I wanted you to meet your great-grandmother. It was for me. Because I was trying to make up for something."

The visit in the Sniders' darkened front room had lasted no more than an hour. The little girls had studied the old woman, their eyes large and wary. At first, Hannah had been moved to pity her mother-in-law, crippled with arthritis and practically blind. The room, its blinds drawn against the August heat, retained the sour smell of her sluggish bowels. At first they inventoried family members. Sam's older brother had retired because of a weak heart. One of his sons had, like him, become a doctor; the other was a farm lobbyist in Washington. Sam's name was not spoken.

"That girl of yours—Miriam. Whatever happened to her?" Greta Snider croaked across the room to Hannah.

Hannah shifted a fold of skirt across her knees and lifted her head. "She teaches at the university. She's an anthropologist."

"Got divorced, didn't she?"

Hannah watched as Deborah scrubbed one foot on top of the other. "Sit up, girls," she said, lowering her voice.

"And your boy. Barton's his name, isn't it? Where's he now?"

Hannah had written her when Barton was buried. "He was killed. Vietnam." This was, after all, what she'd come for.

The croak across the room climbed to a cackle, then broke off abruptly. "So it's your son this time. Now you see what it's like."

"It's worse," Hannah had suddenly heard herself saying, her anger that fast. Blood was pounding against her eardrums. The top of her head felt as if it might come off.

"Worse? What do you mean, worse?" Her mother-in-law shifted forward in the worn recliner.

"Because I love my son," she said. And she felt a chill joy spread through her veins as she stood up and motioned to the girls. It was then that she knew her coming wouldn't count now, wouldn't make any difference. She'd lost Sam, and now she'd lost Barton. How much more would she have to lose before she could ever make up for it?

Maybe coming to see Greta Snider wouldn't have made any difference anyway, not even if she'd sat there and let herself be humiliated by the old woman's taunts. Nevertheless, her angry outburst had made the long trip futile. However much she'd loved Barton, she hadn't loved him enough. She had wanted to hurt Greta Snider more.

"I shouldn't have done it—taken you girls there," Hannah said now. The fingers of her left hand twitched convulsively, and she felt Deb's smooth fingers slide into her palm.

"Once you start trying to undo what's been done, everything starts to come unravelled. It's like trying to escape, to get on the outside of life."

She heard them both make consoling little murmurs. Then Priscilla, her curiosity breaking through, said, "But what were you trying to make up for, Gram?"

She caught the severe look Deborah shot at her sister. "I'm not through yet. Just be still. Priscilla, you sit down over there." Hannah lifted her hand, pointing toward the dark corner. The time it took Priscilla to shuffle around the bed gave Hannah a chance to catch her breath again.

"You know your grandfather and I lived for a while with his people up there in Minnesota after the war." She had always referred to Sam as their grandfather. Even to Miriam she said "your father." Sam was the person only she had known, her secret, the good and the bad of him. She'd never told anyone how reluctant he'd been to venture outside the security of his father's hardware store.

"Times were hard, of course, after the war. Not many jobs for all the soldiers coming home. But I was used to working, in fact, I sort of liked it. And so I went out one morning to look."

Hannah had dressed while the rest of the family was downstairs having breakfast. She took her time making up her face and putting her hair up in a neat roll across the top of her head so that Sam and his father would have already left for work when she came down to the kitchen and asked her mother-in-law if she'd mind looking after Miriam while she went to town. She told her she had a doctor's appointment. Seen one way, it wasn't a lie. She intended to ask about a job there too.

"By noon, I had one firm offer—stocker in a shoe store—and two more possibilities—cashier in the drugstore and the steno pool at a lawyer's office." Hannah closed her eyes and was silent for several minutes. Any of those jobs paid enough for her to rent at least a small apartment for the three of them.

Deborah scraped her chair back, as if to stand up. Hannah raised one hand to stop her, not sure how long they'd been sitting there waiting for her to continue. She seemed to lose whole blocks of minutes now, aware only of isolated intervals instead of time's duration. "Wait," she said. "I'm almost done."

Deborah leaned back. "It's okay, Gram. You don't have to—"

"Hush," her grandmother said. "You don't know. No one knows. Listen." She drew another deep breath.

"About the same time, well, for a couple of weeks anyway, I'd thought maybe I was expecting again. Now here I was with these job prospects. Back then, things were different, you know." She peered at both of them, Priscilla there in the corner and Deborah leaning forward in her chair, to see if they understood what she meant. Deborah was staring at the floor, but Priscilla's eyes were wide enough to catch the reflection from the light above the bed.

"It's not like we were starving or anything," Hannah went on. "But I just couldn't reconcile myself to living in my in-laws' house, eating their food, being beholden to them. And having another baby then was only going to make it worse." She stopped and gestured toward the nightstand. "Can you get me a sip of water, hon?"

Deborah lifted her head and put the straw between her lips, her face a mask, determined to show nothing. Hannah waited till Deborah had lowered her head and replaced the glass on the nightstand, then waited a moment longer before she began again.

"That afternoon, while my mother-in-law and Miriam were asleep upstairs, I slipped down to the living room. In her yarn basket I found an ivory-colored knitting needle—bone she said it was. There were several of that kind, so I figured it was the least likely to be missed.

"I took it upstairs and hid it in the bathroom on the baseboard ledge behind the claw-footed tub."

That night when she had taken her bath, she lay on her back in the water with her knees drawn up, feeling with her finger for the mouth of her cervix. Then she had guided the knitting needle gently inside. Inserting it into the mouth of the cervix hadn't been as easy as she'd expected. The muscle was tough and tight. She tried to go slow, be careful, not push too hard. She'd heard terrifying stories from Lucille about girls bleeding to death. At last, however, exhausted by the tension, she had felt the point of the knitting needle slide in. She noted how much of the shank was still exposed just as it was entering, and when a couple more inches had disappeared inside her, she worked the thin rod carefully from side to side. It felt strange but not painful. She could taste the salt from licking her upper lip. Finally she drew out the needle and looked at it. It didn't look any different.

"Nothing happened, either that night or the next day," she went on, "though I checked every hour."

A flutter was creeping into Hannah's breathing. Deborah had clamped her lips between her teeth.

"In the afternoon I went back to the lawyer's office. The secretary told me it might be a while before they made a decision. Then I went across the street to the drugstore. The manager asked me if I could start that weekend. I said I'd be there.

"That evening I did the same thing I'd done the night before with the knitting needle. My mother-in-law was downstairs crocheting by the radio while the men played chess on the coffee table. I was terrified she might notice that bone knitting needle missing."

This time when she had managed to insert the knitting needle, she had twisted it more forcefully than the night before, making a circle with the protruding end. It still didn't hurt much, though she imagined she could feel small subterranean earthquakes within her.

The next morning, as soon as she waked, she felt the stickiness between her legs. She had hurried to the bathroom and sat crying with relief on the toilet seat. "Thank you, thank you," she hissed in shaky whispers through the tears. Then she stopped with a little gasp and sucked her lips between her teeth.

She slipped back in the bedroom—Sam was still sleeping—and opened the box of gauze-covered pads she'd brought with her from Texas. When she started to crawl back in bed beside her sleeping husband, however, she saw the sheet was stained. She went in Miriam's room, woke her and started dressing her. When she heard Sam get up, she went back and stripped the sheet from their bed.

After breakfast when the men had left for the store, she carried the sheet downstairs to the back porch where Mrs. Snider had a laundry tub, and put it to soak in cold water while she did the breakfast dishes.

Mrs. Snider, coming in from cutting a cabbage from her victory garden, stopped and poked at the sheet in the laundry tub. "What's this?" she called to Hannah, gesturing with the knife.

"What? Oh. I... had an accident. I wasn't expecting, you know... . I should have been more careful. I'm sorry. I think I can get it all out though."

Mrs. Snider tilted her head to one side and looked at Hannah closely. "You went to the doctor yesterday."

She might have meant it as a question, but it came out sounding like a statement, almost, to Hannah's ears, an accusation.

"Yes," she said evenly. She could feel her neck start to turn red. Her hands stilled in the soapy water and she stared at the eggshell china cup that Mr. Snider drank his morning coffee from. She could feel her throat constricting and her eyes begin to sting, but she was determined not to cry in front of this woman.

Mrs. Snider put the cabbage down on the counter by the sink. "You've been vomiting too, haven't you? In the mornings."

Hannah took a shuddering breath and nodded, remembering that the knitting needle was still on the ledge of the baseboard upstairs.

Mrs. Snider sat down at the table, leaning forward over her plump knees, her stockings rolled down just beneath them. "What did the doctor say?" she asked in a subdued voice.

Hannah lifted her eyes and stared out the kitchen window at the bees working a late blooming vine. Another flower she'd never seen before leaving Texas. "He said," she paused, her spine turning cold as she realized she wouldn't have to lie, "it would be a while before he could tell."

"Well." Mrs. Snider patted the oilcloth on the table a few times with her open palm and then stood up and turned back to the cabbage. "You won't have to worry now, will you?"

Hannah looked down and resumed shifting the dishes through the soapy water. "No, ma'am. I guess not."

Hannah was awake all that night with terrible cramps. When she got up, the sheets were spotted again. As she stood by the bed, looking at the stain, already turning brown, she felt sweaty and loose and unstrung. What had she done?

The flow was so heavy, she had to stay in all that day. The day after tomorrow was to be her first day at the drugstore. She hadn't even told Sam about the job yet. Mrs. Snider watched her carefully all day, insisting she keep her feet up.

"Maybe I should call the doctor," she said once.

"No," Hannah said quickly. "It just happens this way once in a while. Some times are heavier than others."

Hannah lay in the bed, staring up at the water mark on the ceiling. Was she going to die? Had she really been pregnant? Maybe this was something else. Tension. What was happening to her?

She closed her eyes and thought of Mrs. McMichaels, beside her hospital bed, the pages of her Bible whispering through her fingers as she searched for a name for Miriam. What would she have said to her? Trust in the Lord with all thine heart; and lean not unto thine own understanding. What would she say to her now?

She thought of Lucille. Cheer up, kid, she'd say. Don't take it so hard. We do what we gotta do to get by. She turned on her side and drew her knees up. Is that what she'd done— gotten by? The aspirins she'd been taking all day were finally taking effect. Gradually she slid off into sleep.

It must have been several hours later when she woke and heard Mrs. Snider's voice next door in the little dormer room. She was putting Miriam to bed and talking to Sam.

"I don't know what you can be thinking, Sam. You can't be having another baby. Not now. You don't even have a job yet."

There was a low murmur that Hannah recognized as Sam's voice, although she couldn't make out the words.

"Of course," Mrs. Snider replied to whatever he'd said. "But things will get better eventually. They always do. You're too impatient, Sam."

Sam broke in here, a little louder and faster, the words still not discernable.

There was a pause while Mrs. Snider spoke instructively to Miriam. Then she sighed and addressed her son again. "All I'm saying is you need to leave that girl alone for now, son. Surely, after all that time overseas, a little while longer... Let's wait and see how things work out."

The next morning Hannah slipped into the living room while Mrs. Snider was hanging out wash on the line in the back yard. She returned the knitting needle to the basket, putting it carefully alongside its mates. That evening she told Sam about the job at the drugstore.

He looked at her darkly, his jaw working beneath the sooty bristles of his day-long beard. "If that's what you want," he finally said, untying his shoes with exaggerated movements. "But you tell Mom and Dad. This was your idea, remember. Don't forget that."

She didn't forget. She had never forgotten.

Hannah felt her granddaughters' eyes on her. She moved her head sideways, hearing the fabric of the pillowcase sizzle beneath her hair. She was so exhausted she could only manage a few words. "I thought for a long time somehow I could pay it off—that debt. I thought, whatever happened, if I was strong and bore what I had to bear, that I could make it up, pay it back. The day I lost Sam—your grandfather—was the first time I thought I'd done that. But I was wrong."

After that fall in Minnesota, Hannah had thought, late the next spring, now would have been the time. But then Barton had come along, and the memory of what she had done to escape from her in-laws' house gradually faded. After all, she told herself, she hadn't been absolutely certain she was pregnant.

But when Sam died the memory had suddenly resurfaced. She tried putting them both away, burying the two losses together. But her memory of Sam remained tinged with a mute and all but forgotten remorse. Whenever difficulties arose afterwards, when money was tight or the children got sick, she found herself accepting the affliction with resignation. Sometimes almost with relief. Now, she thought, at last, it must be done with.

But it was never done, never over, the making up for what you wasted. That was what Hannah had not been able to say to Miriam that night her daughter had brought her own bad news to her kitchen. Because she could never have told her how she'd learned this.

Hannah opened her eyes and saw Priscilla's spiralling tangles next to Deborah's smooth head. "First your grandfather. Then your Uncle Barton. I never have been able to get over the feeling that I tore a hole in the world somehow with what I did. And ever since the things I love have been slipping through it."

18

From the sofa Deborah, still not fully awake, watched the large glass rectangle in the east wall of her apartment growing lighter. It had been after midnight when she finally got home from the hospital. She'd waited to leave till Gram was sleeping soundly, and, to keep from waking her mother when she came in, she'd undressed in the dark and collapsed on the sofa.

Just before she waked she'd been dreaming she was somewhere underground, tunneling furiously through black earth damp with decaying leaf mold. She'd scrabbled at the dirt with her hands, like an animal hollowing a burrow. But the dirt was soft and crumbly, and the tunnel kept caving in behind her, leaving her in darkness, suffocating. Then the tunnel had somehow turned into Buffalo Bayou, snaking its way through the city's core, thick and turgid with mud and trash. She'd struggled toward the surface, her swimming almost crawling, trying to hold her breath till she reached the air, batting at the debris floating overhead.

A large catfish with pale blotches like liver spots had materialized out of the underwater murk, its long moustache-like feelers trailing backward under its belly as it nuzzled the muddy bottom. It came towards her, its round lips pulsed rhythmically. Then, just before it touched her, one goggled eye swelled till it filled her vision and became the sun overhead, penetrating the bayou's viscous sluice.

She lay still a moment, listening to the water running in the shower, her consciousness gradually sorting dream from waking. Then she sniffed at her rumpled slip, almost certain she could still catch the scent of swamp water. Feeling strangely placid, she lay there another couple of minutes, releasing the time like an offering. Finally, she threw back the sheet and padded from the sofa into her bedroom.

Miriam was still in the bathroom; Deborah dressed rapidly in a pair of jeans and a T-shirt. She wanted to slip out to a bakery down the street and pick up some croissants for a peace-offering. She ran a comb through her hair, grabbed a soda cracker from the kitchen, and slung her handbag over her shoulder.

Taking care to shut the door silently behind her, she headed down the dim corridor toward the elevator. Just as she reached it, the doors slid open and Otis Ruffner stepped out.

"Deborah. Miss Estes. I hoped I could catch you before you left for the office." He paused. "I was just coming by to explain."

"Here? How did you know where to find me?"

"I talked to that other lady that works in your office."

"But Arlene wouldn't—"

"Naw, naw." He shook his head. "She wasn't about to tell me where you lived. Which I appreciated, you understand. Good policy. But after I explained..." He spread his hands outward as though the gesture itself would reveal the reason.

"I was just leaving," she said. "My mother... you see, my grandmother—" She broke off. "It's too complicated."

He stretched his eyebrows upward, looked down, nodded.

"But now that you're here," she went on, her peace having dissipated as soon as she saw him, "I've been trying to call you. I'd like to know just what—"

He half turned toward the elevator. "Maybe we could go somewhere? Then I could explain."

They ended up at the coffeeshop on the corner that catered to downtown workers who, for one reason or another, preferred not to eat breakfast at home. He ordered dry toast for them both.

"See," he said, sliding a fork back and forth on the formica tabletop, "I got to thinking. Hoot Jasper and Hank Crawford, well, they been doing work for me off and on for twenty-five years. And I got no complaints, you understand. So far's I know, they always done right by me. But—here, take my jelly—the way I see it, they're no spring chickens anymore. In fact, you may not believe it but them two old coots got a good twenty years on me. They gotta retire one a these days soon or else die in the traces. Either way, I'm gonna be left high and dry."

He stood the fork on end and stared at the tines thoughtfully. "Say I go to court with the feds here about this Alamo Assets business. Then old Hoot, he keels over in the middle of the case. What am I supposed to do then? I don't mean to sound ungrateful, but I'd be up a creek without a paddle. Hank ain't the one been working on this hisself. So he'd have to catch up. And he ain't in no better shape than Hoot."

Deborah kept her expression noncommittal as she picked up another triangle from the plate he'd nudged closer to her.

"So anyway, like I say, I start to figure. Who should I go to? If I'm gonna switch horses, I might as well get a young 'un, someone I can stick with. Don't that make sense?" He laid the fork down and crossed his forearms across his chest. "Then I get to thinking. That Miss Estes. She's young. And she's already in on this. She'd be perfect!"

Deborah pressed the paper napkin carefully to her lips, then laid it down before looking directly at him. "Mr. Ruffner. You must know that what you're asking is unethical. I'm part of the Jasper and Crawford firm. Mr. Jasper is already upset with me because you're leaving the firm. If he knew I was even talking to you now—" She shook her head. "Besides, like I say, it's unethical."

Otis Ruffner spun his knife. "I was afraid old Hoot might make it hard on you. I sure am sorry about that. You gotta understand I didn't intend to get you in hot water. I just got excited though when I come up with this scheme, see?" He gazed across at her, the cross-hatched skin puckering around his small green eyes. "I don't think... that is, Hoot and Hank, they're not the most broad-minded specimens you're likely to run up on. I doubt if they'll be very understanding when they find out about... you know." He brushed a hand diffidently in her direction.

Deborah picked up her coffee cup. "I'll deal with that," she said. "It's not your concern."

There was a long pause followed by a heavy sigh. "I was afraid you'd say that. But, well, you know—oh criminy. I'm not any good at this. Velda always said I—"

"Velda," Deborah broke in. "That's another thing. You never told me that you were divorced. You made it appear that—"

"That's because I never considered myself divorced," he said stiffly, pulling back a few inches from the table.

"Really? Well, the state of Texas granted a divorce."

"The state of Texas can say whatever it dang well pleases. But that don't make it true, ma'am." He clamped his mouth shut in a flat line.

She looked away, shaking her head.

"It was just like I told you," he went on after a moment in a softer tone, "Velda was upset. Disappointed in life. In me too, I guess. Never getting a baby. I don't blame her for what she did, understand. But just because her and her lawyer wrote out a bunch a papers and got the judge to sign 'em, that don't mean I was divorced, Miss Estes. No sir. Not in my own eyes nor in the eyes of God Almighty either. I looked upon myself as married to Velda till the day she died."

Deborah sat back and braced her hands against the table edge. Then she raised her eyebrows as if to set aside the issue. "That may be, but you can't deny you deliberately misled me."

He dropped his gaze now, studying the scraps of crust on his plate. "Misled maybe," he said after a while, "but not deliberately. Least, not like you think."

She waited as his even lips bunched and straightened several times. He was simultaneously so improbable, so earnest. Why did she have this sudden impulse to reassure yet another man who was probably lying to her? "Okay. So what was the reason?" she made herself ask.

He took a deep breath and looked up at her resolutely so that a rim of white showed below his pupils. "Miss Estes. Deborah. The way I see it, we could both of us use some help here. I need me a good lawyer. You need—well, you know better than I do. But one thing I do know, you need to get out of Hoot and Hank's office. As long as you're agreeable to staying there, they just gonna use you. And not the way they would a man."

He sat back and crossed his arms again. "Now I did some checking yesterday after you left. Called up some folks I know over at St. Mary's—"

"How did you know—"

"Never mind. Just listen now. I found out what folks over there thought of you. Which, just as I suspected, was pretty highly. So as you see I've gone about this in a sensible kind of way."

She moved her handbag from the booth seat into her lap.

"Now hold onto your horses. Like I said, you ain't ever gonna get anywhere at Hoot and Hank's. If they let you stay on, which they ain't no guarantee of, they'll hold it over your head the rest of your days how they did you this favor. There wasn't much future for you there to begin with, but after this..." He made the brushing gesture with his hand again. "You understand what I'm saying? I been knowing them two skunks a lot longer than you, Deborah."

"I could still be disbarred for the kind of thing you're suggesting. Besides, I hardly think you could provide me with enough work to keep a law office in business."

Otis reached across the table and patted at her crumpled napkin. "It ain't gonna be unethical either. I even got that figured out. You'll need some time off, right? Fine. How long do you reckon? Six months? A year? By then—"

"Wait." She held up a hand, then looked away, into a dim corner of the coffeeshop. "You're rushing me here. And you're assuming an awful lot."

He dropped his head into his hands and pushed at the spikes of black hair on his forehead until they stood out in a stiff little ledge, then fumbled for her hand and covered it clumsily with both of his. He waited till she had turned to look at him again. "I couldn't help Velda," he said. "Don't you see? For some reason I couldn't give her what she wanted, what she needed. So here's my chance to make it up. Not to her maybe. But I've lived long enough to learn that all the unpaid accounts in this world don't necessarily get squared with the person they're owed to. Still, we get chances, ever' now and again, to settle up somehow. With somebody sometime." He spread his arms wide as if to include the entire coffeeshop, the whole world, in his offer. Then his arms dropped again. "I figure this may be my last chance, Deborah. But I'm at your mercy here. I realize it's up to you. But please. Let me help."

Deborah looked at him a long moment, even after he dropped his own pleading gaze. She thought about her grandmother, using up her whole life to make up for the despair she'd allowed to bully her. After a moment Otis sighed and started to speak again, but she reached across the table with her free hand and laid her fingertips on his lips. "Don't worry, Otis. It's all right." She brushed the straggling hair down across his forehead again. "Everything's going to be all right."

It was Tim's day to drive his work car-pool so Pris had had to get the kids ready, stop by the supermarket for more diapers for Sarah, and drop them at the sitters. By the time she pulled into the hospital parking lot it was almost eleven. Deb's pale green Honda was already there in a slot close to the entrance. Mom must have taken her to work and kept the car today. The hospital drill was becoming routine for them all.

Inside the lobby, people were bunched in front of the stainless steel elevator doors, including a man pushing a woman in a wheelchair. Pris decided to take the stairs. On the second flight, the strap of her left sandal broke. As she limped down the hall to her grandmother's room, it flapped against the tile floor in a staggered slap-and-drag rhythm.

She pushed the door open carefully, wary of disturbing the woman in the bed nearest the door. The woman had grown used to describing the details of her latest tests every morning to Pris. She was gone, however, a naked mattress the sign of her release.

Across the room, the canvas curtain circled Gram's bed by the window. Pris stopped, watching the shadows of several figures moving behind it. Her mother's voice asked "How long will it be?" and another voice, a man's, answered something Pris couldn't make out. Then the movement and voices stopped, as if time had stuttered. When it started again, it was moving faster than she could keep up with.

Her mother backed from behind the curtain, flattening herself against the wall, her right hand, clenched in a fist, striking her chest twice slowly. Then she looked over and saw Pris, still standing in the doorway. She appeared to be neither relieved nor surprised to see her, only blank.

"Go call Deb," Mom said. "See if someone at the office can bring her over here. Right away."

The several legs at the bottom of the curtain stopped moving for a moment. Then someone said, "Now," and the legs all took a step in the same direction. Someone grunted with effort, there was a dull clank, and another voice said, "Okay."

Her mother, who had turned to watch them, looked back at her now. "They're taking Gram to surgery," she said, and flattened further against the wall as the gurney began to emerge from behind the curtain. "Go call Deborah," she repeated.

Pris backed into the space between the stripped bed and its nightstand and watched the gurney roll past. She caught a glimpse of her grandmother's face. Hannah's lips weren't quite closed. Her head rocked, unsupported. An orderly held up an inverted bottle attached to her arm by a tube. Miriam followed the gurney out of the room.

When they were all gone, Pris came around the foot of the empty bed and pushed the curtain back. Gram's bed sheet had pulled loose at one corner. A pillow was on the floor between the bed and the window. Her mother's tote bag, a magazine sticking from one end, sat in the corner. Pris moved aside a ceramic cup, painted to look like a kitten, from its place on the nightstand. The daisies in it were turning brown. She picked up the telephone receiver and held it for a moment, staring at the small card skewered among the dry daisy stems. "From the Rebekah Class. Get well soon."

She punched three numbers, stopped, depressed the buttons in the phone cradle, pushed the nine, waited, then punched out Deb's number at work. "Arlene," she said when she heard the voice on the other end, "can you bring Deborah to the hospital right away?" Even as she spoke she marvelled at her own voice, how it seemed to work of its own volition, without her even having to think.

"Your grandmother's..."

"Worse."

There was a moment's hesitation on the other end. "Okay, honey. Don't worry. I'll see she gets there."

Putting the phone back on the hook, Pris slid open the drawer of the night stand and took out her grandmother's glasses. Then she shut the drawer, picked up the tote bag, and went down the hall to the elevator, her sandal strap still flapping.

Downstairs, outside the swinging OR doors, she found Miriam. "Come on, Mom. There's a waiting room just down the hall." She held out the tote bag to her mother who took it and followed her.

The alcove, its furniture littered with last night's coffee cups and napkins, was deserted. "What happened?" Pris asked.

Her mother sank into a chair, holding the tote bag in her lap as if she were waiting for a bus. "Some kind of buzzer started going off at the nurses' station just as I got here. The monitor, I guess. I couldn't tell anything was wrong. She was asleep. I heard this commotion out in the hall and then they all rushed into the room. It was all confused. Her heart must have—she looked awful, didn't she?" She stopped and stared at Pris. "Did you get Deborah?"

"She's on her way."

"She was up here till late last night. She told me Gram was fine when she left. Sleeping. Breathing better."

Pris only nodded.

After a while Miriam sighed and put the tote bag beside her on the floor. "Have you ever noticed how all the surfaces in a hospital are hard and slick? Everywhere you look. Vinyl floors, glass, formica. Absolutely impervious." She gestured toward the hallway. "How do they expect anyone to get well in a place like this?"

"Maybe I should have taken her home," Pris said. "Maybe she would have been happier there."

Her mother closed her eyes and shook her head. "Don't talk like that. You did exactly right. That's not what I meant." After another minute had gone by, she said, "It's just that people need a certain amount of—something. Sponginess maybe. To thrive, you know? A little give. You know what I mean?"

Pris nodded. She wasn't sure she did. "I think I'll go call Tim," she said.

She went to the pay phone at the end of the hall. The office phone rang four times, then Tim's recorded voice switched on. She left a message and hung up. She wanted him there with her. She was cold.

On her way back up the corridor, she saw Hannah's doctor—young and blond—coming through the swinging doors at the end of the ward. Pris had talked to him a number of times during the past week as she watched him examining her grandmother. She'd been intrigued by the angle and joints of his long fingers, wondering what it would be like to make love to a man with blond hair. Would it be blond all over? She'd asked Tim once, but all he'd said was it depended.

The young doctor had called her grandmother Hannah once.

"Mrs. Snider," Hannah had corrected him.

Pris had watched as the side of his neck turned a faint red. "Sorry, ma'am. Forgot my manners." Then he glanced across the bed at Pris who had let him see her suppressed smile. His eyes had slid to her left hand, then away again.

Seeing her now, he motioned for her to follow him into an empty room. "You're Mrs. Snider's granddaughter, right?" He leaned his elbow against the wall at shoulder height, bracing his head with his fist.

"My mother's here now."

"Yes, I've met her."

"She's been out of the country."

He pushed away from the wall. "Any other children?"

"Just my sister."

"No." He smiled. "Does your mom have any brothers or sisters?"

"Oh. One. Brother. Or she did. He was killed in Vietnam." As soon as she said it, she could see what he'd meant. "There's no one else," she said quickly. "Except my sister. I've called her already."

"Good." He reached out and touched her shoulder. "I'll let you know as soon as she's out of surgery."

She watched him head back down the hall. She could still feel the spot on her shoulder where he'd touched her. For a moment she leaned over the porcelain sink in the empty room, needing something cold and hard.

Her mother stiffened as they heard footsteps come down the hall, then hesitate outside the alcove where they were waiting.

"Deborah?"

Deb stepped inside, glancing briefly back over her shoulder. She had on jeans and a T-shirt. "Mom? What's happening?"

Miriam half rose, and Deborah slid an arm around her as they both sank onto the sofa. "I guess maybe this is it," Miriam said.

Priscilla looked at her watch. "It's been almost an hour now."

A stocky man in a rumpled suit hesitated outside in the corridor, then came in and sat down in the chair nearest the entrance. Leaning on one elbow, he studied the vending machine on the far wall.

"She was fine when I left last night, Mother," Deborah said, her voice hoarse.

Priscilla watched them, almost as if she were viewing a movie. She wished she hadn't seen Gram this morning, not looking the way she had. "It's been an hour," she repeated. "Maybe I should go check."

She bent over and tucked the broken sandal strap under her instep before she stood up. The man across the room raised his head and nodded at her uncertainly. He must be waiting for someone in surgery too. He seemed grateful for their company.

Out in the hall again, she saw the double doors at the end swing open and a surgeon in green scrubs come out, talking and gesturing to the blond doctor. Their steps slowed simultaneously, as if they were dancing, and they turned to face one another, their shoulders angled together, almost touching. The surgeon motioned back toward the swinging doors. He jerked his palm upward, the fingers spread, then let the hand fall heavily. The blond doctor, staring at the floor, nodded.

It had been a long time since she'd felt so light. Not since she'd danced with Sam, with the lights from the pavilion reflecting onto the lake water. But now, just as the music had, she was floating out over the water herself, encased in a transparent membrane. She had only to open her eyes and she'd be able to see everything clearly.

She could still feel the current that had lifted her. It was growing stronger, tugging at her gauzy envelope. For a moment, remembering her scant readiness, she held back.

The air was thickening again. Or was it water? So heavy she could scarcely breathe it any longer. Outside the sheath enclosing her was air. She was certain of that. Lighter air that she could breathe.

"Don't worry, Hannah," Mrs. McMichaels said, drifting beside her. "Now that you're lighter, it'll be easy. Just turn loose and come on ahead."

She closed her eyes and gave herself up to the current. It was rushing now, propelling her out over the water, toward the edge of the world, its quickening surge scrubbing away the thin film surrounding her. Then the membrane was tearing, rippling away behind her, and she was free.

19

It didn't seem right to Pris that they'd left her there. Just driven off and left her alone like that. While he told them in the waiting room, the doctor's eyes had kept drifting to Pris, as if he expected her to act as his interpreter for her mother and sister. "I'm sorry. You understand. It won't take long. I'll have the nurse let you know."

The three women had gone back to the room and emptied Gram's belongings into paper sacks, waiting for the nurse to come tell them they'd finished "cleaning her up." While they were folding Gram's clothes, emptying the vases, and collecting the cards, they'd all avoided one another's eyes, the proximity of strangers making them mute.

After a while a nurse had come and taken them downstairs to an empty room where Gram's body lay on a clean gurney. Mom had smoothed back the hair from Gram's temples, then curved her palm around the upper arm as though to check whether she might need more cover. Finally, her hand trailed down the length of the arm to the fingers. She gripped them briefly, then stepped back.

On the other side of the gurney, Deborah had stared down at the body, her lips parting as if she were about to speak. But instead her mouth compressed suddenly and she bent down and kissed the forehead. After that, she had straightened up and left the room.

"Pris?" Mom had said. "Priscilla?"

And, if she hadn't done that, hadn't used the name, it might have been all right. Already, just looking at the body,

Pris had begun to see it wasn't Gram anymore. In fact, she might have said as much to her mother and sister then, except that the sound of her name—Priscilla—had made the room drop away steeply, leaving her on some unguarded ledge. She took a step backward, away from the body, then mutely followed Deb out of the room and down the corridor to an exit.

Outside in the parking lot, the sun had seemed too sudden and bright.

"You all right?" Deb asked. She was standing in the circle of shade a sweetgum cast near the car. Pris nodded, then tensed as Deb put an arm around her shoulders.

Mom came across the parking lot, shading her eyes with Gram's Bible. "Here," she said as she reached them, fishing in her skirt pocket with her other hand for the keys and handing them to Deborah. "You drive."

Pris had already opened her car door, letting the heat pour out. A cream-colored Lincoln was just pulling out of the parking lot and she saw Deb glance toward it. Pris could see that the driver was the man in the rumpled suit who'd shared the waiting room with them.

"Let's go to Deb's," her mother called to her across the top of Deb's Honda. "It's closest. I'll have to make some calls."

As Pris watched the two of them drive away she almost turned and ran back inside. We can't just leave her, she thought. Even if it is only a body. It's hers—ours. But instead she got in the car and followed them, mechanically shifting gears through the traffic to Deb's apartment.

It was still bothering her as she came through the door with the sack of Gram's clothes clutched to her. "Are we just going to..." She shrugged the rest of her meaning.

Miriam looked at her sharply. "Just what?"

"Gram. Just leave her there." She heard her own voice waver and shrugged again.

Her mother's mouth twitched. "The hospital takes care of it, Pris." She sat down at the small table and started rummaging through her tote bag for her address book.

"But, Mom—"

"Please, Pris." Her mother raised her head and clenched her eyes shut. "It's hard enough, okay? Don't make it any harder." She bent over the bag again.

Pris dropped the sack she was carrying onto the sofa. Deb had disappeared into the bedroom. After another moment, her mother looked up, then took a deep breath and said in a lower tone, "This isn't one of your religious things, is it? Some taboo or something?"

Pris felt her face begin to burn. She lowered her head, pretending to examine the contents of the sack, and started taking the clothes out, one piece at a time, folding them on the sofa. A slip, a bra with thick elastic, a pink blouse, mended under one arm. She began to cry.

Her mother came and sat down on the sofa beside her, putting her arms around her and pulling her head down onto her shoulder. "I'm sorry," she said. "That's the way it is. The hospital takes care of it. I gave them the name of a mortuary. There's nothing more we can do right now."

Pris felt silly. Her head barely fit on her mother's narrow shoulder. She had to bend down a little to reach it. After a minute Pris raised her head and sniffed. "I've got to call Tim. Maybe he's back by now."

Just then the phone rang. She could hear Deb pick it up in the bedroom. "For you, Pris," she called.

She picked up the kitchen wall phone.

"I'll be right over," Tim said as soon as she began to speak.

"No. Wait." She held the phone away and started to say something to her mother, then stopped and raised the receiver to her mouth again. "You know that Kentucky Fried place right off the Tidwell ramp? Why don't you pick something up and take it out to Gram's house? Meet us there."

Fifteen minutes later, on her way out of Deb's building, she saw the man from the hospital waiting room sitting on the slatted bench by a potted palm near the entrance, holding a straw Stetson in his lap. When he saw her he got to his feet.

"Excuse me—Miss Estes?"

"No. That's my sister."

He shook his head, acknowledging the mistake. "Of course. You're married. I forgot."

"Forgot? Do I know you?"

"I'm, oh, an associate of Deborah's. And a friend," he added quickly. "How is she?"

"She can't—"

"I understand," he broke in. "I brought her to the hospital, you see, and—"

"Not Arlene?"

"No. Arlene called me. Anyway, all I want to know is, is Deborah okay? She said her grandmother—"

"She died," Pris broke in. She didn't want anyone else saying it.

"I'm sorry," he said. "Is there anything—"

Pris cut him off again. "You're a friend of my sister's?" she asked, letting her skepticism show.

"Yes ma'am. And, like I said, an associate." He rotated his hat in his hands, his eyes fixed on it.

She took a step toward the door. "Well, she's fine. She's not going to feel like working anymore today though. Or seeing visitors." She pushed the door open a couple of inches before adding, "My mother's here."

The man nodded solemnly. "Good, good. I'm sure you ladies can handle it. But, well, if you need anything." He bobbed his head. Pris nodded in return and stepped out onto the baking sidewalk. The cream Lincoln sat idling in a no-parking zone at the curb.

Why hadn't Deb said anything to the guy in the waiting room at the hospital? she thought irritably as she drove from downtown toward the shabby northeast neighborhood where Gram lived. *Had* lived. She'd let the poor schmuck sit there like she didn't even know him.

But as she pulled into the oyster-shell driveway, the man dropped out of her mind. It would take Deb and Mom a while longer to call all the relatives from the apartment. She had come ahead because she wanted some time alone in the house with no one else around.

She went up the two cement steps of the front stoop, noticing that the four o'clocks under the black-framed front windows were drooping from lack of water, pulled back the screen door, and, stepping inside it, unlocked the front door, deadbolt at the top first, then the knob lock. The door swung inward and she eased the screen shut behind her, careful not to let it slam, the way Gram had instructed them during those long childhood summers. No one even had screen doors anymore.

The air inside the closed house was stifling. Leaving the door open, she went through all the rooms, raising the windows. Sashes, Gram called them. *Raise the window sash, Priscilla. The air's too close and sultry tonight.* Words no one else would ever use again. They were over.

She hesitated before she went into Gram's bedroom, then stepped quickly over the slippery chenille throw rug in the doorway. Thank heavens she'd come back and made the bed after they took Gram to the hospital. If it had still been the way she'd found it that morning—the covers thrown back, the pillow dented—she couldn't have borne the sight. She sat down on the bed, feeling the springs give just the amount she knew they would. She could have picked the wobbly recoil of Gram's mattress out of a million. She ran her hand across the nobbly loops of the white bedspread, the friction from its texture transferring through her fingers to the empty space she had come there to fill.

On the dark walnut dresser, the glass-covered top furred with dust after more than a week now, the neat bottles and bits of china holding her grandmother's small vanities glinted modestly. Her own dresser would never be this tidy, not even when the kids were grown and gone. This ordered kind of womanly embellishment was over with also, done. Try as she might, she would never be able to emulate it. She couldn't even preserve it. She knew what Mom would do— call the Goodwill and have them cart off whatever she and Deb didn't want or couldn't take. She'd keep something for Sarah, a reminder of the great-grandmother she wouldn't be able to remember. But most things in this house would end up with strangers.

She lay back on the bed and stared up at the ceiling. Before the others got there she'd turn on the rattling window units to cool the place off, but right now she wanted to feel the heat like a blanket around her, submitting to its oppressive force by an act of will, trying to make it some kind of homage, feeling it the way Gram had for most of her life. Why wasn't there a way to make it all stand still, some way to save it?

When Tim arrived a half hour later with a bucket of chicken, he found her sound asleep on her side, a pillow with a bird-of-paradise embroidered on the starched case pulled under her flushed cheek. He stood in the bedroom door a moment, staring at her. Then his eyes closed and his lips moved almost imperceptibly. After a moment he set the large paper bucket on the dresser by the door and went to shake her shoulder, brushing the dark disorder of her hair back from her face.

"Pris. Wake up."

She sat up instantly, staring at him blankly. The imprint from a fold of the bedspread caught on the pillow marked her cheek diagonally. She might have been Sarah waking up from a nap, not sure where she was. Wordlessly, he pulled her to him and pressed her head against his shoulder till he felt her shoulders begin to jerk and she raised one hand to wipe her nose.

Tim had moved the bucket of chicken to the formica table in the kitchen and set out some pickles he found in the fridge. No one seemed hungry. Deborah had begun picking up the small bits of clutter in the living room—a two-week-old TV schedule, accumulated junk mail, handwork left beside the recliner. Pris had insisted he sit down at the table and eat before he went back to the office, getting out a plate for him and taking a drumstick herself as if to keep him company. She ate standing at the kitchen sink though, then started cleaning out the refrigerator, making room for the food the ladies from Gram's church would be bringing. Before he left he promised to pick up the kids from the sitter.

Miriam had found Hannah's address book, and Pris waited till she heard her mother talking to the pastor at Gram's church about the funeral. Then she said to Deb who was running water into the sink, "Remember that guy that was sitting in the waiting room at the hospital?"

Deb turned off the water and reached for the dishrag. "Yeah? What about him?"

"He was waiting downstairs when I left your place. He said he was an 'associate' of yours?" She said the word like a question.

"And?" Deb opened the cabinet door under the sink and scraped chicken bones into the garbage.

Pris hesitated. "And a friend, he said."

Deb shrugged and closed the cabinet door. "Sort of."

Pris waited for her to go on, but Deb just looked around the kitchen, as if she were searching for something. Then she pulled the broom from the narrow space between the refrigerator and the wall and started sweeping, making long, slow strokes across the linoleum. Black showed through cracks along the edges.

"So who is he?"

Deb bent over and shoved the broom around under the table.

"He said he brought you to the hospital."

"That's right." Deb straightened up and turned her back to dig at the corner by the stove with the edge of the broom.

"So?" Pris put her hands on her hips.

The broom stilled. "I'm doing some work for him. What's the big deal?"

Pris tried to scrutinize her sister's face, but she was still turned away. "He's just a client? He seemed very... concerned about you."

The broom started moving again. "Yes, well."

Pris threw up her hands, then let them drop with an explosive sigh. "Okay. I can see you don't want to talk about it."

She pushed through the back screen door, letting it bang shut behind her. Crossing the patch of thick Saint Augustine in the back yard, she noticed how much it had grown since the last rain, and, even through her anger, made a note to tell Tim he'd have to get out Gram's old push mower and cut the grass before the funeral.

Inside the carport's shaded interior she sat down on the cool concrete, slumping back against the bricks, her knees raised and her skirt shoved down between her legs. Maybe she should have said yes when Tim had offered to take the rest of the day off instead of telling him there was nothing he could do now. Around Deb and her mother, he was like a shield, setting her apart, putting her in some special zone where they couldn't get to her so bad, where she didn't feel like such a child.

The back door opened and closed carefully again, not slamming, but she didn't look up, not even when Deb stood in front of her, her hands on her hips. "Okay, I'm sorry," Deb said.

Pris took a quick breath and turned her head away, still not looking up.

Deb sat down beside her and leaned back against the brick wall. "I was meaning to tell you, Pris. Really. I was planning to tell everyone today. Make my big announcement." She paused. "Things just didn't turn out the way I'd planned. I guess it was silly to expect them to."

There was silence between them for a while. Then Pris cleared her throat and said, "Tim and I, we could—"

"Please, Pris," Deb said, pinching off her words. "Don't."

Pris blinked and gazed out beyond the back fence sagging under the weight of wisteria. The heat rising from the metal roof of a storage shed in the neighbor's yard made the air and all it held—tree branches, power lines, clouds—swim upwards in shimmering undulations.

Beside her, Deb's rigid back relaxed a little. "I've decided to have it—to keep it. But I have to do this myself, Pris."

Pris stole a glance at her sister out of the corner of her eye. She wished Deb would say baby, not it. But she barely breathed, waiting for her to go on.

"It's something I owe to—any number of people." Deb had closed her eyes but now she opened them again. "And I have... some options."

"Options? You mean you're going to tell Scott?"

Deborah snorted. "I'd sooner die."

Pris was quiet for a moment. Then two vertical frown lines bunched between her dark eyebrows. "Deb? This doesn't have anything to do with that fellow at..." She let her words trail away.

Her sister said nothing, only pulled one knee close to her chest, clasping her arms around it tightly.

"Who is he anyway? Where'd you meet him?"

"He's sort of an entrepreneur."

"Entrepreneur?"

"He's got some money to invest and he wants me to handle the paperwork." She glanced at Pris and then away quickly. "I can manage this, Pris. And for heaven's sake, don't say anything to Mom about it right now, okay?"

Pris stared silently at the sagging wisteria for a few minutes. Finally she said, "But what does this have to do with... does he know about...?"

"He knows." Deb let go of her knee and leaned back again, speaking rapidly. "It means something, don't you think? Him showing up at a time like this?"

Pris felt the world give a little lunge and was suddenly conscious of the gritty concrete under her legs, the spikes of grass at the edge of the concrete. "Means something? What are you talking about? Surely you're not—" She broke off, unwilling even to put what she was thinking into words.

"Well, you've always been the one who believes God makes up little special delivery packages for people, Pris." Deb's voice had grown edged again but when she went on the thin edge seemed to give way as if it were too weak for the weight. "He's the first person who really wants this baby, you know. Not just because he thinks it's the right thing to do or to keep me from going to hell for doing the wrong thing. He wants it."

Deb's face suddenly turned pink and she looked down into her lap as if she were about to cry. What was the word Mother had used in the hospital, Pris thought. Mushy? Spongy? A little give. People need a little give to life. Pris took a deep, noisy breath and let it out slowly. Maybe a lot of give.

"You don't understand, Pris," Deb went on, her voice struggling for firmness. "How could you? You've always been able to make people happy. I never have—at least not like this." Her quick, breathless laugh wavered up with the shimmering heat. "It's all just ordinary to you. You've probably forgotten what it feels like."

Pris had opened her mouth to speak but swallowed instead.

Deb ran her hands through her hair and frowned toward the fence. "Oh, who knows?" She let her hair go and dropped her hands into her lap. "But at least when I woke up this morning, I was glad, happy to be alive." The rush of words broke off abruptly. Deb pulled her knees up and leaned forward over them, rocking gently back and forth. "And then Gram was gone. But now—you know?—it's not the end, is it?"

Pris reached over and tugged at her sister's elbow until she tilted toward her. Then she slid her arm around Deb's shoulder and pulled her head onto her lap, brushing the long damp strands of hair back from her face.

Miriam came out onto the back steps, shading her eyes from the sun. "Girls?" she called, her voice curling uncertainly upward. "Are you out here?" Then she caught sight of them inside the shaded carport. "What're you doing out here? Telling secrets?"

It had been one of her own mother's lines, something Hannah always said when the girls were little and she caught them whispering together and giggling. Hearing herself repeating it, Miriam barely managed to get the words out. The hole inside her, the one she had hoped would fill with sand, had begun to echo like a well again. Her lungs were either going to cave in or explode, she wasn't sure which.

As she came toward them across the thick grass, her daughters scooted apart, making a place for her. She lowered herself between them cautiously, mimicking a decrepit old woman but feeling brittle too. Then she winged her arms around each of their necks, pulling their heads against her own.

How many times had they kept her going, these two? When nothing else made sense, when there was no other reason to get up in the morning. Her responsibility to the bald fact of their existence had always been the one thing she was certain of. Whatever else she was or was not, they had supplied her with at least a basic definition. She supposed she had done that for Hannah. This is the way the whole show keeps on going, she thought. Like stitches, each life pulled through the one that came before.

Deborah edged her head away and began scratching a design on the concrete with a twig. "Mom," she said, and from the way the word broke in her throat, Miriam knew what was coming next.

She caught up her daughter's hand and ran her thumb along the back of the knuckles. "Hush," she said. "Whatever. It's okay."

Deb picked up the twig again, twirling it between her fingers.

"It's all right, Mom," Pris said, gripping Miriam's elbow and jiggling it to get her attention. "Really."

Miriam turned to look at her younger daughter. Pris' face was stretched in a mute grimace, half comical, half cautioning. Miriam felt breath slowly filling the cavity within her. All three of them had taken that step off the precipice, and now, here they were, huddled together at the bottom. But still alive. When you took that fateful step off the edge, the one there was no undoing, it was life you fell into. Out of a dream and into life.

Would she take it all back if she could? Undo the disaster of her marriage, erase all her failures? As soon as she formed the question she knew the answer. However she had failed, whatever had broken, it was still her life. Still her, in fact. And more than just her. Somehow, without her even knowing how, without her wanting such a definite consequence, her life had produced these two other lives. Refusing the mistakes meant discarding them as well. "All right," she echoed Pris weakly, reaching to brush back her daughter's sweat-damp hair where it stuck to her temple. "All right, sweetheart. I believe you."

"Are you going back?" Deb asked suddenly, frowning at them both. "To Israel?"

"After this," Miriam gestured toward the house, "I'll have to go back for a while. I left everything there, you know. And there's a job I was working on that I've got to finish." Yigal and the desert. What would he say when she told him why she couldn't stay?

"But by winter?" Deborah was looking at her anxiously.

Miriam drew another deep breath and held it as she considered the steaming lawn. She supposed she owed it to— whom? Hannah? Her own daughters? Those little bones in Yigal's glass jar? To someone. The worst lie of all was that you owed no one. If nothing else, you owed them for their need.

Miriam slid her other hand through her daughter's arm. "Naturally," she said.